ALSO BY EMILY SNOW

Devoured

All Over You (A Devoured Novella)

Tidal

EMILY SNOW

A Touchstone Book
Published by Simon & Schuster
New York London Toronto Sydney New Delhi

Touchstone
A Division of Simon & Schuster, Inc.
1230 Avenue of the Americas
New York, NY 10020

Originally published in 2012 by Smashwords

First Touchstone trade paperback edition June 2013

For information about special discounts for bulk purchases, please contact Simon & Schuster Special Sales at 1-866-506-1949 or business@simonandschuster.com.

The Simon & Schuster Speakers Bureau can bring authors to your live event. For more information or to book an event contact the Simon & Schuster Speakers Bureau at 1-866-248-3049 or visit our website at www.simonspeakers.com.

Designed by Claudia Martinez

Snow, Emily, 1986–
Tidal : a novel / Emily Snow.
  pp.   cm.
"A Touchstone book."
1. Actresses—Fiction.   2. Hawaii—Fiction.   3. Love stories.   I. Title.
PS3619.N676T53 2013
813'.6—dc23   2013006578

ISBN 978-1-4767-4410-0
ISBN 978-1-4767-4411-7 (ebook)

For Angela,
who reads every book I write at least five times.
You are the best friend a girl could ever have.

Tidal

PROLOGUE

~~~~~~

August 17

My name is Willow Avery.

Yes, THAT Willow Avery—THAT actress. The one who went off the deep end three years ago. The one whose face is plastered all over the tabloids this morning. They don't give a shit if there's more to me than meets the eye, that there's so much more to my fall from grace, even if nobody—other than my parents and agent—knows what that is. Well, at least nobody knew until a few hours ago.

And the thing is I've ALWAYS cared about what everyone thought of me, even when it seemed like I didn't. No matter how much my need for approval has hurt me, there's always been this sick part of me that refuses to let it go. That still desperately craves it. It's just that now, I'm not sure if I mind that everyone knows the truth about me. Now, there's this guy, and he's not waiting for me to screw up. He doesn't care that I HAVE screwed up.

But I guess all good ~~movies~~ stories begin with a guy . . .

CHAPTER ONE

~~~~~~

June 15

The driver my agent had hired for the day slammed on the brakes, squealing the SUV to a halt only a few inches from an orange Metro bus. Behind our Mercedes, someone laid down on his horn hard, blaring it for what seemed like five minutes. I welcomed the sound; it was something other than the excruciating silence that had consumed my life for the last six months. Kevin, my agent, wasn't so appreciative. Beside me in the backseat, he turned and flipped his middle finger up at the rear window, even though the other guy couldn't possibly see through the tint.

"Fucking idiot should get a ticket. Too stupid to see traffic is deadlocked," Kevin muttered. Then, rolling his gray eyes, he sighed. "It never changes, does it?"

I dropped my head back against the beige leather headrest, lolling it to the side so that the air conditioner blasted my face, and stared out the window. Next to us, a couple waited in traffic on a candy-apple-red Ducati motorcycle. Both of the woman's arms were tightly wrapped around the man's waist, and she rubbed her fingertips up and down the crotch of his jeans. He was wearing a huge shit-eating grin. If it weren't for the cop in front of them, they'd probably be completely naked.

"No." I exhaled a whoosh of air. "Never changes. It's insane."

And that insanity was what I loved the most about Hollywood. Somehow during my 180-day stint at Serenity Hills, I'd forgotten just how hectic this place was—how it was all abuzz, even at ten in the morning when most people were just now rolling out of bed. This past round of rehab had been just the opposite.

Serenity Hills was all peace, all therapy, and all "confront your personal demons to save yourself"—all the time.

I had hated it, but as of an hour ago, my six months were up. Freedom had never felt so good. This time, I wouldn't let it go so easily. This time, I'd be smart enough to limit myself and dull my senses just enough to forget, but not to the point of obliterating my reality.

I quickly shook that thought out of my head, ashamed of myself. No, this time—this time I would be different.

I sure as hell would never go back to rehab.

"I am in control of myself," I mouthed before averting my

gaze from the PDA-happy couple. I gave Kevin a sweet smile as I combed my fingers through my long, chocolate-colored hair. "You're taking me to my hotel, right?" I asked.

I was dying to submerge myself back into the chaos and noise. Dying for anything but silence. That moment wouldn't come until I had shaken free of Kevin and his driver, who he said doubled as a temporary bodyguard since my own had quit last year.

Kevin's thin lips parted in surprise, and he stared at me like I was an idiot. My hands froze, tangled in a wavy kink of hair. I sucked in my cheeks as Kevin thoughtfully rubbed his bottom lip between his fingers. I never liked when he did that; it always meant bad news for me. Like he was about to reveal the reason my parents hadn't picked me up was because they were waiting for me in court.

Apparently, getting custody of your adult child is the new thing.

Straining his neck against the collar of his fluorescent-yellow polo shirt, Kevin stopped fussing with his lip to say, "You've got a lunch meeting with James Dickson in forty-five minutes. Your dad said your mom wrote you . . ."

My parents had written me about lawsuits and judgments and more lawsuits, and on Easter they'd sent me a glittery card with a creepy grinning rabbit on the front. Not once had they mentioned anything about lunch with a film producer on the same day I left rehab. This move was so typical of them that I wasn't the least bit surprised, just angry. And hurt.

"Cancel it," I said, pointing at Kevin's iPhone; it was sitting between us in the leather cup holder.

He dipped his head slightly as he shook his head, revealing a thinning patch in the middle. When he had first started representing me ten years ago, he'd had a full head of auburn hair; now, he kept it short-cropped.

"Not smart," Kevin said pointedly.

"I *just* got out."

"People have gone back to work way sooner, Willow."

"I went back to work like this last time and look what happened," I snapped. It had been a sitcom that was panned by critics and charred to a crisp by everyone else. There was nothing like reading about how hollow your acting was, how far you'd fallen. *"Green eyes as flat and lifeless as a porcelain doll, or worse, like a TLC pageant contestant,"* one of the snarky gossip websites had written.

And then I'd relapsed.

"My mom wrote that you guys were booking me a new hotel until I can find a new place to rent," I said in a calm voice.

Sliding across the leather seat so that the sides of our bodies touched, Kevin said in a low, warning voice, "You're almost broke. So if you want to keep paying for your fancy hotels, you'll meet with Dickson." When I began to give him a pissy reply, he flicked his gaze up at the driver, whose eyes were glued to the deluge of traffic ahead, and whispered, "You're on everyone's shit list. You stand Dickson up and you can kiss any acting for this year good-bye, unless you're into taking off your clothes and deep penetration."

"Don't be disgusting," I whispered, swinging away from Kevin. I gripped the edge of the leather seat and focused my attention on the hem of the fitted color-block dress he'd brought me. I'd gained ten pounds while at Serenity Hills and was on the verge of looking like a sausage stuffed inside of a pink, white, and brown wrapper, but I liked the summery outfit. Still, I should have realized when the rehab counselor brought me a Neiman Marcus bag full of clothes to wear home with the price tags still dangling from them that something was going down.

Like a meeting with a producer.

But as much as I hated to admit it, Kevin was right. Dickson or sex was about it for me as far as acting went at the moment. I didn't care whether I ever received a role again, but broke is broke. Acting was quick, easy money. And I already knew my parents weren't about to give me any of the money they'd made off me over the years, or any of the money I'd earned before I turned eighteen nearly two years ago. I wasn't set to receive any of that until I turned twenty-one—in thirteen months.

I pulled in a deep breath. "Do you know what the part is for?" I couldn't imagine it being something big. Nobody in his right mind would offer me a leading role. Late last year, right before I checked in to Serenity Hills, I had bailed on a project that was based on some huge bestselling fantasy book.

I'd never read it, but there was a copy being passed around rehab. Some of the girls had ignored me for days when they found out I was the reason filming had been delayed.

Kevin scratched his chin, cocking his head to the side. "Your father told me they sent you the script."

Of course Dad had told him that. I twisted my head back to the window, glanced down at the PDA junkies, and resumed raking my fingers through my hair—this time so forcefully it hurt my scalp.

"Well, he didn't," I said.

"With that attitude, it's no wonder nobody wants to hire you."

"Screw you too, Kevin," I muttered. But as I pressed my forehead hard against the cold glass, I considered my agent's words. My attitude had nothing to do with my lack of parts over the past few years, though I was on the verge of being blacklisted. I bared my teeth, frustrated at myself for what I was about to do.

"Fine, I'll go," I said.

Kevin was already sighing in relief before the first syllable stumbled past my lips.

We arrived at Junction, one of my favorite restaurants, ten minutes late. The hostess escorted Kevin and me to a square booth adjacent to a towering wine rack. Dickson was already there, sitting next to a guy with tousled blond hair, whose head was down, focused on the menu.

His new assistant, maybe?

No, that couldn't be it. James Dickson was always pretty adamant about his staff dressing professionally for business meetings, especially his assistants. The guy beside him wore a faded lime-green Hollister T-shirt that hugged his biceps and chest— that lean, muscular look I'd always lost my breath over.

Maybe this was Dickson's son. I shrugged off that idea almost as quickly as the last. For starters, I was pretty sure James

Dickson didn't have any kids and once again, he was too professional to bring one to a meeting.

So who the hell was this guy? I narrowed my eyes at the top of his head, wishing he'd shift his gaze up so I could get a good look at him, but he didn't budge.

Junction's menu couldn't be that damn interesting.

Dickson stood, grinning broadly, and he placed his hands on either side of my shoulders, giving them a squeeze. "Willow, it's so good to see you again," he said earnestly as the hostess placed our menus on the table. She murmured that our server would be with us shortly before walking away.

"You too," I told Dickson, returning his smile. "Really, it is."

Out of the corner of my eye I saw a flicker of light—a smartphone. I didn't blink, but I felt the familiar jolt inside that I'd learned to control years ago. The flashing was the one thing I hadn't missed while I was holed up in rehab, but it never changed. That picture would show up on gossip sites before I was finished eating lunch.

What Not to Wear

Willow Avery: The Post Rehab Files
Ten Pounds and Counting as She Pigs Out at Junction

The world would feed off my downfall, savoring every morsel, and there wasn't a thing I could do to stop it.

I pulled away from Dickson's grasp to slide into the booth. Kevin came in right behind me, grinning like the cat that ate the canary.

"You haven't changed a bit," Dickson said, once he was settled into his own seat. As I let his words register, I fought to keep from flinching, to keep the look of defeat out of my green eyes. Because he was lying.

I have changed.

And in more ways than just the tiny frown lines at the corners of my eyes and the thin, silvery scars on the inner elbow of my left arm (from an escape I'd tried a couple of times, over a year before).

The last time I worked with Dickson had been more than five years ago. I'd played the lead in a modern-day Sleeping Beauty, minus the creepy magical fairies. Back then, I had been box office gold and the only thing I'd wanted to do was act.

But now . . .

"I'm not popping gum," I said in a high-pitched voice, and Dickson chuckled. I compelled myself to laugh along with him. The winter we shot *Sleepless*, he'd stayed on my ass about chewing gum during scenes. The guy sitting next to Dickson released an exasperated sound, and my attention wavered back toward him.

As if he finally remembered that we weren't alone, Dickson's eyes widened and he said, "Ah, I've been rude. Kevin, you've already met Cooper, right?"

Kevin bobbed his balding red head. "Last week, at the meeting with Tiff and Jason," he said, shooting me an apologetic look.

My parents and my agent had met with Dickson already, which meant Kevin had lied to me in the Mercedes when I asked him about the lunch date. I pinched the inside of his thigh under the table. He winced, but never dropped the sleazy smile.

Creeper.

"Willow, meet Cooper," Dickson said, motioning to the blond. "Cooper—"

Cooper kept his eyes attached to his menu. "Everyone knows who Willow Avery is," he said, in a quiet voice brimming with sardonic undertones.

Holy hell, he had an accent.

A deliciously sexy one that I suddenly wanted to hear more of, so I could place it.

"I'm Cooper Taylor," he said.

Australian. Definitely Australian.

Extending his hand across the table, he finally peered up to take me in. Even though he was mocking me seconds before, I was mesmerized by his eyes. Fringed in sooty, dark lashes, they were blue—the bluest I'd ever seen, actually—and set in a classically gorgeous face.

I took his hand, sucking in a breath through my nose as his fingertips closed around my palm, as our flesh intertwined. Both our eyes dropped to our hands, and my pulse went from zero to sixty in less than two seconds. When I parted my lips to speak but didn't let go of him, he pulled away. Tilting his head to one side, Cooper gave me a flash of straight, white teeth.

"I'm Willow Avery," I said, stupidly.

"Yeah, I already knew that. Good to know you."

"Cooper is a surf coach," Dickson said, in a voice that made me feel like a second grader.

Cocking an eyebrow in an effort to look indifferent, I asked, "A surf coach?" I locked my hands between my knees, hoping the pressure would erase the memory of Cooper's touch from my skin. It didn't, and I felt his eyes burning into the side of my face.

It's only because I've been in rehab, I reasoned with myself. *That's the reason why I felt that pull toward him.*

"He's a damn good surf coach," Dickson answered.

"One of the best," my agent piped in.

I shifted a strand of my dark hair behind my ear, pausing to rub my fingers back and forth across my earlobe. "And I'm guessing his being here has something to do with a part?"

Dickson grinned. "You always were one to cut to the chase, but yes. We're in preproduction and set to begin filming at the end of the month in Hawaii."

"So it's a surfing movie?" I asked.

"We prefer calling it a"—Dickson raised his fingers into quotation marks—"beach drama. And it's actually a reboot of a popular late-eighties movie." Cooper made a little noise next to him, but Dickson pretended not to hear him.

"Which one?" I asked.

"*Tidal.* It was the movie that launched Hilary Norton's career. I was a production manager on the original."

I'd seen a bunch of Hilary Norton's movies, but not that particular one—though I'd never tell Dickson that. "And I'd be what? The supporting actress who surfs?" I questioned as I rubbed the back of my neck. Kevin made an awkward grunting noise beside me, trying to get me to shut the hell up. I gave him a look that said, *I'll cut you.* Dickson missed the exchange, but Surfer Boy caught it, quirking his eyebrows and lips at the same time.

"Lead, my dear," Dickson said. His answer knocked the breath out of my lungs. I didn't get the opportunity to immediately reply because our server arrived to take our order. Numbly, I asked for a chopped salad and water, and ran my fingertips along the outline of my fork as everyone else ordered. The only person I found myself listening to was Cooper, who wanted a Coke and a burger.

My stomach growled, and suddenly, I wished I'd asked for the same. Rehab food sucked.

"And we would start filming at the end of this month?" I asked, doing the math in my head. I was looking at twelve, maybe thirteen days. That would give me time to see my friends before I was needed in Hawaii. If I was lucky, Kevin would negotiate enough advance money for me to spend those days happy.

"Well, yes, but you'd be going to Hawaii tomorrow evening," Dickson said.

My mouth dropped open. I looked from him to my agent, from Kevin to the surfer. "I have . . . other obligations," I muttered, placing an emphasis on the last couple words. Obligations meaning the community service I was supposed to start immediately, now that I was out of Serenity Hills. Fifty hours, and it would take me at least four or five days working at breakneck speed.

Kevin shook his head. "Already taken care of. Your parents had your attorney file a motion to transfer your community service to Honolulu."

I curled my fingers angrily around the napkin in my lap. Clay, my attorney, had had enough time to file motions, but not enough to answer my letters about a lawsuit I'd filed against a business nearly three years ago. And Mom and Dad weren't too busy to attend meetings on my behalf, but they'd sent my agent to pick me up this morning.

Unbelievable.

"Looks like you have it all figured out," I said.

Cooper snorted. "Right down to you scrubbing graffiti off park benches when you're not with me," he said under his breath. For some reason, the taunt sounded so much harsher coming from him, in his soft-spoken accent. I flipped my eyes across the table at him, doing my best to maintain my clenched smile. His face was red from holding back laughter.

And this was who was going to train me for my role? He could barely get through lunch without laughing at me.

"Back. Off," I snapped. Then, to Dickson, I demanded, "Is he going to do this while he's training me?"

"Of course not, he's only being facetious," Dickson said, trying to console me. Then his voice turned serious. "You're really the only one for the part."

His words were what every actress wanted to hear, even reluctant ones who didn't want to return to work. James Dickson was a fair man; making *Sleepless* with him had been a breeze. And most importantly, I was broke. My agent was right, I needed this part.

"You two will iron out the details?" I asked. The question was aimed toward Dickson and Kevin, but for some reason, my eyes were locked on Surfer Boy. I didn't like the way he was smirking at me. It was unsettling and intense and it made me feel exposed.

And this will be my coach.

"Already working on it," Dickson assured me.

Dragging my gaze from Cooper, I faced my new producer. I tried to think of everything I would gain from doing this job, and not the potential asshole I'd have to work alongside every day while doing it.

Cooper was still there, though, a bronze and startling blue haze in my peripherals.

"I'll do it," I said, my voice shaky. Then, Dickson and I clasped hands.

But later that afternoon, once lunch had ended and Kevin had dropped me off at the nicest hotel I could afford for the evening, I googled Dickson's newest movie. It took two clicks to discover that a starlet—of the mouse-ear variety—had dropped out of the lead role recently due to a scheduling conflict. Staring at the screen until the girl's picture and the adjacent photo of Dickson became a blur, I dialed Jessica, one of my best friends. I caught her voice mail.

"Jess, it's me. I'm out, so call me back," I said. Then I tried contacting everyone else I knew, with no luck, including my parents. Their shared voice mail picked up and my mother's newscaster-like voice answered.

"This is Tiffany and Jason Avery. We're vacationing in Paris, but we'll get back to you . . ."

Frustrated, I punched the end button and tossed the phone on top of the nightstand next to the hotel bed. Mom and Dad *would* be on vacation. I flipped on the TV and settled for reruns of a reality show on MTV, waiting for one of my friends to call me back.

But when I drifted off to sleep a few minutes after midnight, curled into a tight coil of flesh and bone and thinking of blue eyes and an endless blue sea, my phone hadn't so much as vibrated once.

"It's better this way," I said, as I hugged myself. If Jessica had called me back, I would have gone out—I would have gotten high. I couldn't let myself do that anymore. I needed a different escape.

But saying those words, and thinking those thoughts, did nothing to stop the tight pain in my chest.

I had dreams—*nightmares*—about soft, blue blankets.

And when I woke up several times throughout the night, all I found myself wanting was more blue—Roxies, my once-favorite escape of all—to numb all of that away. I cried myself back to sleep, hating my weaknesses.

CHAPTER TWO

~~~~~~

A pounding outside my hotel room door jarred me awake, unraveling me from my fitful sleep. For a moment, I remained still, squinting as the sunlight poured across the bed. There hadn't been a window in my room at Serenity Hills, which I'd shared with a steady influx of other girls—the last being a rocker's kid who was only there for eight weeks. For six months I'd missed waking up to the light. It burned the edges away from the darkness, at least for a little while.

The door shook again and this time a muffled voice on the other side called out my name. Groaning, I rolled over, stumbled out of bed, and crept across the paisley-print carpet. After I wiggled my arms and legs to shake out the stiffness, I leaned forward to glance out the peephole.

Kevin stood in the hallway with his hands in his pockets, biting his lip impatiently. I knew better than anyone that my agent spent more time dealing with me than with most of his other clients, but it still made my throat go dry whenever he dropped a silent reminder that I was *that* client. The nuisance who didn't want to cooperate, despite everything he'd done for me.

Of course, not all of Kevin's suggestions and efforts had had the effect he'd been hoping for.

Sucking in a long breath to force the painful burn in my chest down to the pit of my stomach, I flung the door open. Kevin walked right past me, carrying a folder under his arm and rolling a suitcase behind him. I shut the door and counted to ten to calm myself so I wouldn't say anything I'd regret. When it came to Kevin and my parents, I was prone to doing that.

I turned around to face him wearing a sarcastic smile. "Good morning to you, too," I said, hugging my chest and pressing my back against the wall.

Dropping the bag on the center of the bed, Kevin started, "I'm guessing you—" When he glanced up at me, taking me in, he stopped midsentence. "Is everything okay, Willow?"

So he wouldn't see how much his surprise to see me still clean stung, I rolled my eyes dramatically and shoved myself off the wall with the bottom of my foot. "I don't always have to get high." *But I'd wanted to,* I silently added, feeling my body flush with humiliation. *And nobody called me back.* I slid onto the edge of the bed, curling my toes into the carpet.

He shook his head approvingly. "Sober looks good on you."

I chose not to respond to that. Instead, I flicked the bag's silver zippers with the tip of my thumb. They dangled back and forth, making a tinkling noise as they knocked against each other. "What's this for?"

"Tiff wanted you to have some of your clothes to carry along with you. She's arranged for everything else you'll need, to be sent ahead to your rental house in Honolulu."

"Fun. My mom can call you but can't even leave me a voice mail saying she's glad I'm out of rehab?" My voice broke on the last few words.

"Their phone hasn't been getting half of their calls."

It was a shitty excuse, especially for someone like Kevin who could come up with a lie without so much as twitching, but I brushed it off. He'd only try to maintain the bullshit, and I'd just get irritated. It was way too soon to start up our cycle of butting heads.

"What about—" I began.

"They gave you a twenty-thousand-dollar advance on the two fifty you'll be paid when filming is complete," he said, walking over to the armchair to sit down. "After I took out my percentage that left you—"

"Seventeen grand," I said. I'd been doing this for so long that the 15-percent math was permanently ingrained in my mind. "And it's in my account already?"

Kevin shook his head. "No, but by the end of the week."

I felt my heart sing a little, felt my body come alive as a thrill raced through it. Everything would be better once I was in Hawaii. With Surfer Boy. Sexy and completely hostile Surfer Boy.

I swallowed hard, hoping that the flicker of attraction I'd felt yesterday when we touched was nothing.

I couldn't let him be an obstacle.

"I see the wheels in your pretty little head turning. Don't do anything stupid to ruin yourself," Kevin said, whipping me out of my thoughts. There was a pitying edge to his voice that matched the look in his gray eyes. He'd been looking at me like that for years now, but today when I was so clearheaded—so raw—it rubbed me the wrong way. Today, it was impossible not to vividly imagine the warning Kevin had given me three years ago.

"You're not responsible enough for this, Willow. Any other choice and you will ruin yourself."

And somehow, even after I'd taken his advice, I'd done just that anyway.

"Pretty as she drowns and ruined when she resurfaces," I whispered under my breath, remembering a poem I'd read while in rehab. Kevin cocked an eyebrow, but I shook my head. "What time does my flight leave?"

He held out the folder. When I didn't immediately get up to take it, he jerked it back and forth. Groaning, I skulked over to him and took it, sifting through the contents as I returned to my spot on the bed. There was information about my community service in Hawaii and the probation officer I'd report to, and the address of a personal trainer. Even at my smallest—late last year when I wasn't eating because I'd always forgotten to—I was never Hollywood's definition of "thin."

I was tall and C-cupped and wide-hipped.

"Got to make sure I get rid of the ass fat. Let me guess—it's going to be a part of my final contract," I said, and Kevin made a strangled sound in the back of his throat. "No need to lie to me about this, too. We've been doing this too long."

Thankfully, Kevin opted to keep his mouth closed. I flipped the personal trainer's information over, reaching the last document in the folder. I studied my ticket carefully, silently. In less than four hours, I would take off from LAX, and I was nowhere near ready. As if on cue, my stomach rumbled.

Kevin waved his hand to the suitcase. "I'll settle your bill while you get dressed?"

"Thanks," I murmured, watching him as he quietly left the room.

I showered and dressed quickly, opting for a pair of tiny denim shorts that constricted my thighs, a white tank top that was too tight across my breasts, and an oversize flannel shirt. As I yanked the brush that I found in the front pouch of the bag through my wet, tangled hair, I forced my feet into a pair of black high-top Chuck Taylors. For a long time afterward, I stood in front of the bathroom mirror studying my reflection. It was the look I'd always sprung for before rehab, minus the baseball cap my mother loathed, but it didn't seem so careless anymore.

Now, I felt like I was trying too hard to be myself.

"Suck it up," I whispered to the girl in the mirror with the pale, drawn skin and the green eyes that seemed too big for her face. "Everything will be better soon."

Then, grabbing my bag off the hotel bed, I left the room and went in search of Kevin.

When I asked to go to lunch at Junction, Kevin quickly complied. I wasn't sure if he just wanted to keep me happy or if he was eager to get rid of me. He had driven himself today, in a sleek metallic Audi sports car that I didn't remember his having before. I couldn't help feeling a little jealous when he opened the door for me—I'd lost my license over a year ago, right before I turned nineteen. Getting my driving privileges restored didn't seem to be in my near future.

After lunch, which felt rushed, Kevin and I went to his office so I could sign paperwork. We were halfway through the documents when a giant of a man showed up. As I gazed out the office door, watching him interact with Kevin's assistant, I already knew he was a bodyguard hired for me. My new babysitter. When Kevin caught me staring, he motioned the man inside.

"Willow, this guy's been hired by the studio. Have to keep the rabid fans off, you know," Kevin said.

Which was translation for "evil paparazzi."

"Tom Miller. But everyone calls me Miller," the man said, and I stared up at him and muttered a hello.

Towering over me by half a foot at least, Miller was smooth-faced with a buzz cut and skin as orange as the main characters of those skull-grating shows about the upper east coast, and probably out of his mind with steroids, with what Jessica had always called "bear shoulders." I guessed he was in his late twenties, but I could never tell with the gym junkies.

"Willow," I said at last, half expecting Miller to give me Cooper's smart-ass "everybody knows Willow Avery" remark. He didn't, and I was glad he wasn't a total jackass.

After I finished signing the paperwork, Kevin gave me his "behave yourself" spiel and then volunteered his assistant to drive Miller and me to the airport. We were quiet the whole ride over to LAX, and once I was alone with Miller, I felt intimidated. I should have been as used to strangers being hired to protect me as I was to paparazzo cameras flashing in my face, but it was unnerving to sit next to a stranger who was at least twice my size. It always would be.

As we waited quietly in the terminal, I flipped through an old fashion magazine someone had left in the airport, trying my best to be inconspicuous. Miller's phone rang and he answered, recited a string of numbers and letters, and hung up in thirty seconds flat. I glanced over at him curiously.

"My little sister." Miller shrugged sheepishly. "I had to tell her the password to my bank." Then he smiled, showing off a tiny gap in his top front teeth. His relaxed expression lifted a weight from my chest. He probably wouldn't hover once we reached Hawaii, so long as he was receiving a steady paycheck.

One down, I thought. An image of Cooper flashed in my mind. *One to go. God, one mocking, confident, asshole-ish—*

"Careful, Wills, overthinking is dangerous," someone said from a few feet away. It was that sexy, soft voice that sounded like the love child of a British and a Southern accent. I gasped sharply and every muscle in my body went taut.

Speak of the blue-eyed devil.

My new bodyguard was on high alert and came up out of his seat, but I touched his arm, shaking my head quickly. "He's . . . with us," I mumbled before turning sideways in my seat to get a better look at Cooper.

Standing a few feet away, with a black duffel bag slung over his shoulder, he looked confident and relaxed in a black T-shirt that accentuated his tall, toned body and frayed jeans. And he was smiling—a heart-stopping, panty-dropping smile. I was torn between wanting to pop him in the mouth or kiss him until our lips were so freaking numb I could get this damn attraction thing out of the way.

One taste before I decided whether or not I needed to dull my reality.

I dug my fingers into the wrinkled hem of my flannel shirt. *No*—I didn't need to dull anything except my bad habits. I just needed to get my work done and get on with my life. I could have the chaos I craved in my life without getting fucked-up.

Cooper waited for a noisy, groping couple to pass between us and then stepped closer until he was right next to my seat. I glared up at him. "You could try not to be a dick," I said. He rubbed his tongue over his teeth, and I felt something sharp twist in the center of my chest, between my rib cage.

God, why were all the good-looking ones complete jerks?

"Why? I think I like you when you're all flustered," Cooper

replied, winking. He glided his palm along the high back of my chair, and when the heel of his hand brushed between my shoulder blades, I shivered. "You're less inhuman, much more . . ." His voice drifted off, as if he couldn't quite find the right word to describe me.

Right now, I needed him to say it. Wanted to know what he really thought of me. "I'm much more what?"

He cocked his head to one side, sizing me up. Beside me, Miller snorted but said nothing. At last, Cooper bent down and whispered into my ear, "Beautiful."

I'd been a performer, a liar who could mask her emotions, for as long as I could remember, and yet his words made me burst into flames from head to toe. As he went to sit across from Miller and me, slamming his duffel bag on the resin floor, I gave myself a mental shanking for having yet another knee-jerk reaction to Cooper.

He is an ass. He is your coach. Slow the fuck down, dumb-ass, before you get in trouble again.

So I decided to focus on the negative in what he said. "Glad to know I'm not quite human," I said in an icy voice.

Cooper's smile faded into an apologetic look. "Maybe I worded that wrong. You don't seem so . . . mechanical."

I released a tiny groan from the back of my throat. Where had Dickson found this guy? Narrowing my eyes into tight slits, I leaned forward, resting my forearms on my bare thighs. "Maybe you should just stop using words, period," I suggested.

He raked his hand through his floppy blond hair. "Ah, Wills . . ."

"My name is Willow," I snapped through clenched teeth. He smirked.

"I'm pretty sure I read on Wikipedia that it's Brittany," he said, and I cringed. The only person who *ever* called me by my actual first name was the guy who'd ripped me to shreds three years ago. Cooper didn't seem to notice the change in my expression when he asked in a sincere voice, "So, Wills, why don't we just start over?"

"Whatever."

He bent far over in his seat and stretched his hand toward me. "I'm Cooper Taylor. I'm a Scorpio. I enjoy women, long walks on the beach, and my roommate says I use girly shampoo. Oh, and I generally hate anyone in the film industry because they're total assholes. Guess you could say I'm your Pai Mei."

It was yet another insult to my profession, but for some reason, this time the tease in his voice made me smile. Maybe it was the lack of sleep. Or the fact he mentioned *Kill Bill,* a movie I could watch every day without getting bored. I slipped my hand in his.

"Willow Avery. Actress, Cancer, and according to my team, on my last leg before porn."

The moment the words jumbled from my lips, I realized they were a mistake. I glanced down at a scar on my right knee, but I could feel Miller's curious stare burning into the side of my face and Cooper's unreadable one directed at the top of my head. Cooper cleared his throat and I braced myself for the cruel comment I'd set myself up for.

I swallowed hard; as much as I tried to tell myself it didn't matter what people thought of me, I knew it did. The choice I made a few years ago was evidence enough of that.

"I've seen your movies," Cooper said gently. His grip on my hand relaxed, and when I lifted my head, he gave me an unashamed look. "Guess you can say I like to study up on my clients."

He'd gone through the trouble of finding my whole name on IMDb and seeing my films—I'd say he was the most thorough, and unnervingly sexy, surf coach who ever existed.

"Let me guess—inhuman?" I asked roughly.

He moved the pad of his thumb over my skin, stroking the spot between my thumb and index finger, and I pulled a rush of air through my nose. "No, insanely talented. Light-up-the-fucking-screen talented, Wills."

When I saw a flash, I snatched my hand back. Our heads—Cooper's and mine—turned toward the camera wielder, and Miller was already on his feet, standing in front of me with his arms crossed over his chest. When I peeked around him, I was expecting to see a paparazzo, but it was a kid, probably twelve or thirteen, with her parents. I heard the loud squalls of a baby and dropped my eyes to the covered stroller her dad was pushing. For a second, the blood drained from my face, from my body, but I quickly composed myself, forcing my attention back to the girl. She was bouncing on the balls of her feet excitedly and saying something to her father. He gave me an apologetic look as she dashed forward.

Miller glanced over his shoulder at me. "You want to take this one?" I bobbed my head, even though the sudden pitch in my stomach told me I shouldn't. Miller stepped aside.

"Oh my God, I loved *Sleepless!*" she gushed. The sound of her voice intermingled with the squealing of the baby, and I just wanted to cover my ears. When I didn't immediately respond, the girl backtracked a few steps. "Wait, you are Willow Avery, right?"

As if on cue, my face moved into a tight smile. I swallowed hard to push back the nausea. "Yes! So stoked to hear you love *Sleepless*—it was my favorite to make. What's your name?" My voice sounded sweet and chipper, but inside—inside, I was a mess. I sounded mechanical, just like Cooper had pointed out not even ten minutes ago.

"Lizzie," she said. She held up a wide, thin phone, jiggling it around. "Will you . . . ?"

A few feet away from me the baby squealed. Again and again.

I answered too quickly, too happily. "I'd love to!" Though I was staring right at Lizzie, I saw Cooper's mouth turn downward, into a frown. I would ignore him. I would ignore him and the baby and get this over with. Hastily, I took the phone from Lizzie and jutted it out at Miller. He took it in his giant hand, and I flicked my eyes up to him pleadingly.

"Can you take it?" I begged. *So they can go away? Please?*

Miller gave me a gruff nod. He stood beside where Cooper sat, holding the phone in front of him. Lizzie threw her thin arm around my shoulders and grinned from ear to ear. "This is so awesome," she said, casting a beam over to her parents. Through the haze in my head—the one that was still there because of the conversation I'd had with Cooper only moments before—I wondered how they felt about this. If they were disappointed their daughter idolized someone like me.

Lizzie turned her face to mine. "What should we say?" she asked.

"How about *Sleepless*?" Cooper suggested in a tight tone.

"Yes, *Sleepless*," I murmured.

It took Miller a few times to get it right—his giant fingers kept exiting out of the camera app or showing up in the photo itself—but finally he snapped a few good photos. I sat on the edge of my seat as Lizzie talked excitedly about my movies for a few more minutes. Then finally she left, humming happily, with her mom and dad and the baby in tow.

I sighed in relief as our flight was called to board. When Cooper stepped past me, avoiding my eyes, he said, "Nice way to treat one of your fans, Wills." His voice was hard and unreadable.

I didn't have the balls or the heart to tell Cooper that being so close to Lizzie's family had did me in.

That it reminded me of what I'd given up three years before.

CHAPTER THREE

~~~~~~~~~~~~~~~~~~~~~~~~

Although we immediately learned our seats were booked side by side—Cooper in the window seat, me beside him, and Miller across the aisle, on my right—any headway I thought I'd gained with him inside the airport seemed to evaporate the moment we boarded the flight to Honolulu. Now, as I followed him down the coffee-scented, narrow aisle toward our seats, all that remained was the bittersweet smell of *what-if.* I was more than used to getting my face shoved into could've-been and what-if, but for some reason, this time felt so much worse than usual. I wasn't naive enough to pretend I didn't know why.

Plus, I wasn't high to the point of not noticing.

The first and only other time I left rehab, nearly two years ago after I'd spent ninety days at a luxury program that was like the Four Seasons for addicts, I'd lasted approximately six hours before I caved and bought enough Roxies to last three months. At least, they should have lasted me that long. My best friend Jessica and I had gone through them in a week—seven days I *still* couldn't remember.

"Excuse me," Cooper said in a coarse voice, interrupting my thoughts. He wanted to talk, thank God. I looked up at him expectantly to find him staring over the top of my head, at the overhead compartment. "I've got to put my bag up."

Okay, so he didn't have anything to say to me.

"Sure," I said. As he reached up to store his duffel bag, I slid down into my seat and crossed my arms over my chest. When he sat next to me a moment later, he immediately pulled a magazine—*Surfing*, go freaking figure—from his back pocket and began studying it. Something sharp expanded in my throat, the same constriction I always felt right before I bawled my eyes out, and I slouched down.

You know what, Cooper? I don't give a shit what you think.

Of course that was a big fat lie—I did care if he thought I was an unapproachable bitch. So I sat there, utterly miserable, stuck beside Cooper in first class, silence hanging like stale laundry between us.

After two hours of being quiet and avoiding my gaze, Cooper finally sighed and whispered, "You don't look so good."

Startled, I looked over at him. His eyes were directed at the window, gazing out into hazy white nothingness. He'd spent the last couple of hours dividing his attention between the window and his magazine, unlike Miller who'd fallen asleep and hadn't moved an inch, not even when a flight attendant bumped a drink cart into his seat.

"Are you going to be okay?" Cooper asked.

"And he speaks," I said. "Get tired of pretending I don't exist?"

"Don't throw up on me, Wills," he warned, placing his palm flat on the window, and making no effort to acknowledge what I'd said. Ugh, I was glad I hadn't apologized to him.

I squeezed my eyes closed and counted to three. "I don't like flying over water," I said, and Cooper released a low groan and a curse.

"Please tell me you're not afraid of water."

If we were on the ground, and if there weren't still a razor-sharp tension cutting through us, I might have said yes. It would be worth getting a rise out of him. Instead, I shook my head and whispered, "No . . . just being forty thousand feet over it."

It was the truth. Somewhat. Flying over water had been number three on my list of biggest fears when my rehab counselor had told me to write them out a few months ago. Silence had topped that list, but it was really second—I'd been too afraid to put down number one. Today, I'd faced three of the things that always seemed to shake me apart into a million pieces, and I'd done so unmedicated.

I could do this.

Maybe . . . maybe I wasn't as weak as I believed.

"Get some rest," Cooper said, his voice low, his warm breath fanning my ear, the side of my face. I instinctively shivered, my neck cricking to the side where I felt him. I hadn't realized he'd turned away from the window.

"Why?" I said.

"Because you'll need it when we hit the beach tomorrow." This time when his lips came close to my skin, I didn't show a reaction, though I felt it—a deep burn that started in the center of my stomach, unfurling until it completely took me over.

"I've worked on a lot less sleep," I replied, opening my eyes.

"Not with me, Wills. I'm not going to let you fail."

I snorted. "You get paid regardless of how stupid I look doing this."

"Who said it has anything to do with money?" he asked. Then, he shifted in his seat—moved away from me—and was quiet again.

The plane touched down in Hawaii three hours later, at 7:15 p.m. As we walked to baggage claim together, with Miller a few steps away, I said jokingly to Cooper, "What? No lei?"

He gave me a look that radiated cockiness. "You've got no clue how much I wish there were, Wills."

I'd walked my ass right into that one. Feeling my face light up in mortification, I glanced down at the slick, polished floor to gather my bearings, as he added, "You've got to pay for leis." I looked up in time to see him pointing at a man holding an armful of flowers and a sale sign.

"So much for the welcome they get in the movies, huh?"

"If you want, *I'll* give you a lei."

"I'm sure you will," I muttered, slowing my stride so he could walk ahead of me. I fell in beside Miller. He was all business—stony expression and hulking muscles—and glancing his dark eyes around cautiously, though it didn't seem like anyone was paying us any attention.

We collected our bags without a single camera or phone coming out, much to my relief. Miller went off to a rental car kiosk to pick up the keys for our car, so I followed Cooper out a set of sliding doors, toward the rental car garage. A blast of warm, muggy air hit my face, moistening my skin, and I coughed. Next to me, Cooper pulled out his phone, punching away at the touchscreen keyboard. He still hadn't mentioned what had happened back in Los Angeles, but it was bound to come up at some point during the next several weeks when he bitched about disliking the film industry. What would I even say?

My stomach rolled. I needed to clear the air between us and I needed to do it right now.

"Cooper," I started, and he lifted his chin a little. "Look, I—"

"I don't think it's going to be what you're used to," Miller said loudly from behind us. I turned, shoving away my frustration at having been interrupted, as my bodyguard wiggled a set of car keys high in the air.

"It's a moped, isn't it?" Cooper said, laughing in earnest for the first time in hours. "Fuck me sideways, no private jet and now a moped." Miller shot him a dark glare and shook his head.

"No, it's the—" He punched the key fob a few times, and I whipped my head around to see the headlights of a compact Kia flashing rapidly, illuminating the place. He was right, it wasn't the kind of car I was used to, but I didn't care. There was so much more to worry about than what car took me from point A to point B.

Like the migraine that was gradually forming on the left side of my skull.

Like my parents still not calling me back; like the money that would be deposited into my account in a few days and the fact I was going to start shooting the remake of a movie in a couple weeks.

Like Cooper.

"It's small," I said, sticking my hands into the pockets of my tight denim shorts. I looked up at my bodyguard and cocked my head. "Can you even fit in that thing?"

Miller paused at the curb, lifted his eyebrow at me. "I've fit in smaller." Then he grabbed our luggage and ambled to the Kia.

I didn't know how to take that, so I just nodded.

Cooper began to walk away. Frantic to make things right, I grabbed his upper arm, curling my fingers around muscle. "Wait, I need to talk to you," I said. His eyebrow shot up, but he lagged behind. "Look, what happened in L.A. with that kid . . . it wasn't what you thought, I wasn't purposely being rude," I said.

"I know you weren't. It's not even about that. It's just you. Sorry I overreacted, but"—he paused for a moment and a strained smile quirked the corners of his lips—"you're going to bring out the worst in me."

The worst in him? He was at least a half foot taller than my five-foot-six, so I tilted my head back to stare up into his blue eyes. "Because I'm an actress?" I demanded.

Cooper's halo of golden hair drifted when a hot breeze whispered through the garage, and he moved his head slowly from side to side. He pulled his arm out of my grip and placed his hands on my shoulders. Tossing a quick glance at Miller, who was waiting quietly inside the idling Kia and glued to his phone, Cooper dropped his voice to an uneven whisper. "Because I can already tell you're going to give me a hard time, Wills."

"You don't even know me enough to judge," I snapped. He grimaced.

"Stop jumping to conclusions," he said, his jaw tightening. "I don't care what you've done in the past, okay? I'm worried about what's going to happen in the future."

I scraped the bottom of my foot anxiously across the concrete as I waited for him to explain. It was the least he could offer me since that lip-numbing kiss I'd craved—correction: was *still* craving—was obviously out of the equation.

"I make it a point not to hook up with people I've been hired to work with," he said.

My head spun for a moment, and I just stared up at him. His fingertips dug into my shoulders. Could this guy get any cockier? "Okay, for starters, you've known me for, like, two seconds. Two . . . what makes you think I'd even go for it?"

"Don't be ridiculous. You're Willow Avery—everyone knows you." When I sunk my teeth into my bottom lip to hold back a rude reply, he added, "And besides, you wear your emotions on the sleeve of your"—he dropped his gaze to my blouse, plucking a piece of fabric between his fingertips—"flannel shirt."

I scoffed, finally breaking away from his grip. I leaned back and crossed my arms over my body. "Thought you said I was mechanical."

"Not when you're flustered." He took a couple steps backward, making his way in the opposite direction of our rented Kia. "Good night, Wills," he said once he reached the exit.

"Wait—where the hell are you going?" I called out, frustrated.

He opened the door, glanced over his shoulder, and then said in what could only be described as a Hollywood exit, "I live here, remember? Long-term parking, where I left my car."

No, I didn't *remember* that he lived in Honolulu because he'd never *told* me. Up until now I'd assumed he'd come to Los Angeles from Australia, because of the accent. I watched his body disappear around the corner then stalked across the concrete, to the Kia. When I slammed into the passenger seat, Miller shot me an amused glance that clearly told me what he was thinking.

"It's not even like that," I snapped.

"No idea what you're talking about," he answered immediately, stifling a laugh. He stared straight ahead, but the big-ass smile sliding across his face said it all.

Once we escaped the airport chaos, traffic was scarce. I drank in the sights as the sun slowly set, nervously chewing a piece of gum Miller gave me. Thirty minutes later, he parked the Kia in a driveway belonging to a small, wood-framed home that was more garage than house. I opened the car door and the moment I slid out, I heard the rush of the sea nearby. I could smell and taste the salt hanging in the air, even though this place wasn't oceanfront.

"It's empty," I murmured, feeling a surge of panic rush through me. It was just after eight and there was practically nobody outside, except for a few kids playing basketball at the end of the cul-de-sac. This place was empty and organized with none of the commotion I craved. Pulling in a deep breath, I forced myself to calm down, to focus on the positives. Like the sound of the waves.

Loud and distracting, just the way I liked it.

If I was lucky, that noise would lull me into a dreamless sleep tonight, and every other night I was here. That sound would be just enough to drown out the what-ifs and images that met me whenever I closed my eyes—enough to keep me from sinking myself into something else I'd never emerge from.

No more fucking myself over, I silently promised.

Miller cleared his throat, drawing my attention to where he stood a foot away, leaning against the hood of the car. In the shadows of the sunset, he looked absolutely menacing, but he wore that laid-back smile that had kept me from getting too pissed when he'd silently teased me about Cooper.

"Guess you're not used to this either?" he asked. I followed his eyes back to the front of the tiny house and exhaled.

"At least it's not rehab," I whispered so softly I wasn't sure he heard me.

He walked around the car and opened the trunk. When he closed it a moment later, my rolling bag and his own luggage were enveloped between his massive arms. I tried to take my suitcase but he grunted.

"This is my job," he said.

I led the way to the house. "You make me feel like a runt."

"That's my job too," he replied.

I glanced over my shoulder and nodded my head stiffly in understanding. The sad part was I hadn't always needed a bodyguard. There'd been a time, about four or five years ago, when I was well-known enough to get amazing parts but not so famous that I needed to be protected. To be honest, it sucked to have fallen far enough to get only the parts nobody else wanted and yet still be *that* actress, the one who was so notorious the studio had to hire bodyguards, aka babysitters. Miller was probably getting paid more than I was.

I felt my smile slip.

His own look faltered and he took a hesitant step forward. "Are you okay?" he asked.

Bobbing my head a little too enthusiastically, I turned back toward the front door and opened the lockbox with the code Kevin had given me. There were two sets of keys, and I dropped one into Miller's outstretched palm.

"Don't bust through the ceiling, Lurch. The tabloids would be all over me for trashing a rental house," I said, trying to lighten the mood. Miller tossed his head back and howled with laughter, but the inside of my chest felt hollow, clenched. I focused on unlocking the door so he wouldn't see the look on my face.

"I'll do my best," he replied seriously.

I waited to go inside the house until I heard the sound of his feet scraping on the wooden stairs that led up to his apartment. The moment I opened the door, I felt sick to my stomach. It was suffocatingly hot. I stumbled a few steps backward so I could stand in the doorway and get fresh air. Gripping the wooden frame, I gasped deeply, taking each breath as if it were my last.

I needed to pull myself the hell together.

I needed to walk into that house and go to bed because tomorrow morning, I would have to face Cooper. I needed—

My cell phone vibrated in my back pocket, indicating a text message, and broke my erratic thought process. As I finally stepped inside, shutting the door behind me with the back of my foot, I pulled my phone out. I found the thermostat and adjusted it to the lowest possible setting, then sank down on the worn, brown suede sofa to check my messages.

There were three. Two from my mother—one to tell me the fridge had been stocked with my favorites (I already knew that because Kevin's assistant had told Miller, who had told me hours ago) and the other to say a mover would be dropping off several of my things in the next two days and that she and Dad missed me.

"Phone not working, my ass," I said as I typed a reply, thinking of the lie Kevin had told me this morning in my hotel room.

Thanks. Can't wait to talk.

I expected the other message to be from Jessica since she had yet to call or text me, but it came from an unknown number with an 808 area code. A Hawaii area code, I realized, as I glanced at an outdated calendar across the room that advertised a local insurance agency. I opened the message, 99 percent sure who sent it, despite the fact that I never gave him my phone number.

**8:14 p.m.: Let's try this again . . . I'm sorry,
Wills. Want to do something together?
Neither of us wants to be alone tonight.**

"You confusing, crazy boy," I whispered, shaking my head in disbelief. I positioned my fingers over the smooth keypad, ready to tell him off—to let him know I'd been dealing with his type for years—but then I thought better of it. I called him instead.

"I took you for more of a texter," he said the moment he picked up. I could hear the sound of waves crashing behind him.

"Some things come out better if they're said aloud."

"Like?"

"Like hi Cooper, this is Willow. Thanks for the invitation but I'm *not* fucking you tonight."

A low growl came from the back of his throat, and I heard a thud as he sat down heavily. "That's why I sent the other message, Wills," he said in an admonishing voice. I looked at the screen, and sure enough, there was a second text sent around the time I dialed him.

**8:19 p.m.: That sounded like I was trying to
get into your panties, didn't it? I'm not.**

"I call bull. And besides, I thought you called them knickers," I said. He chuckled. Ugh, even his laugh had a sexy accent. I stretched out on the couch, letting the pitiful AC unit fan my face as I shrugged out of my long-sleeved flannel shirt.

"I don't sleep with clients," he said. "And I've not lived in

Australia for ten years, since I was twelve when my mum and I moved to Hawaii."

"Whatever." I kicked my shoes off. "Good night, Cooper," I said, echoing his final words to me at the airport.

"I'm picking you up in fifteen minutes."

"Wait—what?" I demanded, bolting upright. Suddenly, my heart was pounding wildly and my mouth went dry. I raked my hand through my dark-brown hair. "No. I mean, for *what*?"

"You've got to eat, Wills—nobody wants to pay to watch a sickly looking surfer. And besides, it's my job to look after you."

"Don't you think you're taking what Dickson's paying you to do a little too far?"

"Nothing to do with Dickson."

"What happened to your rule about clients?" I pointed out, my voice coming out in gasps. "You change your mind?"

He paused for a moment, and I heard a door slam shut. His car engine revved up, a Bruno Mars song about getting locked out of paradise blasting my eardrums. I flinched but then he cut the sound so I could hear him laughing quietly.

"Getting dinner with you isn't breaking my rule . . . as long as we both know when to quit," he said.

Hugging my free arm around my lower stomach in an attempt to still the butterflies that were beating their wings violently inside of me, I flicked my tongue over dry lips. "Haven't you heard? I don't know when to quit."

Which was probably why I was having a hard time resisting the urge to flirt with Cooper.

He was silent again. I listened to his breathing, and what

sounded like wind sifting through a cracked window, as I raveled my hands into the fabric of my tank top. Even though I didn't want to have dinner with him, I wanted him to talk. I needed words and noise.

Cooper sighed. "So I lied."

"About your rules?"

"No, about the fifteen-minute thing. I'm pulling into your driveway."

"You're kidding," I said.

"Nope . . . I'm the one who suggested the place to your parents. My friend Paige's parents own it." As if to prove his point, he flashed his headlights multiple times.

Fucking stalker.

Anger compelled me up and off the couch. I reached the front door just as he was lifting his hand to knock. There were tiny grains of sand stuck to the tip of his straight nose and his hair was wet, disheveled. I wanted to tangle my hands into it and pull him inside and—

Thinking like that is what started all your problems three years ago, a nasty voice in the back of my head snarled.

"You're my coach," I said in a warning tone that was directed more at me than him. "And we've already established you have rules. I'm not going out to dinner with you." I disregarded the pangs of hunger in the pit of my stomach. There was plenty of food in the refrigerator.

"Point taken. I just—ah, fuck it." And then, he pulled me to him, roughly, pressing me up against the doorframe and pinning my hands above my head so that the uneven wood scratched the tips of my fingers. His lips were soft and tasted like salt, and I moaned against them as his tongue spread mine apart. When a car crept down the street, the headlights beaming against the sides of our faces for a brief moment, our bodies moved inside in unison, slamming the door shut with our sides.

"Wanted to test a theory," he growled, putting my back up against the door. He raced his hands up my body, leaving a trail of heat wherever they touched, until he reached the sides of my face.

What the hell kind of theory was he testing?

"I'm not screwing you," I groaned. He kissed me again, this time harder. He sucked my lower lip between his teeth, tugging gently until my breath came out in short, choppy pants, until I was about five seconds from coming undone. I reached up and ran my shaky hands through his damp golden hair, and yanked his head back until my gaze was level with his blue eyes. "I'm not going to fuck you," I repeated, my voice stern.

"I don't have any intention of trying, Wills. I just needed to get this out of my head before tomorrow."

My breath caught on an exhale, and I just looked at him for a long moment. I'd wanted the exact same thing and now that I had it, letting go of it was going to be a pain in the ass. He went in for another kiss, but I tightened my clench on his hair. He winced but grinned.

"And now that you've done what you came here for . . . ?" I demanded.

He rubbed his thumb across my lips before reluctantly backing away from me. He sat on the arm of the burgundy recliner a few feet from the door, gazing at me intensely, and pushed his hand through his wavy hair.

"Well?" I asked, as I adjusted my tank top. It had ridden up to my belly button and I pulled it down, stretching it over the waistband of my shorts.

"You taste like bubble gum," he whispered, and I slumped backward. Bubble gum and salt, I thought. What a screwed-up combination. He stood and slowly came back to me. I clenched my fists by my side so I wouldn't reach out to him.

I absolutely cannot get involved with this guy.

He placed a soft kiss at my temple, trailing it across my high cheekbone. I would have called the gesture demure—if he hadn't captured my lips with his one final time, kissing me almost desperately.

But God, Surfer Boy has a mouth on him.

I was the one who pulled away, gasping for air as I shoved him from my body. I kept my gaze directed at the floor when I opened the door for him. I pointed outside. "I think you've gotten it out of your head. Good night, Cooper," I said.

"Good night, Willow. See you first thing in the morning, bright and early."

"I'll be waiting," I said as dryly as possible, wishing my pulse would slow down and that I didn't feel that infuriating pull between my legs.

As he walked out to a newish Jeep Wrangler, I stared after him for far too long. Our eyes connected once more before he

drove off and he gave me a half smile. I slunk back inside, re-
signing myself to an evening of loneliness with whatever healthy
bullshit Kevin had had delivered to the house.

At least tonight, for the first time, Cooper had called me
Willow without mocking me. That had to count for something.

CHAPTER FOUR

~~~~~~~~~~~~~~~~~~~~~~~~~~~

True to his word, Cooper showed up at my rental at five thirty in the morning. Wiping the sleep from my eyes with the backs of my hands, I met him at the door wearing nothing but a signed T-shirt that had belonged to Gavin, my pre-rehab boyfriend. The loser had broken up with me via a letter written by some employee of the network that aired his lame boy-band TV show. The shirt barely covered my thighs and as Cooper's bright-blue eyes combed over my body—starting at my bare feet and working his way up—I snapped completely awake.

Snorting, I pulled the door completely open. "Not very discreet, are you?" It was still dark outside, and I groaned out loud as I gestured for him to come in. He shook his head and took a step backward onto the veranda. I stretched my neck to see his Jeep was still cranked. Frowning, I asked, "In a rush?"

"Overslept," he said. "So yeah, guess we are."

I leaned my weight against the doorframe. "Sleep is good for you sometimes."

He worked his jaw back and forth. "Didn't get too much of that after I left here." Those blue eyes seemed to stare right into me, as he waited for some kind of response. Did he mean that he couldn't get our kiss off his mind or that he went somewhere else? To sleep with someone else?

"Hard night of partying?" I asked in the most nonchalant voice I could muster, pulling my fingertips through my messy hair. Then, I yawned into my palm to show I didn't care. Because I shouldn't care. I shouldn't have been drawn to Cooper when I needed to focus on getting myself back on track.

But the idea of his leaving my place to screw some other girl made my stomach harden.

Crossing his arms over his chest, he shrugged. "Not really. Listen, I'm going to wait in the Jeep. Meet me out here in ten minutes."

I narrowed my eyes and, tugging the hem of my T-shirt down, stalked barefoot across the lanai until I was so close to him our toes touched. Though he sucked in a gasp of air, his relaxed expression never faltered. "You're enjoying this, aren't you?" I demanded. One of his eyebrows lifted up high.

"What?"

I pursed my lip, biting the inside of my lower one. He raked his top teeth over the corner of his mouth, and my mind was immediately pulled back to the way he'd done the same to mine last night. The weight in my stomach changed from jealousy to something entirely different.

Need.

God, I was a wreck. I'd spent so many years dulling away emotions, going through the motions without feeling, that now I couldn't even handle being attracted to someone. "Nothing," I said, spinning around to head back inside. When I turned to close the door, he stood right in front of me, with a confused look on his face.

"What?" he asked once again.

I rolled my eyes. "You figure it out. I'll be out in fifteen minutes and you can—"

Cooper shoved his foot into the house. "Stop," he ordered. He pushed the door open far enough to step inside. Anger mixed with the desire that was surging through my body, compelling me forward.

I pointed past him at the idling Jeep. "I thought we were running late."

He glanced down for a second, as if he were trying to come up with just what to say, and when his head popped back up, there was laughter in his blue eyes. Screw him for mocking me.

"We *are* running late, but the answer to your question about me enjoying this is no. No guy enjoys getting worked up just to have to go home and lie in bed with a hard-on."

My mouth fell open, but I quickly recovered. "That was your own damn fault. Shouldn't have gone testing theories," I said.

He was holding back a grin; I could tell by the way his lips quivered. Giving me an intense look that made the edges of my senses blur, he said, "You're right."

He was agreeing with me. What. The. Fuck? Before I could say anything, he curved his hand around the back of my head, drawing me in to him. "Don't," I whispered. But the sad part was I wanted Cooper to kiss me again, just like last night.

Except, nothing happened. He and I just stood there, our bodies practically wrapped around each other, our lips an inch or two from crushing together. He tangled his fingertips gently into the hair at my nape, and the pit of my belly flooded with warmth. I sighed, twisting my head slightly to one side.

"You're right, I shouldn't. We'll do this when there's not work to be done," he whispered, his breath fanning my mouth. Then he pulled away. "See you in ten minutes."

I watched as he jogged to his Jeep, angry at myself for being so disappointed he hadn't kissed me. When he climbed into the front seat and flashed me a grin, I finally slammed the door, rattling it on the hinges.

Pull it together, Willow, I warned myself.

Twelve minutes later, after changing into a one-piece swimsuit, a neon-green tank top, shorts, and flip-flops, I shuffled outside. Cooper's Jeep smelled like coconut, like his hair, and I shivered at the thought of how I'd pulled my fingers through it the night before.

"You look nice," he said, putting the SUV into reverse and backing out the narrow driveway. When we reached the mailbox, something hit me.

"Hey, stop," I said, and he slammed on the brakes. I pointed up at the little apartment over the garage. "I should tell my body-guard where I'm going."

He shook his head. "I've already spoken to him—we're going out alone." When I whirled on him, he held up his hands defensively. "Look, I want you to be relaxed. I don't want some big-ass bodyguard making you nervous."

He'd gone over my head and talked to Miller?

"You mean he makes you nervous." Annoyed, I crossed my arms. "I'm fine with him being around," I said.

Cooper released a sarcastic laugh. Then he finished backing into the street and put the car into drive. "I should punch you in the face," I muttered as he took off, going ten miles over the speed limit.

"What's stopping you then?"

"I'm on probation."

He laughed again, but this time there wasn't a mocking edge to it. He almost sounded like he felt sorry for me, which only served to make me angrier. "And just so you know, Wills, your bodyguard doesn't make me nervous—not even a bit. I don't think you have anything to worry about here, but I won't let anything happen to you. Not ever when you're with me." There was a roughness to his voice that made it impossible for me to doubt what he'd said.

Not even a bit.

Instead of going directly to the shore, Cooper took me to a two-story beach home surrounded by palm trees. "This is Kailua Beach," he explained as he parked his Jeep behind a Ford Ranger that was probably as old as I was. "And this is where I live . . . and work."

I squinted at the sand-colored stucco house. Sure enough, there was a wooden sign hanging above the front door that said BLUE FLAME SURFING ACADEMY. I raised an eyebrow and he lifted his shoulders. "I forgot to grab our boards," he said. "My mind was . . . occupied."

When he got out of the Jeep, I followed behind him, hot on his heels. "So you live with your boss, not an actual roommate?"

He gave me one of those grins that nearly stopped me in my tracks. There was a deep dimple in his left cheek that I hadn't noticed before. "Well, technically, my roommate lives with his boss."

This time, I really did stop walking. "You own your own surfing school?" I squeaked.

Flashing me a confident look, he said, "I'm the best, re-member?"

He sprinted up the steps and disappeared inside the stucco house. I stood there, staring through the open door into the brightly lit foyer for a few moments. Cooper was twenty-two— he'd said as much last night when he told me he'd left Australia ten years ago when he was twelve. I was sure he made good money competing and teaching people to surf, but this place was amazing. Oceanfront, two stories, and on a private lot—no doubt it cost a fortune.

"Ugh, stop it Willow," I said aloud. Just because I sucked at holding on to money didn't mean Cooper was the same.

Walking up the stone steps, I reminded myself that how Cooper afforded his belongings was none of my damn business. When I reached the foyer, which smelled like sunblock and Clean Linen PlugIns, I followed the sound of voices around the corner into a shop area, complete with T-shirts and surfing gear.

Cooper was on the other side of the most unusual sales counter I'd ever seen—it was made of old surfboards with writing all over them. He was talking to a guy wearing nothing but boxer shorts who was as tall as Miller and probably weighed less than I did. The moment I stepped into view, their conversation faded and the guy dragged his hands through his messy brown hair. He was by no means sexy, like Cooper, or even good-looking for that matter—his grungy facial hair would make Zach Galifianakis weep with pride—but when he grinned at me, I couldn't resist smiling back.

"I'm Cooper's roommate," he said. There was a humorous gleam in his brown eyes when he added, "I used to jack off to your music videos."

Nice introduction.

I'd been a horrible singer and all my music—one album's worth—had been heavily autotuned. At least the music videos were sexy, according to Cooper's pervert roommate. "How'd that work out for you?" I asked, unsure whether I should laugh or run in the other direction.

"Not so bad . . . if you don't count the tanning lotion disaster."

Oh my God—what the hell was wrong with this guy?

Skinny Roommate grinned and walked over to me, holding

out his hand. I looked down at it, disgusted, before I turned my head to the side and gave him a skeptical look. "Oh come on, that was a long time ago," he said, holding up both hands and wiggling them a few inches from my face. "See, no tan streaks."

Gross.

He was totally crass, but for some reason, I started to laugh. It was a welcome distraction from thinking about Cooper. Skinny Roommate pulled me in for a big hug, hunching over so he could inhale my hair. I took a step backward to separate our crotches so he wouldn't get any more strokes of inspiration. "God, who would've thought Willow Avery smelled like peaches. Peaches and—"

"Stop feeling up my client, Eric," Cooper warned. Eric sniffed me a few more times and then, groaning loudly, pulled away.

He gave Cooper a dramatic glare. "You get all the fun ones."

Cooper ignored him. "He's got a girlfriend. He doesn't surf," he said, as he slung a black backpack over his shoulder. He lifted two long surfboards from behind the counter and tucked them under his arm. "And he's a bum."

Eric leaned against the counter, puffing his chest out. "Guess it goes along with being the son of Rick, the resident lazy, pill-dealing douchebag." He turned his gaze on me. "Word of advice, don't buy your shit from him. He'll turn on you like *that*."

As he snapped his fingers to emphasize the final word, my gaze dropped to the floor. I could take jokes about him getting off with tanning lotion without so much as blinking an eye but the moment he mentioned my escape of choice, my whole body burned. I knew it was another joke, that he probably hadn't even thought about what he was saying, and yet I felt like he knew every thought that had crossed my mind in the past few days.

I felt as if I were standing in a room full of people snapping photos of me, judging my every move, my every word. Judging whether or not I'd suddenly cave and wind right back up in rehab.

I wouldn't.

I put on my most convincing smile—the look of someone totally fixed and not screwed-up. It was my best role to date, and a recurring one at that. Then, I lifted my head. "Noted," I said in a confident voice.

Eric's face was red and Cooper was glaring at him. Eric didn't even glance at me when he said, "You kids have fun and no touching in bad places."

"Stay away from the tanning lotion," I retorted, as Cooper motioned for me to follow him out the double doors behind the counter. Eric's laughter made me glance back and he was beaming at me again.

"Is he always like that?" I asked Cooper as we walked down the short, tiled hallway and outside to a beamed wooden deck. There were strings of lantern lights hanging above our heads, but I didn't have time to look at them closely. He was already heading out toward the beach. I left my bag and phone under a chair.

"Eric's like that every day," Cooper answered once I caught

up with him. We trekked through the sand toward the beach, our bodies so close the back of my hand skimmed the smooth edge of one of the boards he carried.

"You're kind of an odd couple."

He grinned and I felt my lips move into a smile too. "The oddest." He stopped, fifteen feet from the shoreline, and I backed up a few steps and watched as he situated our boards down on the sand. When he rose to his feet, he stared out at the sea and said, "Eric was my roommate freshman year at UH and I guess you can say we hit it off. Rick—his dad—kicked him out a few months ago when we graduated and he's been living with me ever since."

"Even though he uses tanning lotion for lube and teases you about your girly coconut shampoo?" I joked.

"He's honest," Cooper said matter-of-factly. He dragged his shirt over his head, and my eyes greedily drank in his bare skin, starting from the small of his back and working my way up to a jagged, diagonal scar that went from just under his right armpit to his left shoulder blade.

When I winced, he turned to face me and gave me a bitter smile. "Ready to do this?" Without another word, he stuffed his shirt inside his black bag, swooped up our boards, and jogged down to the edge of the water.

Sighing, I pulled off my own top and shimmied out of my shorts, rolling them into a wad. Cooper shielded his eyes from the sun with one hand and called out, "Didn't take you for a one-piece type of girl."

As I walked toward him, I found myself hugging my

balled-up clothes tight to my abdomen, creating friction against my own scar until my skin ached. "There's a lot you don't take me for, huh?" I said when I came close enough to touch him.

He winked at me. "Just makes getting to know you more interesting."

CHAPTER FIVE

Cooper didn't elaborate on what he said, not that I expected him to, but that didn't stop me from wanting and needing more from him. Was this how it was going to be? Little comments—offhand remarks—that would haunt me long after they slipped past his lips?

"The sea is amazing this morning," Cooper said at last, breaking the silence. "It's unpredictable and moody—and you never know when it'll try to screw you over—but I can't stay away." He turned to stare out at the unending blue, which gleamed under the clear morning sky. I took two wobbly steps forward, following his gaze with my own. To me the sea didn't seem any different from any other time I'd looked at it. It was still frightening.

But that hazy expression that took over his face, the way

every hard line of his body seemed to gravitate toward the waves . . . I'd be lying if I said I didn't long to feel that passionate about something other than the one thing I couldn't—no, shouldn't—have.

Just as long as that *something* wouldn't drown me, landing me in rehab again.

"It's nice," I said. A blast of cold foam hit my bare feet, causing me to suck in a deep breath, but he didn't notice. He was mesmerized. Too transfixed to realize when I stopped gazing at the ocean to take a few steps backward. So rooted to the spot that he didn't feel my gaze heating the side of his face, peering at the tattoo written across his rib cage—I couldn't make out what it said—and again to the scar on his back.

Had he gotten it surfing?

When I closed my eyes for a moment, I pictured myself getting a similar scar while training with Cooper, and I shuddered.

Not today, Willow. Focus on him, on learning this shit, and not on the what-ifs.

I opened my eyes and sucked in a deep breath. "You ever gotten hurt surfing?" I asked in a husky voice. It seemed better than coming right out and asking how he'd gotten injured. He turned his head a fraction to give me an amused look. I let him study me for another thirty seconds, then I snorted, crossing my arms over my chest. Did he have to make me feel like his blue eyes were burning two holes into my face?

"It's a simple yes-or-no question," I stated.

"You ever gotten hurt acting?" he asked.

All the time. I could have told him what I was really thinking, that acting had hurt me more emotionally than physically, but then I cleared my throat and shrugged. I pretended to be interested in a piece of lint on my swimsuit. "If you count stubbing a toe or breaking a fingernail on a prop, then yeah. Guess I have."

A flicker of disappointment passed over his face but it disappeared almost immediately. He sighed and scratched his head before sweeping his hand out at the ocean. "You're going to get hurt," he said. "A lot. Hell, you'll probably be black and blue by the time the rest of the cast gets here."

"Thanks for the vote of confidence," I replied dryly as he squatted down and repositioned our boards a few feet apart in the sand.

He winked up at me, and I told myself it was because the breeze chose that exact moment to send strands of golden hair into his eyes and not because he was being a sarcastic asshole.

"I'm not being a dick, Wills." He nodded his head at the spot in front of the purple-and-white board as he patted it with one hand. I ran my tongue along the inside of my cheek, jabbing the tender flesh hard, to keep from telling him to fuck off. When he cocked an eyebrow, I sighed deeply and kneeled beside him in the sand.

"Don't tell me we're going to meditate."

"Remember what I said about people in the film industry?" he asked.

"You hate them?"

He looked down at his turquoise-and-red board for a few moments, frowning as if he were trying to make up his mind about something. "Don't fuck with me or I'll drown you," he finally muttered. He was grinning when he said it.

I clenched my fingers into the sand, grabbing up two big handfuls.

"We're starting with some basics," he replied, his blue eyes gazing at me fixedly. "No going out for you today."

"What type of basics?" I released the sand from my fingers and dusted my palms together.

"For some reason I feel like you wanted to throw that in my eyes," he teased. I wrinkled my nose at him. "Lie down on your board, on your stomach."

Reluctantly, I stretched out on the smooth surface, so that my face was an inch from the retro-looking Channel Islands logo. Tossing my long hair over one shoulder, I looked up at him in time to catch his eyes raking over my body. Jesus, this guy wasn't the least bit concerned about being obvious, was he?

"Maybe I should have brought my bodyguard," I snapped.

He shuffled over to me, repositioning me so that my body was completely centered on the board. As he worked, he said, "If we went to bed together it wouldn't be on the beach. Though I do plan on seeing you in that exact position, fully unclothed."

I scoffed, twisting my neck to follow his movements as he crawled around me to examine my form. "Confident, are you?"

He paused. "It was a hypothetical statement, but as a matter of fact, I am."

"Are you this hypothetical about all the girls you train?" I asked.

He lifted one of my feet, spending entirely too long touching his fingertips to its arch, before he placed it down against the end of the board. "Put your other foot just like that," he ordered. I complied, and he added, "And no, I'm not like this with all the girls I train because I don't get involved with my clients. At least, I haven't yet."

Why did that sound so hot coming from him in *that* accent?

"And what makes me different?"

He came around to face me, to study me a little more. I felt totally exposed lying there facedown. I placed my head inside the diamond shape made by my outstretched arms. "Who said you were?" he asked finally.

I didn't immediately lift my head back up because I didn't want him to see the flush that spread across my face.

For the next two hours, we worked on Cooper's basics: popping up on the surfboard and form. After the eightieth time of doing the pop-ups—the point where I felt like my legs and arms were going to fall off from pushing myself up and standing in a lunge in the middle of the surfboard—he looked pleased.

"Did you just fist pump?" I groaned irritably as I turned over onto my back in the sand. I gave the purple board a glare. I didn't want to see the damn thing for at least a day or two— that's how badly my muscles already ached.

Smiling, he said, "Proud of you, Wills. You're getting there."

I rolled my eyes as he began dusting the sand off both our surfboards. "I didn't do anything," I pointed out, hoisting myself up on my elbows so our eyes could meet.

"Sure you did. You didn't flounce, did you?"

At least his standards for giving me praise were low.

He held my board out to me. Grumbling, I got up, grabbed my shorts and tank top, and took the surfboard with both hands. "Here, carry it on top of your head, like this." He flipped his own upside down, and centered it on his head.

"Why?"

He released a loud breath. "Because, you want to look like you know what you're doing when the time comes. And it's not like we've been given a lot of time to train."

He was right, and I felt my stomach twist at the thought. In less than two weeks I'd be filming a movie. A fucking surfing movie that already had a devout fan following.

I shuddered and then balanced my board on my head.

"God, this thing is heavy," I said, as we slogged through the sand in the direction of his house or business or whatever the hell he wanted to call it. "And by the way, you carried them out here in your hands before."

He shot me a cocky grin. "Yeah, you can do it either way." When we stepped onto the deck, he set his board on a wooden bench and lifted mine easily from atop my head.

"So why not do it the other way?"

"Because you're flustered."

"Less inhuman . . . much more beautiful."

Remembering the words he spoke to me in LAX caused the pit of my stomach to tighten but I ignored the feeling. "If only I could fire your ass," I said.

He moved so close to me his tanned chest touched mine. "You can't." Then he lifted a strand of my hair, sliding it back and forth between his fingertips. "And you don't want to."

The sound of the deck door swinging open sent him pulling me to him protectively, and I instinctively lifted my hands to cover my face from the flash I was sure would follow.

Even here, the cameras could find me.

"God, you'd think I had a gun!" a deep female voice said, laughing.

"Paige," Cooper warned through clenched teeth. He stepped aside to reveal a pint-sized woman with tattooed arms, short black hair, and hazel eyes that seemed to pop thanks to jet-black eyeliner. She lifted her eyebrows at Cooper and tapped her foot impatiently. He let out a groan and added, "Wills, this is Paige. She's an instructor here."

Paige. The friend whose parents owned my rental house.

"I'm Eric's girlfriend," she said, grinning.

The Coppertone guy who'd admitted to masturbating to me a few hours ago. Awkward.

"I'm Willow."

"She knows," Cooper said at the exact same time Paige said, "Nice to meet you."

Shooting him a glare, she told me, "I made breakfast."

"I've got to get back to my rental to study my script." It was partially the truth. There was only so much a line prompter could do for me. And of course I wanted to get away from Cooper because I was sure being around him much longer would pull apart my sanity until there was nothing left but a handful of frayed thread.

"Oh come on, you can spare an hour, right?" Paige asked. When I shook my head, she walked across the wooden deck and grabbed my hand. I flinched, but she didn't seem to notice. "I've been dying to meet you, Avery, and I made pancakes."

Paige seemed nice enough—she was smiling at me hopefully—and from somewhere inside the house, Eric yelled, "Tell her I'll eat naked." But when I looked over at Cooper and saw how annoyed he looked, I pulled my hand out of her grasp.

"I think I'll just pass today."

She frowned but seemed understanding as she nodded her head. "Next time, then?"

"Definitely," I said.

The ride back to my rental house was filled with an uncomfortable silence that made me wish the Jeep's floorboard would open up and swallow me or at least spit me out onto the asphalt. When we turned onto my street, I was thankful to see the moving truck parked in the driveway. Miller was directing the guys handling my stuff, and when he saw us pull up, he gave us a little nod of his head and a sideways smile.

I was already trying to jump out of the Jeep before Cooper put it into park.

"Wait," he ordered, and I froze with my fingers wrapped around the door handle.

"What?" My tone was clipped.

He took a deep breath and I waited for a Hollywood-esque apology. For him to ask me to breakfast or make another wiseass, blatant attempt to get into my shorts. When he spoke a moment later, I didn't get either of those. "I'm giving a lesson first thing tomorrow, so have your bodyguard drop you off at my place at nine."

I turned my head to smirk at him. "Why don't you just come

to me and we can practice popping up and down on a surfboard on my front lawn?"

He gave me a slow, lazy grin that managed to dig its way under my skin and rub me raw. "I like you much better in my element, Wills."

Of course he did. I stumbled out of the Jeep, slammed the door behind me, and stalked into the house without as much as a backward glance. The whole time, I felt his laughing blue eyes following me.

For the first time in what felt like ages, my mother kept her word about getting in touch with me. Miller and I were in the middle of going through boxes that had been delivered—a lot of them full of clothes that were too small or too big from my fluctuating weight—when my cell phone buzzed.

"It's my mom and dad," I said, looking down at the screen as PARENTS scrolled across it in neon-green lettering. I sank down on the edge of the couch.

Miller pushed himself up to his feet and started toward the front door. "Want to text me when you need me again?" he asked, glancing back.

I hesitated. Helping me sort through my belongings wasn't a part of Miller's job description. I knew he was only doing it to be nice because he felt sorry for me for being alone, but dammit if I didn't want to keep him with me for the conversation. The phone vibrated on the coffee table, and I felt my ears burn from the sound and the potential humiliation.

This was day four of being out of rehab and my first call from my family. God only knew when or if any of my friends would ever call.

"Willow?" Miller asked.

"I should be okay," I said. "I've got to study my lines and watch the original version of the film." It was a gift from Dickson, my producer, which had come in the mail this afternoon along with a note saying how happy he was to be working with me again.

"I'm going to go work out. You call me if you change your mind?"

"Will do," I said quickly. The moment the screen door shut and Miller disappeared from sight I answered the phone, tucking it in the spot between my ear and shoulder. "Mom?" I asked.

"You sound so good, honey!" she immediately gushed.

"It's good to hear you too."

"Have you been doing . . . well?" she asked tentatively.

Translation: Are you popping a rainbow variety of pills yet? I grabbed a box of shoes from the other end of the sofa, crushing the cardboard between my hands as I carried it to my bedroom at the back of the house.

"No," I said, and then shook my head furiously. "I mean yes. I'm doing great. Rehab worked wonders and I feel great."

Except for every now and then, when I catch myself wanting to reduce every sense in my body to nothing, I silently added.

"How's Hawaii? Do you love it? Are you taking lots of pictures?"

I thought of Cooper and the frustrating insta-lust I felt toward him and threw the box of shoes to the floor. I knelt down beside it. "It's . . . nice."

"I don't like that voice," Mom said. "What's wrong?"

Cooper.

But I wasn't going to get into relationships with my mom because she'd pick me apart with a million questions. Are you taking your birth control? Are you using condoms? You're not . . . *you know* . . . again, right? I changed the subject. "We start shooting in like ten days." It was a lame change of pace, but her voice perked right back up.

"I know, aren't you excited?"

"Why didn't you and Dad let me know you had a part lined up for me?" I asked, shoving a pair of Christian Louboutin pumps to the back of the closet. One of them tipped over to the side, its bright-red sole facing up at me.

"We didn't want to overwhelm you."

"Mom, you sent me details about the gazillion lawsuits against me. I could've handled a damn part or, you know, a script."

She sucked in a deep breath. "Don't be rude, Willow."

But I wasn't being rude. Rude would be asking my mother where she was when I was released from Serenity Hills a few days ago. Rude would be asking Mom where she was right now. I threw another pair of shoes into the closet and gritted my teeth before asking, "Is Dad around?"

"He's getting dressed for dinner, but he wanted me to tell you to take care of yourself."

Meaning he didn't want to talk to me. That had always been

my father's solution to dealing with my screw-ups, and it was one I had never understood. My counselor at rehab had told me he'd come around after I atoned for my failings. Because according to her, proving myself was the best way to win my father's thumbs-up. I couldn't help but wonder how many people left Serenity Hills with even more fucked-up Daddy issues than they'd arrived with.

"You're being too quiet. Is everything all right?" she asked.

I slid into the closet, pulled my knees up to my chest, and placed my forehead against them. "Have you heard from the lawyer about the case against the agency?" I demanded.

"These things take time," Mom said in a singsong voice.

Because apparently, three fucking years wasn't long enough.

After that, my conversation with my mother went by quickly. She reminded me that I needed to get in touch with my probation officer and start my community service. I rolled my eyes and told her I would. When it was time to hang up, Mom gasped and said, "Damn, before I forget—have you started your personal training yet?"

My neck and shoulders tensed up. "Not yet," I replied in a clipped voice.

"You know it's important for you to stay in shape," she admonished, and suddenly, I remembered her putting me on a diet of grilled chicken salads and water a few years back. She hadn't known what was going on then because I'd been too afraid to tell her, too afraid of my parents finding out what I'd done, but it still made me upset to think about it now.

I just wanted this call to hurry up and end.

"Got it, Mom," I said.

"Good. We love you, Willow."

"Uh-huh. You too."

The moment she disconnected the call, I found the manila folder Kevin had given me a few days before. I pulled the personal trainer's information from the back of the folder. And I heard Cooper's words from a few days earlier echo in my head: *"Nobody wants to see a sickly looking surfer."*

After I ripped the paper into shreds, I sent Miller a text.

> **1:43 p.m.: Do you feel like some sightseeing? You know . . . this is my first time in Hawaii.**

He responded five minutes later with a message that made me heave a sigh of relief.

> **1:48 p.m.: Mine too. Got another hour of working out then we can hit the town.**

It was going to be my first time out "on the town" with a bodyguard that I wasn't too drunk or fucked-up to function.

CHAPTER SIX

~~~~~~~~~~~~~~~~~~

Though I was still on the verge of being broke, Miller and I stayed out late into the evening, walking around a cheap amusement park. He was a welcome change from the bodyguards I'd had before. Not once did he give me that look that clearly conveyed he thought I was a dumb-ass, or worse, that he was picturing me naked. I probably would have stayed out all night, but as Miller and I stood in line to ride the only decent roller coaster in the entire park, he slowly turned to me.

I groaned when I realized he was nervously working his teeth back and forth over his top lip and that his skin was flushed beneath his slowly fading spray tan.

"I hate when people look at me like that," I pointed out,

knowing his sheepish expression meant an end to my night and the noise.

I wasn't at all ready for that.

Miller lifted his muscled shoulders. "Don't you think we should call it a night? I mean, this place is thinning out." He gestured around us at the handful of tourists strolling through the muggy darkness. When we arrived—two or three hours ago—the place was in full swing.

Shoving my giant sunglasses up on my nose, I focused my attention on the front of the line and let the sounds around us wrap me up. "It's only nine," I argued.

Miller snorted. "Yeah, an hour and a half ago." Okay, so we'd been here more than four hours. When I held up my hands in a "so what" motion and gave him an irritated look, he said in a gentle voice, "You're the one who told me two hours ago to make sure you went home before eleven to study your lines and go to bed for your lesson with Billabong, remember?"

If I hadn't been so irritated about making that particular promise to Miller, I would have smiled at his nickname for Cooper. Instead, my frown deepened. Thinking about surf lessons with Cooper made my chest hurt. And the last time my heart or chest or *anything* hurt thinking about a guy . . .

Things ended badly.

"One more hour," I pleaded, and though he looked conflicted, Miller dipped his head. He stepped forward when the person in front of us showed his wristband to the attendant.

"You're just like my kid sister. Okay, one more hour and then I'll carry your ass out of here if I have to."

If any of my friends back in Hollywood knew I was hanging out with my bodyguard as a friend, that he was talking to me as if we'd known each other for years, they'd make a smart-ass comment. They'd ask me if we were sleeping together. Luckily, I wasn't in Hollywood. Besides, my friends' opinions weren't exactly at the top of my list of things to give a shit about since I still hadn't heard from any of them—not even Jessica, who was supposed to be my best.

Giving Miller a smile, which coaxed a gap-toothed grin from him, I crossed my fingertip over my heart. "I promise, only one more hour," I said.

Of course, when my phone rang and woke me up at 8:45 the next morning, I immediately wished I'd chosen to turn in much earlier. Apparently, I was losing my party-girl touch. I answered without opening my eyes to check the ID, letting my fingers wander over the smooth surface of the screen until I found the right button.

"Hello?" I mumbled.

"Hi, I'm trying to reach Willow Avery," a female voice said.

I flew up into a sitting position, brushing my hair out of my eyes. "It's me. Anne?" I asked, thinking it was Kevin's assistant on the line. Now, I was fully alert—wide-eyed and expecting good news.

"No, sorry. This is Officer Stewart from probation."

Fuck my life.

"Oh," I said, unable to hide the drag of disappointment from my voice.

"I was calling to set up your first visit to our office—and to confirm your address."

As I copied down the information Stewart gave me on the back of a scrap piece of paper I found in one of the nightstand drawers, and answered all her questions in a monotone voice, I felt a chill claw down the middle of my chest. It wasn't like I was in danger of failing a random pee test—and I'd failed my fair share of those in Los Angeles with my old probation officer, who overlooked them because Kevin represented his son—and yet I felt like the walls were closing in around me. I felt trapped.

"When are you planning to start your community service?" Office Stewart asked.

I grimaced. I should have known that one was coming. Swallowing back the lump in my throat, I croaked, "I'm not sure. What am I supposed to be doing, exactly?"

"You'll be working at Harmony House," she said. Then she gave me the name and number of the person who'd be supervising me. "So, I'll see you Friday morning, at nine thirty?" she confirmed.

"I'll be there," I said slowly, thinking of how embarrassing it would be to have my bodyguard take me to probation because I didn't have a license. It could be worse, I reminded myself. Like asking Miller to escort me to the gynecologist or making him wait for me while I hooked up with someone in a hotel. I'd never been one for random hookups but I had friends, like Jessica, who had no problem having sex with a new guy every weekend while her bodyguard waited in the car or outside her hotel door.

I looked down at my phone, wincing when I saw the time.

It was 8:58 a.m. and I was supposed to meet Cooper in two minutes. I shot him a message letting him know I was running late, then I sent Miller one telling him I'd be ready to go in five minutes. I changed quickly—today in a modest two-piece that had been delivered with my things yesterday. Somehow, it managed to hide the telltale scar and accentuate my boobs at the same time.

One of my hands was working on the button of my tiny yellow shorts and the other was cramming my face with a whole-wheat waffle that tasted like overcooked cardboard as I ran outside to where Miller was waiting by the Kia. He shook his head, grinning, and got into the driver's side. My phone vibrated in my pocket and I held my waffle between my teeth so I could check it.

Cooper had messaged me back.

> 9:08 a.m.: You know that James Dickson won't be so lenient when you stay out too late partying, right?

I didn't want to care what he thought I spent my spare time doing, but I found myself hesitating before getting inside the car to text him back.

> 9:09 a.m.: Thanks for the heads-up, smart-ass. If my body wasn't so tired from your "basics" I'd probably have gotten up on time.

I slid the phone back into my pocket. The look on my face must have said it all, because when I dropped down next to Miller he cocked a dark eyebrow and scratched the back of his buzz cut. "You look like you just told someone off," he said, as he began to drive.

"Oh, I did."

"Let me guess, Billabong?" he asked, chuckling. When I shot him a look, he cringed and said in a serious tone, "Sorry, I keep forgetting that you decide whether I have a job or not. You're just not what I—"

"Expected?" I asked. My phone buzzed against my thigh again, and I felt my heart jump.

"You can say that," Miller said.

"I'm actually quite charming," I said. Then, I gave him a grin that was forced but sincere. "And you don't have to worry about getting fired. As long as you don't try to sell my dirty panties to *Sleaze Police,* we're good."

"Gross."

"It's happened before," I said as I fished my phone out. It was still buzzing from incoming text messages. "You wouldn't believe what some of these dickwads will pay for." I didn't add that the panty incident had happened to Jessica and that she'd been sleeping with the bodyguard who did the deed.

I was more interested in Cooper's newest responses.

9:15 a.m.: So you're saying you spent the night in bed with sore muscles, thinking about me?

**9:16 a.m.: I've got to say Wills, I'm pretty
turned on.**

I rolled my eyes, ready to let him have it, but then another
text came in. This one was from a familiar old contact whose
photo popped up when I clicked on the message. Strawberry-
blond hair, blue eyes, a giant grin, and a shot glass lifted up
high. I still remembered bits and pieces of the night I took this
picture of Jessica.

**9:18 a.m.: Where are you staying??? I was on
vacation in Ibiza. I want to see you, bitch!!!**

I began typing a response to her, barely listening when Miller
said, "Hey, Willow . . . I was wondering if we could talk about
days off."

"The weekend," I blurted, and I heard him shuffle around,
probably to turn his head in my direction. "The weekend because
I don't need to go out. Seriously, if I ask to go out, stop me."

Because my text to Jessica read:

**9:20 a.m.: I wish we could hang out but I'm in
Hawaii for a part! Sorry. :(**

"What? With physical force?" Miller asked, snorting.

"I'm weak," I said, adjusting my ringer to silent. That way
she couldn't tell me about what she'd done, and who she par-

tied with, in Ibiza. That way I wouldn't get jealous. That way I wouldn't wish I'd been with her, getting so fucked-up the universe failed to exist for me.

"I don't want to go back to rehab or jail or any of that. I'm *not* going to go back," I whispered.

There should be other reasons why you don't want to get screwed-up, my conscience muttered to me.

I paid attention to the winding road ahead.

"Nobody wants you to either," Miller said quietly. But I closed my eyes and saw the flashing lights and the headlines behind my eyelids. He was wrong, so I didn't respond.

When he parked the car beside Cooper's curb, I hesitated before getting out. I pulled my hand away from the door handle and gazed back into Miller's dark-brown eyes. "What are you going to do when you're off?" I asked.

He looked surprised. "Something part-time . . . to help with the expenses when I move." Yesterday, during our all-day tour of Honolulu, he'd told me about his girlfriend. The assignment as my bodyguard would be his last before he moved to live with her on the East Coast.

My gaze slipped to the front of Cooper's stucco house and then back to Miller's face. "Another security job?"

Miller opened his mouth to answer me, but then seemed to think better of it. His face wrinkled into a frown and he flicked the tip of his tongue over the tiny gap in his front teeth. "Willow, are you stalling?"

Yes. And I wasn't about to admit aloud—or even to myself— the reason why. Letting my shoulders sag, I pinned on a smile that was probably more creepy and robotic than bright. "I'll text you when Surfer Boy and me are done."

A second after I stepped inside the empty shop area, Eric padded in through the doors behind the surfboard counter. He had a half-eaten energy bar in one hand and a giant bottle of water in the other. "What if I said you're stuck with me today?" he asked, hitching an eyebrow.

I pretended to be interested in a T-shirt for sale, though I could still easily see him out of the corner of my eye. "What exactly are you going to teach me? And by the way, I met your girlfriend."

He took a long gulp of water and then shrugged his shoulders. "Paige knows my flirting is harmless." When I rolled my eyes, he added, "What can I say, I'm starstruck. What would you do if Brad Pitt walked into your house?"

I scrunched my face. "Not shit because he's two years older than my dad." Then a thought hit me, and I shifted an eyebrow up. "You're not much of a bum if you're up this early each morning."

"It's to see your beautiful, famous face. But really, not even I sleep past nine thirty. I've got to polish those"—he pointed to three surfboards resting against the wall on the far side of the room—"and go to the grocer. I'm kind of your boyfriend's bitch."

"There is nothing going on between me and Cooper," I said through gritted teeth. Then, taking a long, calming breath, I walked over to the counter, leaned my elbows on the smooth boards, and asked, "Where is Cooper anyway?"

Eric scratched the back of his head and yawned. "He's a glutton for punishment. He's out on the beach because he swears it de-stresses him." He bent down close to me as if to share a secret. "And believe me, you stress the hell out of him."

"Thanks for the heads-up. Good luck with your . . . bitch duties."

He sighed. "It's not an easy job, but somebody's got to do it."

Shaking my head, I left Eric standing there grinning like an idiot. I went out to Cooper's backyard, the way we'd gone the day before. He was wading toward the shore, his golden hair wet and clinging to his forehead, his board tucked between his arm and body, his expression relaxed.

The moment he saw me, though, that look changed to a cocky half smile, then surprise when his eyes dragged over the black halter top of my swimsuit. He gave me a little wave. I pressed my fist to my mouth to hide my smile and steadied myself against the outside of the deck for a moment. Then, I slowly sauntered down the beach toward him.

He met me halfway.

"Trying to get out of work by looking like that?" he asked.

"Oh, please. It'll take a lot more than a two-piece to convince you to go easy on me."

"Mmmm . . . good point, Wills. I will never, ever go *easy* on you."

My body heat jumped, but I radiated perfect confidence as I stepped out of my yellow shorts and shoes. I tossed them in a pile a few feet from my board, which he must have brought out with him earlier.

"How will you torture my ass today, Boss?" I asked.

The corner of his mouth tugged up. "Didn't take you for that kind of actress, Wills."

My torture turned out to be the same as yesterday, but I was determined to show him I could handle his training. I spent the next hour and a half working on my form and asking him questions about his history as we worked.

"How long have you been doing this?"

"Since I was six, so sixteen—almost seventeen—years," he responded. He stood in front of me, tilted his head to the side, and then motioned for me to move my left foot back a little. I slid it back on the smooth surface of my purple-and-white board until he held up his hands for me to stop.

"How many competitions have you won?"

He pretended to think and then he asked, "How many movies have you starred in?"

I narrowed my eyes. "Too many to count."

"Well, there you have it." He walked in a circle, examining me, and let out an annoyed sigh before coming up behind me. Placing his left hand on my hip, he touched the inside of my right thigh, moving it forward. My mouth flooded with moisture as I glimpsed his fingertips gliding across my bare skin. "There, perfect. Now, bend your knees." I didn't miss the hitch in his voice, or the way his touch on my skin felt too gentle, too lingering, for someone tasked with teaching me.

I thought of the way his hands and mouth had felt on mine that night in my living room, and I traced the tip of my tongue over my lips, dampening them, before I cleared my throat. "So why'd you move from Australia?"

He pinched the bridge of his nose, which was slightly chafed from spending so much time in the sun. "Show me everything you learned, starting with getting up off your board."

This was the first question of mine he'd ignored, so naturally, I wanted him to answer it. "If you tell me about Australia."

"Why? Planning a visit?"

I shrugged. "Who knows? Maybe."

"Just . . ." He dragged his hands through his hair, a look of frustration suddenly clouding his features. "Go through the fucking basics, Wills." The last few words were clipped and every muscle in my body went tense.

This was a different side of Cooper—a vulnerable side—and to be honest, I was kind of turned on by it. Maybe I was more sadistic and screwed-up than I originally believed myself to be, but if this was what he felt when he tried to fluster me, no wonder he did it.

Keeping my eyes locked with his, I showed him everything he'd taught me over the last couple days. I lay down on my stomach, keeping my toes at the edge of the board, and then popped up, centering my feet expertly in the middle of the board.

Tilting my face up at him, I smiled despite the painful burn in my arms and ass. "Now, why'd you leave Australia?" I demanded. I stepped off the board and crossed my arms over my chest, shaking the soreness out of my legs.

"My parents divorced when I was twelve," he said with a little shrug. "My mum was from America so . . ."

"You moved here," I completed and he nodded. "I bet she knows how many competitions you've won," I added. My mom might not pick me up from rehab, but she could easily tell you my first movie, the last, and every role in between.

But when Cooper looked up, and I got a good look at his face, I felt a lurch in my chest that had nothing to do with attraction or my own personal shame. His expression was blank and I already knew what he was going to say before the first word was spoken.

"She died when I was seventeen, Wills."

"Oh," I whispered. I lowered my gaze to the sand, digging my foot into it. I'd spent so much time being around other people—*being* other people—and I still didn't know what to say when facing someone's loss. "Cooper . . . I'm so sorry."

"Don't do that," he said, but I shook my head. A moment later, we were toe to toe, with his palms pressed gently to either side of my face as he forced me to meet his gaze. When he looked at me like that, I forgot there were other people on this damn beach with us. And when he touched me, I almost forgot that I didn't want to get involved—emotionally or physically— with this guy.

"I'm not angry at you for mentioning my mum. It was an innocent question—no harm, you know," he said.

My shoulders deflated. "I'm really—"

"Drop it," he said, this time his voice hard. I flinched but said nothing.

Our lesson ended a few minutes later. Paige met us out on the deck again as I was putting my clothes back on, and this time when she asked me to eat with her—correction: told me I was going to—I accepted. She clapped her hands happily.

"I've got to give a lesson in half an hour but we've got a little time. Holy crap, I'm going to eat lunch with a celebrity," she said. Cooper wiggled his fingers in mock enthusiasm and she rolled her eyes at him. "If you want to fire this dumb-ass and hire me, I could use the cash. My shitty Grand Caravan is dying!"

I didn't know anything about this woman other than the fact she was a surfer who dated a horndog, and that her parents owned the place I was staying in—but for the first time in what seemed like years, I felt a pull toward another female that had nothing to do with getting fucked-up or blowing money. I cleared my throat. "I should call my bodyguard and let him know."

She opened the door for me, ushering me inside, and then lifted her eyebrow to Cooper. "Are you coming?"

He shook his head. "No, you guys go ahead . . . I'm going to go back out for a few minutes. I'll be back to put up your board and take you home in a little," he said. When he saw me hesitate, he gave me a strained smile. "Don't worry, she won't bite."

"Not too hard," Paige added, coming in behind me. I walked forward, dragging the soles of my rubber flip-flops across the tile floor. There was a part of me that wanted to turn back around and cast another glance at Cooper, to see if what we'd talked about was still bothering him, but he was probably already in the sea. De-stressing.

We walked through the hall into a small laundry room. Paige moved past me and motioned me through the door, into an open kitchen that looked like it belonged on an HGTV show. "You go ahead and sit down over there." She pointed to a counter with a row of stools in front of it. As I crossed the room, sending Miller a text message as I walked, I heard the refrigerator open. "So how are you liking it?" she asked.

I glanced over my shoulder. "What? Surfing?"

She laughed, probably because my irritation was obvious. "It'll get better. I sucked when Cooper started teaching me."

I slid onto the first stool and leaned forward, supporting my elbows on the granite countertop. "How long have you been doing it?"

"Six years."

Cooper had been a surf instructor since he was sixteen—practically a kid. I wanted to be surprised by that, but for some reason, I wasn't. Suddenly, though, I wanted to know if he'd made Paige work on form and popping up on a surfboard for two days straight. When I came right out and asked her, she threw her head back, so that her short black hair brushed her shoulder blades, and laughed.

"He made you do that both days?" she asked. She brought two plates with subs over to the counter, placing one in front of me. Then she bent down and fished two bottles of water out of a cabinet. She handed me one. "Does he not want you to walk tomorrow or something?"

I opened the warm water and chugged quickly to flush down the string of curses I wanted to direct at Cooper. When I was finished, I glared at the window. I could see him—or at least what I thought was him—a tiny dot riding a wave somewhere in the distance. Maybe if he'd shown me more than standing up on a surfboard in the sand I could've floated out there to push him down.

"You're going to be good for him," Paige said, tilting her head to one side.

"What? The paycheck for him training me? Right about now I'm tempted to ask Dickson to hire *you*."

She gave me one of those pointed are-you-fucking-kidding-me looks and then a half smile. "Sure. The paycheck. But if you want to hire me I'd be cool with that."

We ate and talked about surfing for a few more minutes before Eric popped his head in to say her client had arrived. She hopped off the counter, keeping her eyes on mine. "Gotta go give this group surf lesson, so make yourself at home until he's done. Good luck with studying your script!"

I waited to pull out my phone until she and Eric had disappeared. If I waited around for Cooper, I was bound to say something screwed-up that would only make working with him even more difficult. I sent Miller a text asking him to come pick me up.

But before I went to the front of the house, to the shop area, to wait for Miller, I left Cooper a note using the blue Post-it pad on the counter.

Hypothetically . . . it's kind of hard to get me into your bed if I'm too sore to make it there in the first place. Thanks for spending two days torturing me for nothing.

-W

Then I folded it, scribbled his name on the front, and tucked it under the purple-and-white surfboard, which was still out on the deck. Later that night, as I watched Dickson's DVD for the second time, studying the way Hilary Norton made the role of Alyssa look as natural as breathing, and waited for a call from Jessica who'd texted she wanted to talk, I received a message from Cooper.

> 10:53 p.m.: I'm perfectly capable of carrying you to the bed and doing all the work.

> 10:54 p.m.: And before you bring up my little rule again . . . you won't always be my client.

This wasn't the first time a guy had been so blatantly obvious about wanting to sleep with me, and it wouldn't be the last, but I climbed into bed with my script fifteen minutes later wearing an enormous grin. I lay in the dark with my phone mere inches from my face, wondering if he'd text again. Wondering what he was doing. Wondering if I'd make a fool of myself with him, and screw up all over again.

All I knew was that when I fell asleep, it was the fourth night in a row with no bad dreams.

CHAPTER SEVEN

June 21

"... *available balance is twenty thousand, one hundred and eighty-nine dollars, and seventy-three cents,*" the automated banker droned. This had to be at least the twentieth time that I'd listened to my account balance since Miller and I left the rental house nearly half an hour ago to head to my probation meeting, and yet adrenaline still prickled through my body, making my face and hands numb, clumsy.

Yesterday evening, I'd come home from a full day of training with Cooper—stand-up paddleboarding at early dawn followed by waxing our regular surfboards with coconut-scented gunk for what seemed like an eternity—and had thrown myself into studying my script. When I'd finally dragged myself into bed a little after eleven, I had fully expected to wake up in the morning to the shitastrophic bank balance I'd had for a while now.

Before I'd fallen asleep, I'd made up my mind. In the morning I would call my mother—wherever the hell in the world she was right now because she hadn't been in touch with me since her call—and if necessary, I would grovel for some of the money I'd earned before I turned eighteen.

Instead, I'd awakened to find that Kevin had come through. My advance had been deposited at some point this morning, long before I'd rolled myself out of bed.

"You look dazed," Miller said, his deep voice yanking me back into the present, into the cramped interior of the Kia.

I let the monotone voice tell me my balance one final time before I hit the end button on my phone and dropped it into my cluttered bag. "I'm good," I answered.

But even as I spoke, I could hear my breath coming out in choppier gasps. My hand slid up the front of my light-blue sundress to pull at the neckline. God, why did it feel like it was slowly closing around my throat to choke me?

The answer was clear and it had everything to do with my own issues and what I'd just heard on the phone. I'd spent so much time stressing over the advance money that I hadn't stopped to consider how I would react once it arrived. I should have been ecstatic. My jumpiness should have stemmed from feeling happy about working and getting paid again, not from memories of blowing all my money on Roxies and booze even before the online deposit status changed from "pending."

But I wasn't stupid. I knew better than anyone that telling myself I was too strong to mess up again wasn't enough.

I smoothed back strands of dark-brown hair from my damp forehead and said aloud, "I'm fine." Because that was the only thing I could be, right?

"*Right,*" Miller drawled.

I shrugged and sucked in another long breath, wheezing as soon as the chemical taste of air freshener collided with the back of my throat. "You know you'd accomplish the same thing with *one* of those, right?" I jabbed two fingers at the pine-scented clips crammed into the center air vents.

"I only bought them because the car was—" Miller paused midsentence, and though he kept his gaze focused on the highway, I saw his brown eyes narrow into thin slits. "For an actress you're not too subtle at changing the subject. Or keeping up the poker face."

So I've been told, I thought. I checked my reflection in the visor mirror so he wouldn't see me cringe. "How's the porn-star dancing gig going?" Miller had landed a second job as a bouncer at a strip club without even trying, and I'd heard him dragging into his apartment at some point in the middle of the night.

"At least you're not denying that you're purposely trying to change the subject." Smirking, he added, "If lessons with Billabong are getting to you this bad, why not ask for a day off, or better yet, a slower pace?"

My feet froze midshuffle, and my toes curled. Miller thought my sudden discomfort was only because of Cooper. A quick flush raced through me, eventually settling in my ears until I felt like flamethrowers were being held to either side of my head.

Was it that obvious I was attracted to the guy?

"It's got nothing to do with him," I said hotly.

"If you say so."

Miller and I said little else, because a minute later he pulled the car into the parking lot of the probation office and nudged the Kia into a spot between a police car and a giant Hummer. "See you in a few," I muttered, grabbing my bag.

Although the outside of the building was a lot smaller than the ones I'd been to before, the moment I stepped inside, shivering under the cold blast of air-conditioning, I felt disgustingly and completely at home. I checked in with the woman at the front desk—who looked at me curiously when I whispered my name—and then took a seat on one of the vinyl chairs in the waiting room.

"You don't look like you belong here," a croaky female voice said from beside me. Startled, I turned my gaze on her. She was young—maybe a couple years older than me—but with a faded look in her eyes. She raised one of her thinly plucked eyebrows and said, "Let me guess. Drunk in public at your country club?"

By the way she was looking at me, it was obvious she didn't know who I was, and more than anything else, I was relieved. The anonymity I'd found since coming here was the best thing about doing this movie.

Besides the money, I thought.

And your hot Australian surf coach, the voice in the back of my head added.

The girl's eyebrow cocked even higher, and she twisted her head forward, as if she were waiting for an answer.

"Sure," I said. "Why not."

She raked her bottom teeth over the corner of her upper lip and tilted her head to the side, the motion sending her dyed-red hair flying backward and with it the odor of sweat and stale cigarettes. "There's no point lying to me. I mean, we're both here, right?"

Yes, and probably for the same reason, I wanted to say. Instead, I shrugged and said, "You called it. Just giving you what you want to hear."

Her lips curled into a sneer and I saw her dig her shimmery-painted fingernails into the armrests. She glared at me for another few seconds, then turned her head and slammed back in her seat.

A moment later, my name was called. As I walked to meet the man waiting for me in the open doorway, I felt the redhead's dark eyes following me. I caught her confused expression just before I disappeared behind the door. She was mouthing my name slowly, squinting and wrinkling her nose.

I hoped she wouldn't make the connection until much later, if she ever did.

"This is Officer Stewart's desk," the man said, tapping the top of the fifth cubicle we came to. "You can go ahead in."

I was surprised to find that Officer Stewart was years

younger than my probie in California and model-pretty, with light-brown hair styled in a knot on top of her head, a starched white shirt, high-waisted pants, and pumps that made me feel like I was going to fall flat on my face just looking at them. She gave me a bored once-over as I took a seat on the other side of the desk, and a few minutes later, stared at me entirely too long when she escorted me to pee in a cup.

After I passed the drug test—to her surprise I was sure, because she glanced between me and the cup several times before tossing it in a huge trash bin—we returned to her desk. She opened her laptop and began asking me a series of questions.

"Your full name is Brittany Willow Avery?" she asked, lifting her eyebrow slightly as she read my first name.

"Yes."

"And your birthday is July 15, 1993?"

"Uh-huh," I said.

"Are you still living at the same address as the other day?"

I shook my head, only murmuring a "yes" after she glanced up at me impatiently.

"Are you actively employed?" she asked. I knew these were standard questions—I mean, I'd heard them dozens of times—but that didn't stop me from gritting my teeth. Officer Stewart lifted her gaze as I was rolling my eyes. "Is there a problem with your employment, Miss Avery?" she asked, emphasizing each and every word.

"No, I'm . . . working," I said, but I couldn't hold back the exasperation in my voice. Suddenly, I felt defensive—like I had to prove myself to this woman I didn't even know because of the way she was staring at me.

Officer Stewart tilted backward in her rolling chair, so far that it touched the two filing cabinets behind her. She linked her fingertips, rubbing them back and forth and picking me apart with her blue-green eyes. I just knew a question that would make me feel like shit was coming, and I braced myself for it.

Sure enough, a moment later, she said, "My case notes say that you're not scheduled to begin shooting your film until"—she took her eyes off mine long enough to squint at the laptop screen—"July first."

"That's right."

"So why are you here so early?"

Glancing at the clock as if it would help this meeting go by faster, I clenched my hands together between my knees. "Because I'm training with a surf instructor for my role." I flicked the tip of my tongue nervously across my top lip and dropped my gaze to my lap. "I play, ah, a surfer."

Saying it aloud sounded like such a fucking joke.

"Original," Stewart murmured. Sitting forward again, she typed something into her computer, her fingers making a rapid *click, click, click* noise that annoyed me. I imagined what she was typing, but then I stopped myself. I shouldn't care. I'd be done with probation soon enough and I'd never have to see Officer Stewart again. "Who are you training with? Lots of good ones in Honolulu." She never looked up or stopped jabbing at the keys.

"Cooper Taylor at Blue Flame Academy," I said. Stewart's shoulders stiffened and her fingers clenched. A second later, she regained her composure. What the hell was that about?

"You're filming the remake of the"—she coughed—"Hilary Norton movie, right?"

I was pretty sure she already knew that, but I nodded anyway. "Yes, I'm her—I mean, I'm playing the character she played."

"Ironic," she said, and tilted her head to the side. I flushed. It didn't take a genius to figure out she was comparing me to Hilary Norton. The woman who'd originally played my part had been a class-A junkie. I was dreading the day the gossip columns would point out that similarity. "And you're working with Cooper. He's a good one, that's for sure," she added, a tight smile clawing at the corners of her mouth.

And though I knew it was bitchy and childish, I half grinned and said, "Definitely. Cooper's the best." There wasn't anything suggestive to my voice but Stewart must have taken it that way, because she looked up and gave me what could pass for either a nod or a twitch. Before I could stop myself, I asked, "Do you take surf lessons with him?"

Grabbing a Styrofoam coffee cup off the corner of her desk, she downed a long gulp and shook her head. "He and my kid sister dated for a few years. They're still . . . *friends*."

I didn't like the bright-red spots that pranced in front of my vision any more than the way she cleared her throat before saying "friends." Pressing my lips flat, I sat back, wanting this meeting to end as quickly as possible. Stewart had known exactly what to say to get to me, and I felt like an idiot for trying to one-up her. Now the only thing I'd think about during my les-son with Cooper was whether or not he was sleeping with my probation officer's sister.

At least that would keep my mind away from the money in my account and what disasters I could blow it on.

The meeting with Stewart lasted another few minutes, and then she set up our next appointment in a month, on—no surprise—my birthday. As she walked me toward the front of the building, she turned to me and said, "I called Dave to verify your community service hours this morning and he said you haven't checked in yet."

When I didn't reply, instead feigning interest in a tattooed guy slurping down water at the fountain outside of the bathroom and sweating profusely, Stewart handed me a business card with an address scribbled on the back.

"I've set you up an appointment with him today at noon." She shrugged and gave me a little smile. "Just so you can meet him."

"I've got a surf lesson," I said automatically, and her polite smile faltered a bit.

"I'm sure Cooper will understand. He's the best, after all."

Right. The best. With her sister.

But when I gulped in the taste of fresh air a few minutes later, not sparing the probation office another glance as I rushed to the Kia, I didn't know what Cooper would think. Yesterday during our lesson, he'd been quiet, focused only on work. There had been no flirting, very little touching, and I'd found myself confused and wanting both.

Today, the moment I stepped into the front of his shop and

he gave me a dizzying smile from behind the counter where he was going through a surfboard catalog with a couple around my parents' age, I realized I would leave just as frustrated as I'd been yesterday.

"Give me a few," he mouthed, gesturing his head to the back of the house. I nodded. I walked out to the deck, where I began stripping down to my suit.

I was unbuckling my Steve Madden wedge sandals when I heard him walk outside. I didn't immediately acknowledge him, but I could feel the heat from his gaze running from my ankles and up my bare legs. When I felt it skim past my breasts, I lifted my chin. If he was ashamed at being caught watching me, he didn't show it. Instead, I was the one who blushed all over as I folded my sundress into neat creases and set it on the deck bench.

"I'm impressed, Wills. You're on time and I didn't even have to ca—"

I cut him off. "I've got to leave early today."

I expected a smart-ass would-you-leave-shooting-with-Dickson-early response, but he slid down on the bench next to me, draping his arm around the wooden handrail, and looked into my eyes. "You're all right, aren't you?" There was a genuine concern in his voice that caught me off guard. Nodding, I tucked a loose strand of hair behind my ear, suddenly conscious of his scent—coconut and sunblock.

My voice was husky when I said, "I had my first probation meeting this morning with Officer Stewart." I paused to let her name sink in, but his expression didn't change and his body stayed relaxed. "I've got to go meet my community service boss this afternoon."

He nodded his head slowly and started to drag his shirt over his head. "What time?"

"Noon."

He half laughed, half groaned, shrugging his shirt back down. I gave him a blank look and he said, "Then why did you have your bodyguard drop you off? It's ten forty-five now."

Honestly? Because I hadn't paid the slightest bit of attention to the time. I'd been too rattled by the meeting with Stewart and the money in my account. I reached for my bag where I'd slid it under the bench. "I'll call Miller and—"

Cooper's hand closed around my wrist. A shiver raced through me and my fingers tightened. I took one breath—and two more just to be sure of myself—then I met his gaze full on. The way his blue eyes alternated between confusion and want and astonishment made me want to melt into him.

Made me breathless all over again.

His lips parted. "Don't."

"Why?" I whispered in a voice that was too heavy and pleading for my own good.

"I'll take you."

Our lips were inches from connecting. I glanced away and tried to focus on the vacationers lounging in beach chairs several feet from his deck, but even then the sound of their radio became fuzzy, the sight of their Corona bottles clinking together became a haze. The only thing that was vivid was Cooper's face when he tucked his finger under my chin and compelled my gaze back to his, whispering my name in that accent.

"You've got work," I said, but my words were more for myself. He had a rule about clients. I was his client, and at the end of the summer my movie would be shot and I'd have to leave. I couldn't want him like this or my heart would get ripped out when that time came.

Holding my chin steady, he traced his other hand from my wrist up to my elbow, and from there to my shoulder. He bent forward, dipping his head a little, so that I could feel his breath hot against my throat.

"I'm my own boss, Willow." One of his fingertips brushed over my lips, and—I couldn't help it—I flicked my tongue out over the rough skin. His grip on my shoulder tightened and he cursed against the delicate skin at my collarbone.

"I can call Miller."

"I'm taking you." His voice was more determined than before.

"What the hell makes you think I want you to take me anywhere?"

He drew away from me and my chest deflated. I struggled to keep the uninterested look on my face as he linked his hands behind his head. I was anything but bored and by the way he was grinning, he knew that too. "Because of the way you're looking at me right now."

"And how is that?"

"Like if Eric and Paige hadn't come back just before I walked out here, I'd have your legs wrapped around my waist in five minutes."

"Your confidence makes me want to blow chunks all over you."

He dropped his hands from behind his head. "Get dressed before—"

"Before what?" I challenged.

He pulled me down onto the deck floor with him, like he didn't care if anyone could see us or that he'd known me for all of a week. And while his lips and tongue probed mine, my brain screamed at me, begging me to remember that it *had* been only a week.

Shoving his chest hard with my hands, I stumbled backward and to my feet. Turning my back to him, I grabbed my clothes from the bench and began yanking them back on. My breath came out in ragged little gasps and I was trembling. I was mad at him for making me want more and with myself for being stupid enough to let him affect me.

When I was calm enough to face him, he was still on the floor of the deck and his eyes were gleaming.

"Why are you laughing?" I snapped, plopping down in a patio chair to shove my feet into my sandals.

He stood, staring down at me like he wanted nothing more than to tear my clothes off. "Because you didn't puke on me and because you're going to break your neck cleaning gum from park benches in those shoes."

I rose to my feet and smoothed down my sundress. His

breath hitched as I shook my long, dark hair out before knotting it at the top of my head. "Ready?"

"You're not going to argue with me?" he asked and I glared at him, evoking a grin that made me want to run my lips across the dimple in his left cheek. "God, I love when you come undone, Wills."

CHAPTER EIGHT

~~~~~~~~~~~~~~~~~~~~~~~~~~~~~~~~

Cooper was wrong about me having to clean gum off park benches—the card Stewart had given me directed us to a homeless shelter for women and children—but he sure as hell was right about the shoes. While I found out that I wasn't scheduled to do any community service today, Dave, my boss, took me on a two-hour orientation of the shelter. By the time we went through our third rotation of the grounds, I was caught between wanting desperately to kick off my shoes and wondering if Cooper had given up on me and gone home.

I hoped not, because I'd stupidly left my bag and phone sitting on the front seat of his Jeep.

"So do you think you've got a grasp on what you'll be doing?" Dave asked.

I nodded. "Kitchen duties." Cleaning, serving, and helping unload deliveries, to be exact. I glanced around the massive dining room one final time as we shuffled through it. To be honest, it reminded me of the one at my court-ordered rehab—bleach-scented, with three rows of plain, scuffed wooden tables and chairs, and a kitchen with a serving window at the front of the room.

Thinking of rehab brought a swell of hysteria into my throat, but I gulped it back when I spotted a group of kids huddled at the end of a table at the other side of the room, staring at Dave and me, whispering loudly. I gave a tiny wave in their direction.

"It seems you have fans," Dave said, as we left the large room. The sound of excited giggling followed us. "We've got quite a few of your older movies on DVD."

Back before you turned into just another party girl, I added for him.

"It's the first time I've been recognized since coming here," I admitted.

He belly laughed, and walked me outside to the front of the building. Cooper's Jeep was still parked across the street, thank God. "With your movie about to start filming, I'm sure you'll be recognized everywhere you turn," Dave said.

I knew he didn't mean anything by it, but my muscles went rigid anyway. "I can't wait," I said in a voice that was detached. *Robotic.*

"Do you have any idea when you'll be able to begin working at Harmony House?" Dave asked.

"Monday," I answered quickly. I wanted to knock out my

community service as quickly as possible. And I wanted something to focus my attention on other than surfing and work and Cooper. "I'll have my bodyguard drop me off after work."

He looked pleased with my response. Pumping my hand in his, he said, "We'll see you then." As I walked to the edge of the sidewalk, he cleared his throat. I turned, shifting one of my eyebrows up. "You should probably wear . . . work clothes."

I nodded my understanding. "I will." When I got into Cooper's Jeep, he cast me a questioning look. "How do your feet feel, Wills?"

"Like I could paddleboard all day, Billabong."

A grin crept its way across his face, and his shoulders shook slightly. "Nice, but I'm canceling the lesson for today."

"What—why?"

He raked his hand across his chest, ruffling the front of his gray Alternative Apparel shirt. "Because I've been thinking about you too much."

"You're getting paid to train me," I pointed out.

He merged onto the highway, seemingly absorbed in the Incubus song playing on the radio. I crossed my arms over my chest; I was more interested in hearing what Cooper had to say than listening to Brandon Boyd sing about picturing someone's face in the back of his mind. The lyrics were way too close to my own dilemma with the guy sitting beside me. When the song ended, and a commercial for a nightclub replaced it, Cooper sighed.

"There's a forty-year-old cougar paying me to train her and I don't give her a second thought after our lessons," he told me.

"Cooper, I—"

"I'm not going to beg you to be with me, Wills. I'm not going to chase you or do any of that. But just know that I want you, and before you say it—fuck the rule." He cast a tight grin in my direction. "Not that I've broken it."

"You don't know anything about me," I said. *Just like I don't know anything about you other than I want to throw myself at you every time we see each other,* I thought.

"And I've told you before that I don't have to know you to want you. Sex between us would be . . ."

When he didn't continue, instead clenching his hands on the steering wheel and squinting at the road as he struggled to come up with the perfect word, I was sure he was thinking the same thing I was.

Amazing.

Shattering.

Catastrophic for my heart.

A moment later we were parked in the empty driveway of my rental and he turned off the engine. "Cooper, what exactly do you want from me?" I asked. He offered me a strained look that made my chest ache and my throat tighten.

"Nothing. Dammit, everything. I needed to get it out there, Wills—how I'm feeling about you. Yeah, I'm your coach but I'm also a guy and you're digging your way under my skin." He laid his head back on the cloth headrest, lifting his chin and squeezing his eyes shut. Before I could stop myself, I was out of my seat belt, pressing my lips to the column of his throat. He groaned. "Don't. Fucking. Tease."

"I'm trying to spend this summer focusing on my career," I whispered, and Cooper opened his blue eyes to take me in. He brushed strands of my hair back from my face. "I just got out of rehab and I'm not—"

"I get it."

"You don't," I said firmly. "I don't like being attracted to you. And if you think I'm getting under your skin, just imagine what you're doing to me. I haven't . . . I've not been in a real relationship in a long time, Cooper. But here you are and you scare the shit out of me."

A look of understanding and then pity entered his eyes. A deep burn scorched its way through my stomach, up to my chest, and I reached for the door handle. He closed his hand around my wrist, jerking me back to him.

"Somebody fucking hurt you," he said in a dangerous voice.

"Yes."

"Who?"

"Why does it matter? You going to break his legs with a surfboard?" When Cooper pressed his lips together determinedly, I heaved a sigh. "Tyler Leonard." Even now, three years later, my voice cracked whenever I said his name. I didn't watch his movies. I pretended not to notice whenever his picture made the cover of *Us Weekly*.

And yet I still couldn't let him go.

"The actor?" Cooper asked.

I nodded, using every acting chop within me to hide the disappointment. "We met during filming." *Into the Dark*. My first and only horror movie and my last successful film before my fall.

"He's what—ten years older than you? What, did you have a crush on him and he turned you down?" Cooper's voice was hopeful, and for a second, I thought about telling him what he wanted to hear, but then I gripped my free hand into the fabric of my dress.

"When you're in Hollywood, you've got all these people who think that you're so fucked-up, that you're so jaded, even when you're just a kid, you know? But I wasn't back then. I mean, yeah, I went to parties with my friends, but I hadn't . . ."

"He was your first." When I didn't answer, he growled a curse. "And that's what started . . ."

The drugs.

"No. And yes. Part of it was what had happened between me and him. And part of it was just myself." I'd wanted a permanent anesthesia to numb away the short memories of what I'd given up.

"Willow," Cooper said, dropping his fingers from around my wrist so he could rake his hands through his blond hair. Anxiety pulsed through my veins again, but this time, instead of making a run for it, I pulled him close to me, dragging his lips down on mine to hush out any more pity.

We were in the most awkward position imaginable—with the center console acting as a frustrating barrier between our bodies—but all I could think about were Cooper's fingertips cupping my face and caressing my skin. His lips on my mouth.

"Wills, don't do this if—" He started to pull away, but I shook my head and wrapped my arms around his neck, pulling him into me. As his tongue parted my lips and his hand squeezed my breast, I skimmed my fingers beneath the top of his gray T-shirt. My hand brushed over the scar on his shoulder, and he shivered.

He pulled back and the light filtering around him made him seem so ethereal my head spun. "Why are you doing this?" he demanded in a low voice against my mouth.

You take the nightmares away, I wanted to tell him. *Because I don't fucking know you but when I'm with you, I want to feel again. I don't need pills or noise or a distraction.*

Instead, I whispered, "Because you said you'd always look after me."

His Adam's apple bobbed. "I'm not going to take advantage of you."

"Because of what I told you about Tyler?"

"Because you're using me to flush him out of your system. When you come to me, when we do this, I want it to be because you're thinking about me. Not some perverted shit who fucked you over when you were a kid."

I straightened, smoothing my dress and keeping my eyes wide so I wouldn't cry. I refused to. "You sound like a movie," I said in a thick voice.

He raked his hands through his hair and held it back for a long moment before releasing it. Then he gave me a long, hard, unnerving stare. "Good. Guess sometimes Hollywood does make sense."

"I'm going in now, Cooper."

He didn't argue or beg. He wasn't going to chase me. Before I reached the front door to the rental house, his Jeep was halfway up the street.

The rest of my weekend was quiet, slow, but full of dreams that rocked me so hard, I woke up screaming. The first one, Saturday night, Miller had come bolting down the stairs, barging in with the spare set of keys to find me hunched over the toilet.

"I'm fine . . . just go away," I'd muttered, placing one cheek on the cool surface of the tile floor. But leaving the bathroom to get a drink of water, I'd found him sitting on the brown suede couch, with his elbows resting on his thighs.

"I said I'm fine," I barked, clenching my hands, and he glanced up at me, his eyes tired and full of worry.

It was weird to see someone as tall and muscled as Miller look so helpless, but he did. "You're . . . *sure?*" And I knew what he was implying. He wanted to know if I was high. Sighing, I sat down next to him.

Drying the dampness from my face with the back of my hand, I nodded. "I swear I am."

But I wasn't. Because the entire time I'd had my head in the bowl, I was trying to remember Eric's father's name. The resident lazy, pill-dealing douchebag, Eric had called him on the day we met. But as I vomited, I didn't care what he was—only that he had something to help me.

It wasn't until now—the ass-crack of dawn on Tuesday morning—that I was reminded of his name, as Cooper and I sat side by side on our boards, our legs outstretched, paddling through the flat water.

"Where's Eric at?" I asked. He hadn't been around yesterday and his truck wasn't in the driveway when Miller dropped me off earlier.

"Someone broke into Rick's house, so he's been trying to help him find a new place."

Rick. If I had remembered that a couple nights ago, what would have happened? Would I be here now or would I be catatonic, watching my world float by in slow motion?

"Oh," I said, switching my paddle to the other side and flexing my foot. A cramp was running up the side of my leg, and I wanted to straddle the board, but every time I did that Cooper shook his head. He claimed it was because it would take us forever to get where we were going, but I swore it was because he wanted to torture me. Yesterday had been our second day of stand-up paddleboarding and we'd rowed through still water until every inch of my body burned from the workout.

"Thought Eric hated his dad," I said at last.

"Relationships are complicated," he replied, giving me a meaningful look. I curled my toes and tried to tell myself he wasn't talking about ours. Despite our conversation before the weekend, he still made no effort to hide the fact that he wanted me. He was respectful, but at the same time, gave me looks that undressed me and made my legs, and the area in between them, feel weak.

"Okay, we're out far enough. Up you go," he said.

He stood up effortlessly, and I felt a stab of jealousy at how easy he made it seem. Groaning, I placed the paddle between my legs and pushed myself up, wobbling a little as I quickly grabbed it again. Some greater power must have felt sorry for me, because I managed to balance myself without nearly toppling over like yesterday. The form was different from surfing—my feet were positioned on each side of the board instead of in the middle—but Cooper swore up and down it would all click together once we took on actual waves tomorrow and next week.

"Very nice," he murmured.

"Do you think I'll be ready in time for the movie?" I asked. I felt my heart drop a little when he laughed and shook his head.

"Not even close to it," he said. I started to give him an earful but he narrowed his eyes. "Getting good at anything takes years. And it's not like you'll be doing the big stunts, Wills. Dickson just needs you to look like you know what the hell you're doing for the pivotal scenes. Trust me; I'm not going to let you fail at this."

I moved the paddle to the other side of the board, rowed four strokes as he'd shown me, and then switched sides. "I don't want to fail," I said, but it was more directed at the thoughts I'd had about giving in to pills over the last few days.

"Dickson has faith in you," he said.

"What about you?"

"I don't think you'll let me or yourself down."

That didn't answer my question and, frustrated, I sucked in air through my teeth. After that, the conversation shifted to the cast of the movie—a bunch of relatively unknown actors if you didn't count my love interest, who starred as a dreadlocked werewolf on some CW show—and Cooper's next surf competition in October.

When the waves picked up soon after, we sat down and paddled back to shore, where the beach was slowly beginning to fill up with the morning crowd. I slipped my enormous sunglasses from the top of my head over my eyes and grinned up at him.

"Do I not look like Willow Avery?" I asked in a teasing voice.

He shot me a sideways grin. "Hottest tourist I've ever seen. But even if you were"—he winked—"Willow Avery, nobody would bother you here."

I sniffed. "Are you kidding?" Lifting my board and paddle, I followed him through the sand. "You don't know how it is. Being noticed."

He stopped halfway up the beach, just feet away from sunbathers soaking in the hot morning sun. "Tell me then." He tossed his board and paddle into the sand and I gently placed mine next to it. He held up a finger. "I'll be right back."

He ran through the sand toward his house, disappearing inside, and came out less than a minute later carrying a bundle of towels in his arms. He grinned as he sprinted down to where I was sitting on the gritty ground, shook out the towels, and motioned for me to lie down with him. I complied, stretching out on the soft fabric and letting the sun warm my damp body.

"I've got community service today," I reminded him.

"Stay with me."

I groaned. "Why do you have to say things like that?"

"Telling you what I want?"

"Yes," I said through clenched teeth. "I thought you didn't

want to do this with me . . ." My voice trailed off because neither of us had mentioned what we'd talked about in his Jeep last Friday, and I didn't want to bring it up.

"I don't want to do this with you if you're not willing," he corrected. "It's just that I'm still kind of shocked by this." I cocked my eyebrow and he sighed, rolling over onto the side where his tattoo was. Propping himself up on his elbow, he explained, "I've not been the best boyfriend in the past."

I made a strangled noise in the back of my throat. "Let me guess. Perpetual cheater?"

He frowned. "I don't cheat, Wills. If I say I'm with you—if we agree that we're together—I am. I just tend to sometimes . . . put other things first." He stared out at the sea as he said this, and my eyes followed his.

I understood what he was saying. I'd had boyfriends after things had gone to hell with Tyler—some of them good and some of them so bad I would have broken into a million and one pieces if I hadn't already been so screwed-up—but in each relationship, I was the one to ruin things. I'd put my desire to drown out the world over everything else.

Cooper rubbed his tongue back and forth over the center of his upper lip and curled strands of my dark hair around his fingers. Staring down at it, he continued, "But the thing is, I've known you for a little over a week, Wills. I think about you more than surfing. I think about you when I wake up, when I'm giving someone else a lesson. Fuck, I think about you when I'm in the bathroom."

"Nice to know you shit while picturing me," I said, cocking an eyebrow.

He let go of my hair and stroked the back of my neck, staring me directly in the eye. "No, what I'm saying is I can't get you off my mind. I've never felt like this over a girl."

My heart felt as if it were shrinking because I'd heard that before many times. The only difference now was that I wanted it to be true.

Finally, I found my voice. "Not even my probation officer's kid sister?"

He laughed, plopping his head back on his towel to gaze up into the clear sky. "Nice to know Miranda's sister is professional, but to answer your question—no, I didn't. We were high-school sweethearts, Wills. Love—relationships were different then."

"Were you about to say you loved me?" I joked, leaning over him to stare down into his eyes. My hair fell in a canopy over his face and he inhaled the scent of it—some Victoria's Secret shampoo my mom had mailed me. I shivered. "Because just so you know, I don't believe in love at first sight," I whispered.

"Neither do I."

I dropped flat onto the towel, barely breathing when I asked, "Then what are we going to do?"

"Be honest with me for a second, Wills."

"Yes."

"If things were different, would we have already given in to this?"

He was asking me what would have happened if Tyler hadn't jaded me, and I answered without missing a beat. "Yes."

Cooper groaned, and out the corner of my eye I saw him rub his hands over his face. "I'm still trying to figure you out." His voice was lulling but powerful enough not to be drowned out by the roar of the sea and the piercing screams of kids playing by the shoreline.

Closing my eyes, I shook my head. "I'm not that difficult." I slid toward him until our bodies touched—shoulder to shoulder, hip to hip. Our towels had separated, leaving my right side exposed to the coarse beach floor, but I didn't care. I needed this closeness. He smelled like warm air and salt water and it intermingled with the scent of coconut wax drifting from our boards a few feet away.

Cooper turned his face, gazing at me intensely. "Are you kidding, Wills? You're the most difficult person I've ever met."

But he was wrong, I wasn't difficult.

I was just cautious.

CHAPTER NINE

"So, did you ever kiss him?" a soft voice asked, and I stopped in the middle of swooping the mop across the linoleum floor to face the little girl it belonged to. Her nose wrinkled as she waited for me to answer.

I switched the mop to my left hand, and then flexed the right to get rid of a sharp cramp. "Who?"

"Gavin Sawyer."

It was Wednesday evening, a little after six, and I'd been at the homeless shelter since before noon. Cooper had called me unexpectedly this morning, moving our early-afternoon surf lesson to eight o'clock this evening. When I'd asked why, I could practically hear his shrug through the connection. "Got an appointment," he said.

If I had been the one making the request, he'd have asked me a hundred questions.

"Well, did you?" the girl asked, dragging my mind back to the present. She'd been in here for at least an hour, sitting at the end of one of the D-hall tables, writing in a spiral notebook as I scrubbed the place clean.

And now that I was mopping just a few feet away from where she sat, she was asking me about my pre-rehab boyfriend, Gavin.

Plunking the mop down inside the yellow bucket full of murky water, I bent over and scooted it up against the wall. Wiping my hands on the front of my dark jeans, I slid over across from the little girl. "Why would you think I ever kissed him?" When I gave her a serious look, she rolled her dark-brown eyes and tossed her curly chestnut-colored hair over one shoulder.

"Because I'm eleven and I'm not stupid. Besides, I saw you on the Teen Music Awards with him last year before my mom and dad . . ." She looked down, playing with the corner of the notebook, bending an unraveled bit of spiral with her fingers. Her unspoken words lingered in the air, so heavy that my world felt as if it were spinning off its axis. When she took a deep, shaky breath and raised her eyes back to mine, my chest clenched, hurting for her. What had happened to her parents in the last nine months for her to end up here, in a homeless shelter meant for women and kids?

Why the fuck was life so unfair?

"I adore his band," she said in a lisp. "'Green-Eyed Girl' is my favorite song—I bet it was about you."

No, it wasn't. Because everything about Gavin, from his

catchy pop music to his perfectly coiffed, highlighted hair, was manufactured by the network his show aired on.

"So," the little girl said, folding her hands together and tilting her body forward, "stop avoiding the question. Did you ever kiss him?"

"Only once," I replied, my voice gentle. Because, to be honest, I couldn't tell her that the guy she worshipped—the boy-band, teen-magazine prince—was nothing more than a coke-snorting, fan-hating shitbag. Hoping to steer the conversation away from Gavin and back to something that would make her smile, I pointed down at her notebook and peered over. She lunged forward to cover the page with her hands and chest. I drew back, holding my hands up in front of me. "Just wanted to see what you were writing," I said defensively.

She cocked her head to the side, pursing her lips together as she decided whether or not to tell me. Finally, reluctantly, she said, "I'm drawing."

"Can I see?"

She looked surprised—wide-eyed and cherry-red-face surprised—before she mumbled, "It's not very good." But she sat back, pushing her notebook in my direction, keeping her fingers at the edges like she was too afraid to let go. For a long time, I stared down at the drawing—a princess made out of bubble gum from a cartoon I was guilty of watching a few times.

"This is awesome! Got any of Marceline?"

Her mouth dropped, and I held back a grin. "You like *Adventure Time*?"

Nodding, I started to quote a line from the show—the only

line I actually remembered—but the sound of a throat clearing startled me. The girl and I both turned our heads to where Dave was now standing at the foot of the table, smiling.

"Willow, can I speak to you?"

My face sunk into a frown as I pushed away from the table and followed Dave out of the cafeteria, down a wide hallway, and into his office, which was cramped by stacks of books, paperwork, and at least a hundred pictures of his family. I sat on the other side of his desk, scraping my hands together in my lap, and waited for him to tell me what the hell was going on.

"Willow . . ." Dave began, and it was in one of those exasperated voices that automatically made me sink my teeth into the inside of my lower lip. He was frowning, as if he were trying to find the right thing to say, and then he sighed. "We almost declined your lawyer's request to allow you to work for us, but we believe in second chances."

Well, thanks for letting me know that.

I started to speak, but when I opened my mouth it was impossible to talk past the giant lump in my throat. So I nodded my head slowly.

"A lot of our residents are children, like Hannah, who have been hurt. The last thing we want is for them to get their hopes up."

"I wasn't making her promises or getting her hopes up. She had a question about a band she likes. I"—I bit my bottom lip— "know one of the members pretty well."

"We'd prefer you not answer questions like that."

And then it hit me. Dave wasn't just admonishing me; he was

asking me not to have contact with the residents of the shelter. I didn't want to be affected by what he was requesting, and yet it felt like someone was punching my chest from the inside.

It seemed like the shittiest second chance ever.

I struggled to keep my body, and my voice, calm as I told him, "I'm not going to tell her I won't talk to her." I didn't care if that meant I'd lose my job or lose the sixteen hours I'd worked so far—I refused to ignore anyone like that.

Coming to this conclusion made my heart race because the other Willow—the Willow Dave was basing this conversation on—would have shrugged it off even if it made her feel like shit. Apparently, there was less of her in me than I'd realized.

"I won't refuse to speak to Hannah if she talks to me," I said, this time my voice steely.

Dave gave me a courteous but frustrated smile. "We wouldn't dream of asking you to do that. Why don't you call it a night and we'll talk to everyone staying here with us this evening?"

He wasn't firing me, but it still felt like I was losing. "Sure," I said.

"Willow," Dave said in a soft voice. "We're not trying to hurt your feelings, but at the end of the day, our top priority is helping the women and kids who come into our shelter."

"I understand," I said. And I did. To him, I was the flighty actress with two trips to rehab before the age of twenty under her belt. I could see why Dave wouldn't want me to be around the residents of the homeless shelter.

Understanding the reasons behind his decision only made the pressure in my ribs squeeze harder, suffocating me.

As I did the march of shame to the exit, I sent Miller a text message.

6:38 p.m.: Come pick me up please.

He wrote me back almost as soon as I hit send.

6:38 p.m.: Already in the parking lot.

Even though he was especially chatty about a fight he'd broken up at the strip club he worked at, I didn't talk much as Miller drove me across town to my lesson. I nodded in the right places and laughed when he said something funny, but I was barely listening.

I was still thinking of Hannah, the kid who liked cartoons full of adult innuendo and had a tween crush on my ex-boyfriend, and how my boss had slapped my wrists for talking about both with her.

For the first time since my surf lessons began, nobody was in the shop area at Cooper's place or coming out of another part of the house to greet me—probably because it was so late in the evening. When I stepped inside and the little bell hanging over the doorway rang, Paige yelled from the kitchen, "In here, Avery."

Following the mouthwatering scent of marinara sauce, I found the three of them—her, Eric, and Cooper—at the round kitchen table with heaping bowls of spaghetti in front of them.

"You're early," Cooper pointed out, but there was a smile on his face, extending all the way to his clear blue eyes. For a brief moment, my throat felt dry and all the stress from this afternoon started to blur. Then he linked his fingers, slid them behind his head, and asked, "How goes the toilet cleaning?"

Way to yank my ass back to reality, I thought as I gave him a sarcastic smirk. I crossed the room and sat on one of the stools behind the granite counter. "At least I don't have to practice popping up to grab the cleaner and toilet brush."

"Careful or I'll send you out back to practice now," Cooper said, his blue eyes issuing a challenge.

Eric snorted. "Cooper's bedroom is upstairs, second door on the right. I'll totally give you guys all the condoms I've got if you take your verbal hate-fuck up there," he said, and Cooper and I broke eye contact to glare at him. "What? That's what you're doing."

Paige smacked the back of his head, hard, and practically knocked over her seat jumping up to make me a plate. "Come sit with us. There's plenty for—"

"You don't have to do that for me."

But she was already standing on tiptoe, rifling around in a high cabinet. "Don't tell me you're on a low-carb diet or something." She closed the cupboard door, holding a red plate in front of her like she'd go all *Tangled* on me and hit me with it if I argued with her.

I thought of the whole-wheat waffles I forced myself to eat every morning and the personal trainer I'd never called, despite Kevin constantly texting me about doing so. "No, no diet."

"You should call Hulk back and see if he wants any," Paige

said, as she spooned the pasta onto my plate. When I told her that Miller was probably already in the gym, she motioned her head to the table. I slid in the spot between Cooper and Eric.

"You look like you lost your best friend," Eric said.

I held back a snort. Jessica was still the only friend I'd spoken with since coming to Honolulu and contact with her had been sporadic at best. She was in the middle of filming a pilot for a new TV show—at least that's what she swore whenever I called and she rushed off the phone a few minutes later.

"No, I . . ." I was grateful that Paige chose that moment to slide the plate of spaghetti onto my placemat. My stomach rumbled; it smelled so good and I hadn't eaten anything since my waffle and egg whites this morning. Three sets of eyes burned into the top of my head as I dumped a bunch of Parmesan cheese onto my pasta and then dug in.

"We've got seconds, Wills. And thirds if you're that hungry," Cooper teased, and I shot him a look. When he flinched, I groaned.

"Sorry, it's just been a bad day," I said.

He frowned, sunk his fingers into his blond hair to scratch his head, and then said hesitantly, "Did someone say something to you?" The dangerous tone that had been in his voice when I told him about Tyler had returned, and out the corner of my eye, I saw Paige's and Eric's eyes dip to their laps.

"No, not like you're thinking," I said, part of me surprised at how honest I wanted to be with him. Even with other people around. It was his eyes, I decided. The way he looked at me made me want to spill my every secret. "I, um . . . my community service boss basically told me to stay the hell away from the residents today."

"Why?" Paige asked.

At first, I had no plans to tell them any more. I was fully prepared to shrug it off. But then I realized that I was already in too deep—that I'd already peeled away several vulnerable layers of myself. As I sat there stuffing my face with Paige's cooking, I unloaded everything that had happened today on three people I'd barely known a week.

When I was finished, Eric's usual lopsided, playful grin had turned into something thoughtful and he was scratching his out-of-control beard. I was grateful that he didn't say anything, especially since I'd probably just solidified myself as the Psycho Sally of the year, actress edition.

"It's still pretty light out," Paige said, breaking the silence. I flicked my eyes across the table to find her glancing out the window. She met my gaze with a big smile. "And I've got the coolest boss on the planet who's going to go easy on his client today so she can soak up the rest of it with me. She's looking pretty pasty."

"She looks perfect, but whatever," Cooper said, his words causing my heart to hammer wildly.

A few minutes later, Paige and I carried our boards out to the deck. She was right, it was still sunny out, but the beach was empty, save for a few people playing a horribly uncoordinated game of volleyball.

Before she hopped off the deck, she said, "Just so you know, I love *Adventure Time*, too." When I leaned over the railing and raised my eyebrow, she shrugged, adding, "What's not to love about a show with a hug wolf?" Then she took off into a sprint toward the sea. Halfway there, she turned, cupped one of her hands over her mouth and yelled, "Come on! I'm going to show you what Coop Taylor wishes he could do."

He chuckled behind me. I turned, pressing my back against the wooden banister. Our gazes tangled. And it wasn't until Eric's tall form shuffled past him, toting a beach chair, that we looked away.

As soon as Eric was out of earshot, Cooper pushed away from the opposite side of the deck, reaching me in two long strides. He grabbed my face between his hands, pushing back wisps of my dark hair that had fallen over my eyes.

"You're not a bad person," he said.

They can see us. They can see what you're doing to me!

I swallowed hard. "Don't think I ever said I was."

"You didn't have to."

I jerked away from his grasp, feeling a tingle on my face where his fingertips had touched. "I better get down there with Paige before she comes to drag me." I raked my hands through my hair and skimmed my body past his. Cooper opened his mouth to say something, but I shook my head and cut him off. "You don't know me."

"I know that the media turns everyone who makes a mistake into a monster," he said, with a bitter edge to his voice.

Hugging my arms over my lower abdomen, over the fabric of my T-shirt and the stretchiness of the one-piece I wore underneath that, and the scar that symbolized the only secret of mine the media had never gotten their hands on, I matched my smile to his tone of voice. "I deal with it."

"I bet you do."

"Stop trying to figure me out," I said, remembering his words from the other afternoon when he'd called me difficult. If I was so difficult, why wouldn't he just let this thing with me go? Hell, why couldn't I just let this thing go?

His eyes challenged me. "You can't take it?"

"Just . . . stop," I whispered.

He shook his head to each side in amazement. "Fine. When you want to give this thing between us a go, you let me know. You be the one to change the game." When I didn't say anything, he motioned out to where Eric was sloshing through the waves, with Paige sitting on his shoulders, her short legs wrapped around him and her tattooed arms flailing wildly. They looked happy. So fucking happy I felt my stomach burn.

"You should probably go before I change my mind about doing what Dickson's paying me to do," Cooper said.

For a moment—hell, longer than a moment—I wanted to turn and tell him I didn't want him to just do what Dickson was paying him to do. That I wanted so much more from him. By the time I'd worked myself up enough to speak, the door to the house was clanging shut.

Swallowing hard and cursing at myself for being so difficult, so afraid of starting a new relationship, afraid of happiness, I grabbed my board and joined Paige and Eric.

CHAPTER TEN

If Cooper was in a bad mood, he didn't show it Thursday morning during our lesson. Maybe it was because for the first time, we took on real waves and he could tell I was scared shitless. Or because he knew that after the weekend was over, shooting would begin—which, to be honest, also made me scared shitless. When I spoke to James Dickson and Kevin that evening on a conference call, Dickson told me that some of the crew had already started arriving.

"Yay for me," I said; I knew the film crew and their cameras would attract the paparazzi. Nikons and Canons would suddenly become my worst enemies again. I was ecstatic (and shocked) that I hadn't been photographed, and I didn't want it to end just yet.

"How's the training going?" Dickson asked, changing the subject.

I decided not to tell him how Cooper had made me practice pop-ups for days and switched the game on me with paddle-boarding at one point. "We tackled small waves today," I said. It was the truth and I'd only fallen once, taking in a mouthful of salt. Cooper had told me I looked better than some of the people he'd trained for months, and I'd blushed like an idiot.

No matter how much I pushed him away, that guy was slowly unraveling me.

"Small waves are good," Kevin said enthusiastically, and I imagined him fidgeting with his lower lip as he prayed I wouldn't say anything screwed-up during this call.

"I completely agree," Dickson said. He hesitated for a moment, then asked, "And you've got the script down?"

"Not only have I watched the original like twenty times now, I know Alyssa Mayer better than I know Willow Avery," I said, referring to the girl I was about to become for at least the next month and a half of my life, maybe even more. I liked the escape of being someone else for a little while, even if that imaginary person had already been played by another actress.

Dickson sighed. "Perfect. I've got to go to dinner with my wife, but I'll see you at the end of the weekend. You be good, Willow."

"Can't wait," I said. As soon as the conference call was disconnected, Kevin called me back and asked a million more questions. I answered them as I shuffled around the kitchen preparing my dinner—mahi-mahi and half a sweet potato.

As I stared at the fish in my plate, I found myself wondering what Cooper, Paige, and Eric were eating tonight.

"Willow? Willow?"

I sat down alone at the kitchen table and pulled a rush of air through my clenched teeth. "Yes?"

"You're distant tonight. You're not . . . doing anything, are you? Tom Miller refuses to answer any of my messages so . . ."

Dropping my fork onto my plate, I demanded, "You're pumping my bodyguard about me?"

Kevin was unapologetic. "We need you at your best for this film."

"Thanks for fucking believing in me, but the answer is no, I'm not on anything. Leave Miller alone."

When we hung up shortly thereafter, I hoped Kevin wouldn't call back anytime soon. I knew he meant well—in his own way—but space from him was often a good thing.

The next morning, when Miller came downstairs to take me to surf lessons, the conversation with Kevin was still fresh on my mind. "Not quite done dressing," I said, holding the door open for him to come inside. He sat in the recliner close to the door, staring at the toes of his white K-Swiss sneakers as I rushed to find the black tank top I'd picked out for myself earlier. When I located it between the couch and one of the side tables, I heaved a sigh.

"I need to clean up," I muttered and Miller nodded in agreement. After I pulled the top over my head and tied my dark hair into a high ponytail, I sighed. "Miller, I'm just going to get this out right now—thank you."

He cocked an eyebrow and tilted his head to one side. "For what?"

"For making these last several days not completely suck. For not wanting to . . . well, you know. For not reporting my *every* move to my agent."

Miller had tanned recently at the nearby gym he'd joined, but his flush was still vivid. He shuffled his feet together. "Have to say, Willow, you're creeping me out."

"I know that I can be . . ." The words Cooper had used to describe me played in my mind again, and I trembled before slinking down on the edge of the couch to put on my shoes. "I know that I'm difficult, but thanks for not talking to my agent about me."

Miller lifted his giant shoulders. "I'm here for *you*. Not your agent or your parents or James Dickson. And truth be told, I'm doing a shitty job."

Biting my lip, I frowned and clutched my flip-flop, bending the rubbery material. "What do you mean?" Had I misread him?

"You're not exactly hard to guard. You go to your lessons, to your community service, and you go home."

Relaxing, I slid my shoe on and grabbed my bag from the floor. "Thanks for reminding me how boring I am." When I winked at him, he chuckled. "Ready?" I asked, walking to the front door.

"You've got it, boss."

When we arrived at Cooper's place, not only was Paige's gray Grand Caravan there, parked behind Eric's truck, but when I went inside, Cooper met me in the foyer with his finger over his mouth.

"They're asleep in the den," he mouthed, sliding his hand

into mine to guide me outside. Delicious tingles crept up my arm, through the rest of my body, and as the warning bells in my head went off, I ignored them. "Ready to bomb?" he asked once we were on the deck. I cocked an eyebrow and he laughed, shaking his head. "Shit, surfer talk. Um . . . you ready to try a big wave?"

"Totally amped," I said.

As he turned to pick up our boards from the deck floor, I stopped him, wrapping my fingers around his forearm. He stared at me with questioning eyes as I leaned in close to finally read the tattoo running up his side. *"And quiet sleep and a sweet dream when the long trick's over,"* I murmured aloud.

"It's a quote. John Masefield."

Nodding, I took things a step further, reaching out to touch him. He went still, but he didn't stop me as I traced my fingertip over each intricate letter.

"If that were only your tongue," he said once I was finished. He grabbed the boards and stood to face me. Even though there were several inches of fiberglass wedged between our bodies, I could practically feel his on top of mine. I wet my lips, and he groaned. "I wasn't exactly talking about on your own lips, but that works."

I pulled my board out of his grip, my fingertips skimming his, and balanced it on my head. "I'm sorry," I said, as we padded barefoot to where the waves were crashing more violently than any day I'd been here. He gave me a look, waiting for me to elaborate, and I sighed. Why did he have to make it so hard? "About the other night. Being so . . ."

"Difficult?"

"Don't be a dick."

"I'm not the one apologizing for being difficult."

I sighed, shaking my head, and shuffled my feet, kicking up sand. "I'm not good with relationships," I said.

"We could learn," he said, and I shivered. "But for now, let's just enjoy this."

We pushed our boards into the sea, sloshing out past the white water. Once the water came up just under my breasts, Cooper nodded. "Okay, push off the floor with your feet and—"

Before he could finish speaking, I kicked off the sand with the balls of my feet and easily slid my body onto the purple-and-white board. I looked over at him, grinning, as I began to paddle my arms through the water using long strokes. He was right behind me.

"Confident much?" he asked.

"I've got the best teacher, don't I?"

He tilted his head back. "Well, yes, but I don't want you to get in over your head."

"You said you'll look after me," I said teasingly, but the fiercely protective expression that took over his face made some of that lightheartedness disappear. When he looked at me like that, I felt like the sea could drain dry and he wouldn't even notice.

"Always," he said. Then he frowned, breaking our eye contact, and shook his head. "We're too far out, Wills. Let's go back some."

"Lame ass," I said, but I began to paddle my board around to take his advice. I expected him to come back with something witty and sexy or so intense it made my stomach and between my legs hurt. "What, no comeback?" I asked.

"Paddle back," he said. "Now!"

It was only then that I saw, and heard, the giant wall of water coming toward us. My heart hurled itself into my throat, choking me, and my body went numb. For a moment, I couldn't move or breathe—all I could do was watch the wave get closer, bigger.

Cooper's accented voice finally broke through my haze, shouting over and over again for me to paddle.

I pumped my arms hard, drifting my board over the first wave. When I popped up, taking on the second, I could have sworn I heard Cooper say something. But then the next swell came at me, knocking me off my board. The sea crashed over my head, dragging me beneath the white water, and the only thing I heard was the sound of my heart exploding inside of my ears.

I fought the sea—tried to use the surfboard string attached to my ankle to claw myself back to the surface—but all that did was yank me down even farther. When my feet touched the bottom, terror ripped through my body.

Then, a pair of familiar arms wrapped around my waist.

A moment later, Cooper and I broke the surface, both of us gasping for air.

My head was spinning as he whispered repeatedly, "You're all right."

I was numb as he helped me climb onto my board. He pushed me back to shore in silence, but once we hit the sand, and he stood over me, examining me, all I could think about was how he'd saved me. How he'd found me.

But a moment later when I wrapped myself around him, seeking out his tongue with my own, he pushed away from me.

"You almost drowned, Wills," he said through clenched teeth.

He was rejecting me. Holy fuck, he was actually rejecting me after all the effort he'd put into telling me how much he wanted me.

I wouldn't let him know how badly that stung. Trying to seem nonchalant about the fact I'd almost drowned and he'd shoved me away only moments later, I said, "Thanks for looking out for me." I turned away from him, yanking my hairband out, releasing my dark hair to tumble down my back in a mess of tangles. When I faced him again, his body tensed up, and I mentally slapped myself.

"What I mean is—thank you for pulling me back in. I don't want to drown before . . ."

Before what, Willow? Before you can fuck up again?

I ignored that voice, bending down when he did to help him pick up our boards. Our hands reached for my purple one at the exact same time and he had no other choice but to look up.

"I'm okay," I whispered, unable to form any other words.

He laughed, shaking his head, as he tugged the board from my grip and stood up. "When you're like this, I can't—"

"Can't what?"

He started the trek back to his house, so I scrambled to my feet, ignoring my aching muscles, and caught up to him. He looked down at me and gave me a tortured smile. Didn't he know I was a sucker for angsty, tortured looks?

"I want to kiss you. Again and again," he said in a hoarse voice.

"You had your chance, so why didn't you?" I demanded. He gave me a dark look and started to turn away, but I grabbed his free arm, forcing him to look at me. "Don't be fucking wishy-washy, Cooper."

He threw both the boards down. They fell into the sand, clanged against each other, as he yanked my body against his. I stood my ground and dared his blue eyes with my own, even though my chest felt like it would burst from the pressure. Screw Cooper. Screw him for making me feel like this over and over and over again.

"I'm not wishy-washy. I know exactly what and who I want, but I'm also smart enough to know when that person isn't ready or willing. You tried to kiss me because you wanted to pay me back for saving you and I refuse to take advantage of that." I opened my mouth to argue, but he hushed me, catching my lips gently between his thumb and forefinger. "When you went under, I freaked out. I don't want you to get hurt out there but I can't stop you from falling."

No. God, no—how did he expect me to respond when he was talking about falling and getting hurt? How the hell did he even expect me to catch my breath when his words had so many meanings? I nodded, and he dragged his fingertips away from my mouth, sliding them gently down my chin, down the column of my throat, stopping right above my heart.

"We should head back," I said in a cracked whisper. "I've got community service."

I walked away, pretending not to hear what he said next:

"That's the only thing stopping me from taking you inside to show you I'm not the least bit unsure of what *I* want."

The moment we stepped into the house, Cooper headed upstairs to his bedroom, stripping away his swim trunks and wet T-shirt along the way. I gripped the banister to keep myself from following him.

"See you in two days, Wills," he yelled, disappearing around the corner. I sighed, and then shuffled into the shop area. Miller was already there, leaning his massive frame against the surfboard counter, and he and Eric were laughing about something.

"You look like a wave beat the crap out of you," a voice said from the far corner, and I spun around to see Paige sitting in front of a T-shirt display, carefully folding promotional tees for the shop. I gave her a dark look and her smile faded a little. "Oh . . . guess it did."

I lingered a few steps away from the door and shot my bodyguard a pleading look. "You ready?" I pressed the tiny button on the side of my phone to illuminate the screen. "I'd like to get to the shelter in the next thirty minutes."

He gave me a tiny nod and swiped the keys to the Kia off the counter. As he came toward me, his expression changed to worry, but I pursed my lips and shook my head. "I'm fine," I said. To Paige and Eric, who were now organizing sunblock bottles in the compartment behind the counter, I said, "See you guys soon."

"Get some rest. You don't look like yourself," Eric said. When I turned around to glare at him, and Paige snorted in disgust, he shrugged. "Do you want me to lie to you?"

"Bye, guys," I said, this time my voice final, and I walked with Miller into the foyer. Paige stopped me halfway to the car, her short black hair flying around her face as she bounded down the steps.

"Hey! You're coming to Cooper's party tomorrow night, yes?" she asked, bobbing her head up and down as if it would help me make up my mind. I hadn't even known there was a party, so I shook my head, frowning.

"Wasn't invited."

I didn't know why saying that bothered me, but it did. Quite a bit.

"Don't be stupid—of course you're invited. It's for a competition he won a couple months ago," she said. Then, her eyes widened and she tilted her head to look at Miller, who was climbing into the Kia. "You're worried about being safe? Because there's nobody coming you'd have to worry about."

"No, I mean . . . I doubt Cooper wants me to come." Not when there were a million pounds of frustration between us.

Placing her hands on her hips, Paige glanced at me, then back at the house, and finally at me again, all the while keeping her face completely blank. I started to walk away toward the Kia.

"Well, Cooper can suck it the fuck up," she said. "Eric and I are hosting it and you're coming, even if I have to drag your ass out of my parents' rental house."

"We'll see."

"I'll come and get you," she warned as I got into the Kia.

I gave her a thumbs-up as Miller pulled away, heaving a sigh of relief when we were out of sight. "Tired?" he asked.

I gazed out the window, letting the beach houses become a white-and-brown blur. I thought of the painful nightmares I'd had several days this week and waking up with that need to drown my sorrows. I thought of how the sea had pulled me under this afternoon and the way Cooper had found me, his hands tightening around me, saving me, pulling me back in.

Cooper was wrong.

I knew exactly what I wanted. It was him.

Over the next twenty-four hours I knocked out ten hours of community service. This time I followed Dave's directions not to communicate with the residents at Harmony House, thanks to the iPod I borrowed from Miller that was full of angsty music—Five Finger Death Punch, Puddle of Mudd, and Saving Abel, to name a few. The work was monotonous and boring, but it kept my thoughts off Cooper and the fact that shooting was scheduled to begin in a few days.

I hadn't acted in what felt like an eternity and the more I thought about being on camera again, how much I still needed to learn from Cooper, the more anxious I became.

When I texted Jessica on Saturday evening, I mentioned how nervous I was and she responded almost immediately.

6:36 p.m.: WTF? You'll be fine. You always are.

6:37 p.m.: Please tell me you're coming back to LA for your birthday? We'll celebrate in style! ;)

I reread Jessica's last text repeatedly, letting the meaning sink deep enough into my brain to give me a headache, allowing the shame and frustration to ooze through my veins. No matter what she thought, I wasn't going to spend another birthday so fucked-up that I could barely think or move. Cooper managed to do that to me every time I had a surf lesson with him but at least I didn't wake up unsure of what I'd done the night before.

I wasn't going to message her back, but then she sent me a series of question marks, and I gave in.

6:43 p.m.: No. I'll probably have to work on my birthday.

6:43 p.m.: Filming has never stopped you before . . .

Dot, dot, dot. Jessica had to know how much that irritated me because of the implications behind it.

She didn't text back—not that I expected her to since she'd gotten in the last word—so I set the phone screen-side down on the table, beside my empty dinner plate. Placing my elbows onto the wood surface, I leaned forward, rubbing my face with my palms. Like it would help scrub the dirty feeling away from my skin.

Why had I texted Jessica? It wasn't like she and I had ever had a healthy or decent conversation since we reconnected. But even as I questioned myself, I knew the exact reason why I messaged her. I'd been in Hawaii for two weeks and aside from Cooper and his friends and Miller, I was alone.

Pulling a deep breath in through my nose, I gripped either side of the table and shook my head. I wasn't going to be alone tonight—not when I had an invitation. I grabbed my phone and texted Paige, asking if she'd pick me up.

She called me fifteen minutes later, as I was taking a shower. "Hey," I answered breathlessly, leaning my head against the shower wall farthest from the steady stream of water. "Does that invitation still stand?"

"Yes, why wouldn't it—hey, is that running water?"

I laughed, but my voice caught. "I'm showering."

"Oh baby, that's hot," she said dryly.

"Hoebag."

"You bringing the bodyguard?"

"He has a second job."

She must have heard the hesitation in my voice because she was silent for an uncomfortably long moment before she said, "You don't have to worry. It's just going to be a bunch of us sitting around the beach, playing some music." I sighed and she added, "And you'll be with Cooper. Not that that means anything, of course . . . just saying since you know him, you know."

I could hear the smile in her voice.

"I'll be ready in half an hour," I said, pushing past the lump in my throat.

I dressed slowly, carefully, in a white eyelet dress that probably wouldn't have fit as well two weeks ago, and the wedge sandals Cooper teased me about when he caught me wearing them to community service. I wore makeup for the first time since I arrived—red lipstick and dark eyeliner that made my green eyes stand out against my pale skin. As I applied a shimmery bronzer over my skin, I realized that this was the first of so many makeup sessions in the coming weeks. On Monday the cameras would come, the rest of the cast, the paparazzi.

But tonight, I'd have fun with people who weren't waiting for me to fuck up.

And I'd be with Cooper.

CHAPTER ELEVEN

An hour after we hung up, Paige pulled up in her Dodge and blew the horn. Though I'd checked my appearance at least a dozen times since getting dressed, I studied myself one more time before I grabbed my bag and cell phone and locked up behind myself. I'd already sent Miller a text telling him where I was going for the night, but I quickly ran up the outside steps to his apartment and slipped a note beneath his door, just in case, before I climbed into Paige's van.

Miller would probably message me back soon and tell me what a shitty bodyguard he thought he was.

Paige turned to me, her face pulled into a dramatic pout. "Sorry I'm so late. Had to go play shuttle for a few friends."

I shook my head. "Not a big deal." Dragging the seat belt

across my body and buckling it, I continued, "I mean, I've only been dressed an hour and the AC unit in your parents' house sucks, but whatever."

She nudged my bare shoulder softly with her knuckles. "Smart-ass," she said, her face lighting up as she grinned widely. "I'm DD, so you know how that goes."

My toes curled. "Not really. I lost my license for running into a building while I was fucked-up on methadone."

The van swerved a little over the yellow line, and Paige flinched. I saw her mouth move into something that looked like "Holy crap." She glanced over at me, her face full of remorse and said, "Oh my God, Willow, I didn't—"

"Ugh, if you apologize I'll punch you in the boob," I said. "I'm not proud of what happened, or what I did, or my fuckups, but it's public knowledge." Still, I had to take a deep breath to put myself back together. Saying those words aloud just reminded me that so much of my life was a book, left wide open for anyone to skim through.

"Yeah, but I don't want to seem so—"

"What? Insensitive? Don't worry, I'm pretty sure if you Google me, my lawsuits come up before any of the good I've done." *All except for one.*

I shook that thought from my head because I didn't want to think about any of that tonight. I wasn't sure if that was selfish and fucked-up, but I needed this night for myself.

"Oh, Willow . . ."

I turned my body in the seat to give her a firm look. "It doesn't bother me. Let's just have fun and celebrate Cooper's win." I wouldn't add that this was the first party I'd gone to since the one more than six months ago. The party I'd left on a stretcher. The party that ended my last role and landed me in Honolulu in the first place.

Paige sighed and nodded, but she didn't loosen her grip on the worn leather wheel. We'd managed to make the atmosphere inside of the van entirely toxic, and by the time we pulled into an empty spot in Cooper's driveway, I felt like I'd die if I didn't get fresh air. I stumbled out of the vehicle, nearly twisting my ankle in the process, and inhaled deeply. I squatted in a position that would have the paparazzi shitting themselves to take a picture, rested my forearms on my knees, and counted, slowly, to ten.

After a minute, I heard the driver's-side door shut. I straightened, smoothed out the wrinkles in my dress, and walked confidently to the front bumper, where Paige was leaning against it, pulling her black hair into a short ponytail.

"I feel overdressed," I said dryly, taking in her plain green T-shirt and tiny denim shorts.

"You are." Then she smiled and stuffed her hands into her back pockets, leaning back to give me a once-over. "And God, you look like an accident waiting to happen. A thousand bucks you'll ruin that dress by the end of the night," she said.

I snorted. "I don't think I have a thousand bucks to spare," I replied, but I couldn't help thinking of my advance deposit, money I still hadn't touched.

She winked. "I don't either."

Letting an Ed Sheeran song and the sound of laughter act as our guide, we walked around the house to the backyard. The moment the beach came into view, I felt like I was in paradise. Someone had turned on the strings of lantern lights hanging above the deck, and they cast a faint, multicolored glow on the sand. A small throng of people huddled around a bonfire in a circle of beach chairs, and my eyes immediately settled on Cooper. He was shirtless—but what else was new?—and talking to a pretty blonde girl in a bikini who was making the kind of wide-ass gestures with her hands that drove me crazy. And he was laughing. The pit of my belly churned, and I quickly looked away from him, to the sea.

Paige slipped beside me, tucking her finger under my chin to close my parted lips. She stretched her arms, linking her fingers behind her. "Beautiful, huh?"

My gaze drifted back to Cooper and the other girl. "Every time I see it."

"I'm talking about the ocean at night," Paige said. "But yeah, he's pretty nice too if you like blonds. Me? The skinnier and scruffier, the better."

If Cooper hadn't glanced up then, catching my eyes with his, making me feel like I was the only person on the beach, I would have been able to keep my voice even. Instead, I said in a gasp, "I'm not talking about him."

God, where was Willow Avery, the actress? Where was that girl who didn't give a shit? Wherever she was, she was laughing at me.

"Fucking liar," Paige said, shaking her head in undisguised amusement.

I pretended not to watch Cooper excuse himself from the

chick in the bikini. He made his way toward Paige and me, and for a moment, I couldn't read the expression on his face. It was blank, and I felt something sink in my rib cage. Maybe I'd been wrong for coming here.

I was invading his personal time.

I was his client.

I was—

He was smiling, a slow, heartbreaking grin that pulled me forward on wobbly legs until we met halfway. "My favorite movie star," he said teasingly.

"You hate film people," I pointed out softly.

"Not when they show up to my house looking like you do."

"Going to find my boyfriend," Paige said in a loud voice, breezing past us. "Oh no Paige, don't go!" she squealed. "We love when you're the creepy third wheel." She glanced over her shoulder at us and winked. "No, but seriously if you need me, I'll be keeping Eric from the lure of doing a naked keg stand."

I followed her finger to the keg on the deck. Eric was sitting beside it holding two cups of beer as he talked to another guy. I returned my gaze to Paige and pressed my lips into a fine line. "If that happens I'm walking home," I said. Once she was out of earshot, I glanced up at Cooper. "Sorry for interrupting your conversation with . . ."

"Miranda."

Miranda. As in Officer Stewart's sister. As in his ex-girlfriend. I peeked over his shoulder, not quite caring if anyone saw me, and he laughed.

"Who knew that a surfer from Hawaii could make *the* Willow Avery jealous?" He started to walk away from me, toward his friends. "Come on, I'll introduce you to everyone."

I caught up beside him, cursing myself for the wedge sandals. "This place looks amazing," I said, as we stood on the sidelines of the bonfire. I pointed down at it. "And I'm pretty sure that's totally illegal."

He lifted an eyebrow. "Studying up on local rules?"

"My script," I explained. "Alyssa . . . gets in trouble for having one."

"That wasn't in the original," he said.

My head jerked up in surprise. "You've seen *Tidal?*" When he lifted his chin slightly, I released a little laugh. "Sorry, just didn't take you for the romantic movie type."

He clutched his muscular chest and pretended to look hurt. "Wills, you don't give me enough credit," he said, before pushing his way through a couple of his friends. They turned to grin at us as he gestured for me to sit in an empty beach chair. He took the one beside me, taking a red plastic cup from someone when they offered it to him.

A moment later, his friends started to gravitate toward us. I held my breath as he introduced me as one of his clients, and I half expected someone to make a joke about the drugs or ask me a question about Hollywood, but nobody did.

"Did Coop tell you I'm an extra in your movie?" a guy named Knox with spiky red hair asked me when Cooper disappeared to refill his beer. Nobody else had noticed, but I'd seen him dumping the contents of his cup—all of his beer—into the sand a few minutes before.

I shook my head. "No, he didn't." Up until tonight, Cooper hadn't mentioned any of his friends aside from Eric and Paige.

"They tried to get our boy here," Knox said, nodding to my other side where Cooper was sitting back down.

I focused my attention on Cooper when I asked, "Why'd you say no?"

"You know how I feel about Hollywood, Wills," he said, and Knox rolled his eyes before pulling a girl who was passing by into his lap to take a chug out of the drink she was holding.

"I've got to go to the bathroom," I told Cooper as I stood up, and he got up next to me. I gave him a sideways look as we walked inside the house. "You're coming in with me?"

"Are you inviting me?"

"Absolutely not."

Someone was already inside the bathroom next to the laundry room, so I stood with Cooper in silence, crossing my legs together tightly as we waited. He was biting the corner of his lip and pretending to look down at a doorstop extending from the baseboard, but I could feel his gaze heating the side of my face. I started to tease him about it, but then the bathroom door opened. I almost groaned when Miranda stepped out, wobbling a little. She looked surprised for a moment, as she glanced back and forth between my face and Cooper's, but then she smiled. A genuine one at that.

"All yours," she said, before disappearing down the deck hallway.

I honestly wasn't sure if she was talking about the bathroom or the boy beside me, but when we went back outside I didn't see her and I realized she must have already left. Cooper caught my wrist when I started to gravitate toward the bonfire and gave me a tiny smile. "Let's get away."

"Yes."

We walked with a couple inches of space between us as we headed away from the party, but when the sides of our bodies brushed, he reached between us, lacing our fingertips. A tingle raced up my arm.

"I should've said this before, but congrats," I said, trying my best to ignore the pressure weighing down on my chest, making it difficult for me to breathe around him.

"For what?"

"The competition you won. That's what this party is for, right?"

"And here I was thinking you were congratulating me for finally getting the girl," he said, and when I inhaled deeply, he ducked his head and added, "But thank you."

The sound of the party slowly faded as we walked farther away from his house. Away from the lights and his friends. Away from turning back.

"You've got guests," I said at last, stopping beneath one of the palm trees peppering the beach.

"It's my party," he pointed out, "and besides, it's thinning out. They'll probably be gone before we get back."

"And you're leaving it to break your rule about clients," I whispered.

He froze, and my lips dragged up into a satisfied smile. Cool,

calm, and collected Surfer Boy was frazzled because of something I'd said. It didn't last very long. Tightening his grip on my
fingers, he closed the space between our bodies, keeping each
movement controlled. His lips parted, and I expected him to
question me like he always did, to ask me if he was what I really
wanted. Instead, he backed me up against the tree, pinning my
hands over my head so that the bark scratched my palms.

Everything touched—our bodies and lips and tongues. He
smelled like coconut and salt water, and more than anything I
wanted that scent on my own skin. I was hardly aware when he
took me down with him to the ground, pulling me on top of him.

His thumb pressed against the center of my panties—against
the center of myself—and I about lost it.

Breaking away from his mouth, I whispered, "I haven't done
this in a really long time."

He pulled his hand from my panties, cupping my face and
tangling his fingers into stray strands of my hair. "I know."

"Cooper, I'm not going to have sex with you—at least not
out here."

"Jesus, Wills, we've been undoing one another for days. The
last place we're going to tear each other apart is right here, in
the sand. Guess you can say I'm greedy because I want to be the
only one who hears you come," he whispered in a harsh voice,
hushing my gasp with his tongue, his lips, before it even had a
chance to surface.

When I came up for air this time, I tightened my knees
against his sides and raked my fingers through his blond hair.

He squeezed my bottom and grinned, but it wasn't easygoing or teasing, like usual. It was brimming with frustration.

"You never talked to me like this before," I said.

He gave a husky laugh and then sat upright, gripping me like he'd never let go. "You coming here tonight was the game-changer."

CHAPTER TWELVE

≈≈≈≈≈≈≈≈≈≈≈≈≈

In the two weeks I'd been taking surf lessons with Cooper, I hadn't once seen the inside of his bedroom or any area of his house other than the laundry room, bathroom, kitchen, and shop. Until tonight.

By the time we'd returned to the beach, the party was over and everyone had scattered. I had a feeling that Paige had something to do with that, but I didn't say anything as Cooper guided me inside through the deck door, locking it behind us.

His fingertips pulled gently on my own as he walked backward, guiding me toward the staircase. He dropped my hand and motioned for me to go up first. I moved slowly, feeling my heart pulse a little harder with each step.

"You're quiet, Wills," he said.

"I thought you liked it when I was quiet," I teased, grinning. Spinning me around to face him, he ran the tip of his tongue across my bottom lip. My hand flew up to touch that spot as we climbed the last six stairs.

"I don't want you quiet tonight," he said.

The second Cooper closed his bedroom door he lifted me up, gripping my thighs through my white dress. I wrapped myself around him, crossing my feet behind his back, draping my arms around his shoulders.

"Do you want to hear something, Wills?" he asked in a low, sexy whisper, his accent clipping every other word.

"No," I said honestly. I just wanted him to kiss me until I couldn't think.

He pinned me hard to the wall, and the dresser a few feet away shook, rattling the items strewn across it. "I've wanted to do this since night one."

"When you came back here with a hard-on?" I asked breathlessly.

He coaxed one of my hands from around his neck, grinning when I tightened the grip my legs had on his body, and kissed the inside of my wrist. "Further back."

I moaned as he skimmed his other hand along the low-cut, elastic line of my panties. "That was our first night," I pointed out. I ignored my conscience when it yelled at me that that night was only twelve days ago. People screw a lot earlier.

Yes, they do. So fuck off, conscience.

"We had to meet, right?" he asked.

"Lunch?" I squeaked, and he nodded slowly. He drowned my

surprise out, slanting his lips over mine, demanding that I open them for him. I did.

"I want to be inside of you, Willow. I want to watch your face when I'm inside of you, when you sigh, when you come for me. And Willow?"

He was using my whole name again.

"Yes?" I said.

He released me, standing me up, with his hands on either side of my shoulders to steady me. I automatically moved toward him, as if a magnet pulled me, but he shook his head, keeping me in place.

"You're going to tell me right now if you're not for sure," he said.

"I want you, Cooper. I don't know what the fuck else I want anymore, but I want this right now."

That's all it took. He gathered me in his arms, holding me close as he carried me to his king-size bed. He sat me on the edge and I scooted backward until I was in the center with the blankets bunched around my hips.

"You look so sweet," he said. The way his body moved as he crawled up to me was the most sensual thing I'd ever seen, and I gave a hoarse cry as he pulled me beneath him, kissing my lips until they were sore. "Relax."

"What are you going to—"

"Just . . . do it, Wills."

His fingers scorched my skin as they traced up my legs, inside my thighs, stopping at my center. I gasped and bolted up when he stroked the outside of my panties, but he squeezed my thigh.

"Relax. I'm not going to hurt you."

Not my body, but my heart?

I fell back against the pillows, closing my eyes as he dragged my panties off, shivering when the cool air from the ceiling fan above us hit my bare flesh. He made a rough noise in the back of his throat, and I felt the corner of my mouth tug up. "It's cold."

"Open your eyes, Wills."

The moment my eyelids fluttered apart to meet his gaze, he dipped his head between my legs, pushing his tongue against me. "Mmmmm," I moaned. I started to lift my hands from where they were bunched in the covers, but he locked his fingers around my wrists.

"We're alone and I need to hear this from you," he growled. "Let go for me, Willow. Please?"

I had a feeling those words would stay with me for the rest of my life, regardless of what happened after tonight, so I nodded. "Yes."

And then he bent down again, with my legs draped over his shoulders and the soles of my feet sliding up and down the hard lines of his back. When my body went rigid, he groaned; when I relaxed, he sighed; and when I tensed up again, finally going limp beneath his hot mouth, he released a low, sexy moan.

"Cooper?"

"Yes?" He traced his lips up the center of my body, as he slid my dress up along with his kisses.

"Kiss me again," I said.

When he reached my lips, I tasted myself and mint, and I shivered as I sat up a little so he could drag the white dress over my head. I heard it fall beside the bed. He shrugged my lacy strapless bra down around my waist, and the cool breeze from the fan made me shiver once again, but then he covered my breasts with his mouth, warming me, driving me crazy.

"Cooper, please?" I gasped, and he groaned against my damp skin. He started to pull away from me, from the bed, and I fell back against the soft sheets. "Where are you going?" I murmured.

"The lights. I told you I wanted to see all of you."

My heart raced, but for all the wrong reasons.

"Don't turn them on!" I whispered frantically, scrambling up on my knees, the mattress sinking a little. He turned back to face me, and I grasped his wrist. "Please . . . no lights?" I pleaded, surprised at how desperate my voice sounded.

He leaned in to kiss me, in that sensitive spot beneath my breasts, and brought my hand between us, wrapping my fingers around him. "You're beautiful, Wills. I *want* you."

He was wrong.

I wasn't beautiful.

I was damaged.

I felt stupid for letting myself forget that.

"I can't do the lights," I whispered.

Gripping my hips hard with his hands, he laid me back down, kneeling over me, and mumbled against my skin, "Do you know what this is doing to me? You naked and so fucking shy?" Whatever he was feeling, it wasn't anger. His voice just sounded amazed—broken and sexy and just a little rough.

I didn't have the heart to tell him that I hadn't always been shy like this. That if things had gone different, if my body weren't scarred, I probably would be the one jumping out of bed to flip on every light in the room.

He trailed kisses down my belly—so soft they felt like feathers teasing my skin. Reflexively, I wrapped my arm around my lower abdomen, even though my bra was already pushed down to hide the vicious scar, the reminder of what had happened the last time I fell so hard. When his lips brushed across my wrist, he looked up into my eyes.

I moaned—a mixture of need and frustration.

Why did this have to be so difficult?

"Willow . . . are you okay?"

"I know that I want you," I said firmly.

That must have been enough for him because he dug a condom out of the nightstand drawer, sliding it on before he lay back against the pillows. He motioned me to him and I gasped when he dragged me onto his lap, burying himself inside of my body. Cupping my face gently between his hands, he drew me closer to him until our chests were pressed together, until our foreheads touched.

"I don't want to let you go, Wills," he whispered, releasing my face to encircle me with his arms.

I was going to die. From the way he smelled and the way he felt inside of me. From the sound of his breathing.

I dug my fingertips into his shoulders, feeling his scar beneath my fingers and his heartbeat beneath my own. "I don't want you to," I gasped.

And then we became a tangle of skin and sweat, of mouths and tongues and hands. Of bodies and beating hearts.

Afterward, we clung together, strands of my hair stuck to his body and his arm wrapped protectively around me. His eyes were closed, and I stared up at the ceiling fan, watching it spin, and I tried to figure out whether I was dizzy from watching it or from Cooper. When I caught my breath and gazed over at him again, I decided it was because of him.

Always him.

I slid away, determined to find my clothes, and he rolled over, skimming his hands across my hips to stop me. I stood anyway, breathing heavily, with the backs of my legs pressed to the side of the bed as he placed a kiss at the small of my back.

As he slid his tongue up the curve of my spine.

And then he pushed strands of dark hair away from my nape, so that he could touch me there too.

"Where are you going?" he murmured.

"To put on my clothes . . ."

He spun me around to face him, searching my eyes in the dark. "Why?"

"So you can take me home."

"Do you want to go home?"

"No, but—"

"Then what's the problem?" he asked in a rough voice. When he saw me flinch, his blue eyes softened and he pulled me back onto the bed with him, one knee at a time, until we were kneeling together. "I'm not one of those guys, Wills. You're with me now."

I didn't know what that meant. I didn't know what any of that meant, but I heard myself laugh and ask shakily, "Who said anything about being together?"

We hit the pillows with our arms tangled around each other and he sighed into my hair. "*You* did, beautiful girl."

CHAPTER THIRTEEN

~~~~~~~~~~~~~~~~~~~~

I couldn't remember the last time I woke up next to someone where the details of the night before weren't a fucked-up haze or an altogether void. But when the sunlight filtered unsteadily through Cooper's bedroom window, pulling me awake, and I felt every inch of his body pressed up against mine, every touch and taste and sound from last night came rushing back to me.

So I decided to count this Sunday morning in Cooper's bed—in his arms, with my fingertips carefully tracing the text of his tattoo—as my first time being wide-awake since what had happened with Tyler years ago.

And quiet sleep and a sweet dream when the long trick's over.

Cooper didn't open his eyes until after I'd moved my hands past his chest, to his shoulder, where he caught my fingers before I could touch the scar on his back. He stared at me for a long time, before I murmured the same thing he'd said to me in his Jeep when we talked about Tyler. "Someone hurt you."

His gaze dipped to my mouth and he brought my fingers to his lips. "Just an accident from when I was a kid," he said.

"In Australia?" I asked, and he lifted his chin slightly. He raked his teeth lightly over my thumb, sucking the tip into his mouth. "You're lying."

Reluctantly, he pulled my finger out of his mouth, rubbing the tip of it across his lower lip, wetting it. It was so sexy that I felt my breath leave my body. "Why do you think that?" he questioned.

"Because of your eyes."

He cleared his throat. "What about them?"

"They're not looking into mine."

That brought his gaze back up. Groaning, he raked his hands through his hair. "Do you really want to know?" he demanded, and I gave a little nod of my head. He scooted himself upright, pressing his back up against the headboard as he squeezed the bridge of his nose. "All right."

There was so much emotion in just that one phrase that I immediately faltered. Fuck. I'd pushed too hard. I rolled over onto my belly and propped myself up on my elbows. "Cooper . . . you don't have to tell me," I whispered. I shivered as he reached out to skim his fingertips along my face. "You don't have—"

"Shhh, Wills," he murmured, leaning over to stroke his lips across my temple. When he pulled away he was smiling. "I was ten and my dad hit me with a fishing rod."

"I can see you're going to joke with me, so—" But then I looked past the dimple and the grin, past the relaxed expression on his face, and what I saw in his eyes stabbed me in the heart. They were vacant.

He wasn't fucking with me.

I swallowed hard, glancing away, but he quickly maneuvered my chin so that I was forced to face him.

"I didn't tell you that to make you feel sorry for me. It's just a fact. My dad hated me . . . I wasn't something he wanted." The way he said it—in the same easy tone he used when we discussed whether to go surfing or paddleboarding—made my stomach feel sour. A strangled sound burst from the back of my throat. "And there you go again, feeling bad," he muttered.

"How the hell do you expect me to feel after you tell me your dad hit you with a fishing pole?"

He narrowed his eyes. "People have way more fucked-up childhoods than I did. My mum loved me. That's all I needed—fuck, it's all I still need."

But his mother was gone. He'd said as much to me before. "I'm sorry, Cooper. So fucking sorry."

He slid down in the bed, straddling me, pressing his erection against my bottom. He murmured something about how inconvenient it was that I had the sheet draped across me, and then he kissed the spot between my shoulder blades.

"You have the sexiest—" Cooper started, but then he paused. His fingertips were gentle as he swept my hair away from my left shoulder. Then, carefully, so as not to press too much of his body weight down on top of me, he bent over to examine me.

"It's amazing what you find when the lights are on," he said in a low voice, before tracing the tip of his tongue along the small tattoo that ran across the soft skin behind my left ear.

I trembled and curled my hands into the sheets.

"*Five, nine, ten*," he whispered. "What's it mean?"

I twisted my head to glance over my shoulder into his eyes. "It's a date. When I lost someone that I loved." I was surprised I was being so honest with him.

I'd gotten the tattoo when I was high, and my mom had flipped out about it.

"*You can't have both, Willow. You can't keep a secret and then go and get a goddamn prison tattoo advertising his birthday*," she'd hissed.

"*It's not a prison tattoo*," I'd retorted. "*And nobody knows what it means.*"

"*We went through so much trouble making sure this didn't get out*," she'd said, reminding me of how she and Dad had sent me away from Los Angeles for months to live with her stepmother in Bumfuck, Oregon. "*Please be a bit more grateful.*"

"*Grateful? You let me sign a screwed-up agreement and I don't even know what happened.*"

After that, I hadn't talked to her for nearly a month, and I'd spent the majority of those thirty days forgetting that I even got the tattoo in the first place.

Cooper pulled me away from the bitter memory. "What are you thinking about?"

I shrugged. "Nothing."

"You're going to rip my sheets," Cooper said in a soothing

voice, taking his mouth, and then his hands, away from my flesh. I focused down at the cotton clenched in my hands and released it. "I'm not going to push you to talk, Wills. I'm not going to push you to do anything. But at the risk of sounding like a total pussy, I'll listen to anything that comes out of your mouth."

Burying my face into the sheets, I nodded. When I lifted my head a moment later, there was a tiny smile curving the corners of my lips. "Your sheets smell like your girly-ass shampoo."

"Smart-ass," he said, rolling me over. Our tongues and lips tangled together and that familiar ache crept from my stomach, in between my legs. I wanted to get lost in him again.

And again.

We stayed in his bed until I could no longer ignore the sound of my cell phone vibrating inside of my bag. There were a couple missed calls from Kevin, but the newest was a text from Jessica.

10:39 a.m.: I've got to tell you what I did last night, you busy?

Cooper rolled out of the bed, flashing me a knee-weakening smile over his shoulder as he disappeared naked into the enormous master bathroom. I heard the whistle of water running from the pipes a moment later. Exhaling, I cocooned myself in the sheet and messaged Jessica back as I waited for my turn to shower.

10:40 a.m.: Will call you later, okay?

She texted back with a wink smiley, and I rolled my eyes.

Half an hour later after we had both taken our showers, Cooper offered to make me breakfast.

"I'm not a very good cook," he explained, as he prepared a feast of Toaster Strudels and fresh fruit. "And Eric is probably going to bitch about me touching his strawberry strudel stash." He tossed the empty box into the trash can before handing me my plate.

"I basically live on a diet of organic waffles and grilled chicken and fish. I'd say this is pretty fucking awesome." I sat down across from him at the table and he smiled. "By the way, where *is* Eric?" The house had been quiet all morning, and I was half expecting Eric to pop around the corner with a video camera attached to his hand.

I shuddered at the thought.

Cooper took a drink of his orange juice. "Staying with Paige at her apartment. He, um, wanted to give me the house to myself for the weekend."

Luckily my phone buzzed right then and interrupted us before I could start freaking out about the possible implications behind Cooper's words. I picked up the phone and stared down at the screen, groaning when I saw a text from Kevin asking me to call him ASAP to iron out the details for tomorrow. I replied that I was working out and would call him as soon as I was finished.

It wasn't exactly a lie.

Cooper and I finished breakfast quickly, and though I

wanted to climb back into his bed, I asked him to take me home to my rental. When we reached the house and I stepped out of the Jeep, a thought hit me, and before I could stop myself, I asked, "Cooper?"

"Mmm?"

"Why'd your dad do it?"

He leaned his head on the headrest and gave me a hard look. "Because mum loved me and everything I represented more than him." I didn't know what that meant and he chose not to elaborate. "Willow? Tomorrow, when you're that girl again, will I just be the surfer bum from Hawaii?"

Though his words were teasing, there was a serious edge to his voice that made my throat go dry. I slid back down into my seat and gazed straight ahead until the sun turned the kids playing basketball at the end of the street into a dusty blur. No, I couldn't imagine Cooper being a just *anything* after last night.

And after this morning.

"I'm not good with relationships," I said, and I heard his breath catch. "And from what you've told me, neither are you. But that doesn't stop me from wanting more of you."

He moved closer, despite the center console separating us, and stroked my cheek. Every nerve in my body tingled as his blue eyes connected with mine. God, when had this happened?

When had I started wanting him like this?

When had I started caring whether he wanted me back?

My voice was heavy when I spoke. "I . . . know you hate Hollywood. You'll be ripped apart if we make this public, so—"

He shook his head, moving his hand from my jawline to hold my chin. "I'm not hiding. And I'm not fucking afraid of some douchebag with a camera."

"You've got no clue."

Tilting his head to one side, he rolled his lips together. "I can handle whatever they do to me. It's you I'm worried about."

"It doesn't bother me anymore," I said.

Liar.

If it doesn't bother you, why haven't you googled your name since coming to Hawaii?

I took a deep breath to ground myself. "Let's just get through the first week of shooting, okay?" Reaching up, I touched his face with the back of my hand. "And just enjoy this?"

For a moment he looked like he was about to argue with me, like he was going to laugh at me and tell me to piss off, but then he nodded slowly.

He kissed me again before walking me to my front door, and as I watched him go, I realized this was another first for me:

My first normal relationship in my adult life.

When I finally got in touch with Kevin toward the middle of the afternoon, I found out I was expected to attend a press conference the next morning with some of the key members of the cast. This was the second time in my entire career that I hadn't met any of the people I'd be working with. Usually, I was sick of the rest of the cast by now after multiple screen tests for chemistry and meet and greets.

Apparently, James Dickson had a shitload of confidence in me.

My mother called me shortly after I spoke to Kevin. I was in the middle of studying my script, with the original version of the movie playing quietly in the background for inspiration, when I answered.

"Have you checked Leah Dishes Hollywood today?" Her voice was brimming with excitement when she referred to the infamous celebrity blog that hated me.

I rolled my eyes. "Nice to hear from you too, Mom."

"I'm guessing you haven't looked." I could picture her face falling just by the way her voice had dropped.

"I'm not in the habit of reading about myself being mocked." But for some reason, I'd already pulled my MacBook off the coffee table and was trying to find the website she was talking about. When it loaded, I saw myself, standing next to Tyler at the premier of *Into the Dark* almost four years ago. Same dark-brown hair, same green eyes, same pouty lips, but the look on my face was so alive, so in love with the guy on my right side, that it made my chest burn.

Avery Surfs into Hilary Norton Role

Directly below the headline was a film still of the gorgeous actress who'd starred in *Tidal* in the late eighties, grinning at the camera and gripping a brown surfboard as her blond hair blew around her shoulders.

I skimmed the page as my mom chattered on, telling me how thrilled she was about the film. Certain words in the blog post jumped out at me, like "rehab" and "lawsuit" and then of course there were the comparisons between Hilary and me.

Overdose.

The article ended on what my mother claimed was a positive note—the writer mentioned how excited she was to see the movie since she'd been such a fan of the original. Then she'd added that she hoped to every higher power that existed that Avery didn't "dumb down" such a classic.

"Nice," I said, closing the MacBook before curiosity got the best of me and I scrolled down to look at the comments. They were never pretty, and the last thing I wanted was to let them get to me and tear up the high I'd gotten with Cooper.

"People are talking about you again in a good way," Mom said.

"Yeah, I guess," I said. There was a knock at the front door, and I peeked up to see Miller standing on the other side of the screen. I motioned him in and pressed my finger over my lips. "Hey Mom, sorry, someone from wardrobe just showed up to—"

She gasped. "They're sending them to your house now?"

"That's what happens when you're washed up," I replied sarcastically.

"Don't be ridiculous, you're nineteen."

"Twenty in two weeks," I pointed out. I wasn't sure if she remembered, so maybe this would serve as a reminder for her not to miss my birthday. When we disconnected seconds later, I pushed my hair out of my face and gave Miller an apologetic smile. "Sorry about that. My mom is . . ."

Scratching the center of his close-cropped hair, he chuckled. "You don't have to tell me, I've got one too." We sat there for nearly a minute, in one of those awkward silences, and then Miller said, "So you're ready to go?"

"What?"

He frowned for a moment, checked his phone's screen, and then answered. "You said you were doing community service this afternoon, right?"

Fuck.

Of course I'd told him that yesterday afternoon, before I'd changed my mind about going to Cooper's party. "I've got shit for brains today," I explained.

He flushed and looked down, and then I groaned, because he knew exactly where I'd gone last night.

"I'm just going to go die now," I murmured, before skulking back to my bedroom to throw on some old clothes.

Miller was good enough not to say anything about Cooper, but when we arrived at the shelter he took a deep breath. "I know I'm just the guy hired to watch out for you . . ."

I rolled my eyes. "If you give me that 'I suck at my job' thing, I'll cut you."

He laughed. "Oh, don't worry; I'm on high alert when it comes to you right now." I lifted an eyebrow, and he added, "I like to think you won't need me, but people are . . . crazy."

I buried my face into my hands. "Don't remind me."

"But what I was going to say," Miller said, steering the conversation back on track, "is to be careful. I've told you this before, but you remind me of my little sister and I don't want to see you hurt."

It took me a second to realize he wasn't talking about the paparazzi or getting knocked in the face on set with a surfboard. He was blatantly referring to the thing I had going on with Cooper. Whatever the hell that was. I dragged my hands away from my face and smoothed back my hair.

How did I even respond to what he just said?

On one hand, Miller was someone hired to work for me. If my old bodyguard had warned me about a guy I was sleeping with, I would have flipped out on him and fired him on the spot. But on the other hand, Miller wasn't my old bodyguard. He was the man who'd taken me to the lamest amusement park ever when I was alone. He'd sat with me after I had a nightmare.

So, I told him what I would tell any of my friends if they gave me non-shitty advice. "Thanks for the heads-up, Miller."

"And now you're going to fire me."

Shaking my head, I climbed out of the Kia. I turned to face him, supporting myself by holding on to the edge of the door and the roof of the car. "Nope. I'm trying to keep from hugging you for giving a fuck."

All these feelings today—they were going to be the undoing of me.

CHAPTER FOURTEEN

"Skye from Las Vegas asks, 'Willow, how did you feel when you learned you were cast in the reboot of the movie?' " the moderator said.

Like if I didn't take the role, I'd never work again, I thought.

I cast a glittering smile in his direction and lifted my microphone to my mouth. "Excited and—don't laugh at me, guys—terrified. I'm not sure if you've ever carried a surfboard, but"—I sighed and rubbed my forehead for dramatic effect—"it really, really hurts when it knocks you in the head." The crowd of fans lined up in front of the outdoor stage rolled with laughter and hundreds of smartphones flashed simultaneously.

"But really, I can't wait because this cast is amazing and the script is so incredible. I can't wait to work on such a kick-ass movie," I said.

How many more adjectives could I use this morning without sounding like an idiot?

We were twenty minutes into the beachfront press conference and for the last ten of them, Justin Davies, my leading man, had kept trying to touch my thigh beneath the table. Once again, I leaned close to him, keeping my smile plastered on my face, and muttered, "It would be a shame if I break your fucking nose with a surfboard when we start shooting tomorrow."

He skimmed the back of his hand across my cheek and the flashing cameras went berserk.

Asshole.

"Uh-oh, is there more than an on-screen romance blooming between Justin and Willow?" the moderator asked the fans, and they cheered wildly.

I twisted Justin's fingers tightly in mine, and he winked a hazel eye at me.

Once the crowd quieted down, the moderator said, "Mitchell from Greenville, Texas, asks, 'How are you training for your role?' We'll start with Justin."

I nearly rolled my eyes when Justin tilted his dreadlocked head to the side (he'd told me shortly after we met that there were fan pages dedicated to his hair), stared confidently into the crowd, and said, "If you've seen the original you know of course that Chad is a photographer. James Dickson and I thought it would be interesting if we added a little twist to the story line and put me out there with Willow."

I kept the surprise out of my face when I turned to look at him. Had he trained with Cooper too? As if to answer my question, Justin winked and said, "I'd done a little surfing when I was a teenager, so it was easy to jump back in. By the way, let's give it up for Willow Avery. She's gorgeous today, isn't she?"

Never in my life had I wanted to drown someone as much as I did right now.

The moderator turned his attention on me. "What about you, Willow?"

I raked my hand through my brown hair, which the stylist who'd shown up at my rental house at the ass-crack of dawn had artfully tousled for at least an hour. "I didn't have it quite as easy as Justin. I've spent the last couple weeks training with a really incredible surf coach here in Hawaii—Cooper Taylor. I've gotten to the point where I can actually take on a wave or two. Of course, I fall flat on my butt two seconds later, but it's a work in progress."

That comment evoked more chuckles and flashes from the throng of people, so I gave them the pretty smile they expected.

"Speaking of Cooper Taylor," the moderator started, and I felt my breath catch. "How does it feel to be working with Hilary Norton's kid?"

I blinked. And for a moment, I was left utterly speechless. *How does it feel to be working with Hilary Norton's kid?* And he was talking about my Cooper?

A shiver raced up my spine the moment I thought of him as that.

When I answered, I never faltered. "He's got this insane

work ethic. We train for three or four hours a day." And not once did he tell me I was playing his deceased mother's role. "We still have a ways to go, but I'm confident that all the stunt work you see me actually doing is going to look fantastic."

The moderator turned his questions on Justin then, and after that on one of the supporting actors, but the sharp tingles creeping down my face and throughout the rest of my body made it nearly impossible to hear anything that wasn't aimed directly at me.

Cooper was Hilary Norton's son.

The sad part was that as I sat there, becoming angrier, I wasn't sure if I was even supposed to be pissed. It wasn't like it had ever come up in conversation, but God, it was hard not to feel duped.

Because Hilary Norton—Cooper's mom—had OD'd on the same crap that sent me to rehab.

By the time I reached Cooper's house for my lesson, which Miller insisted he had to stay for now that the press had me on their radar, my anger had reached the boiling point. As Cooper and I strode out to the beach, with Miller trailing behind us a few feet, I put as much distance as I could between our bodies.

He gave me a sympathetic smile. "I'm guessing your press conference went badly?" he said.

Narrowing my eyes, I snorted and picked up my pace. "Where should I start? First there's my horny costar who intro-duced himself by asking if I'd fuck him in his trailer to test out the new couch."

Cooper caught up to me, his face dark. He placed his

board down by the shoreline in slow, controlled motions. "He touched you?"

"Don't worry, I threatened to hit him with a surfboard on set," I said. Cooper smiled, murmuring something under his breath. Crossing my arms over my chest, I stared down at him and asked, "Why didn't you tell me who your mom was, Cooper?"

His toned body went taut and he glanced down at the emblem on the head of his board before meeting my gaze. "Because it's not a big secret," he said, shrugging indifferently.

I sank down on my knees beside him in the sand, not caring that Miller was lounging close by or that there were other people around us on the beach. I squinted at him and realized it wasn't because the sunlight was beating down on my face—it was to hold the stupid tears back.

I pretended to clean something off my board with the end of my beach towel. "I didn't know," I finally said in a low whisper.

He scoffed. "Then how's this? Hilary Norton was my mum but I don't broadcast it. Because I don't like talking about her. Because they tore her apart until she tore herself down."

"I don't know who *they* are."

A sound of frustration bubbled up in the back of his throat and he leaned close to me. "Don't be ridiculous, Willow. You of all people know exactly who they are."

"And Dickson knew who you were?" I demanded.

He scoffed, nodding.

"God, I feel like an idiot," I said.

"Why?"

I stopped fidgeting with my board and looked him directly in the eye. "Because I've been studying your mom's movies and working with you and—"

He touched his fingertips together in front of his mouth and shook his head. "It doesn't change anything."

So why did it feel like it did? When I started to push my board out into the water, he caught up behind me, tugging on the strap of my swimsuit. I whirled on him.

"Who my mum was doesn't change anything," he repeated.

"Why'd you agree to train me?" I demanded. "You hate Hollywood and I'm working in your mom's most popular movie. That's got to hurt, Cooper. I mean, *fuck,* I hurt *for* you."

He started to speak and then hesitated. When I tightened my hold on the edge of my board and nodded for him to continue, he demanded, "You want to know why I agreed to train you?"

"Please."

"Because Dickson said nobody else wanted to work with you."

I felt as if someone had struck a hand across my face. When I flinched, he muttered a string of curse words. "Look, Wills, that didn't come out like I wanted it—"

"No, I appreciate your honesty," I said, shoving my board farther out into the white water.

"Where are you going?" he called after me.

"We've got a lesson, don't we?"

CHAPTER FIFTEEN

~~~~~~

The tension between Cooper and me during my lesson was almost unbearable, and when Miller waved at me from the beach a couple hours into training, I was relieved.

"I've got to go," I said to Cooper, lying down on my board and maneuvering it around to face the shoreline. "It's almost five and I've got this meet and greet with the crew and cast tonight at seven—"

He came up beside me, so that our elbows knocked against each other. I gripped the sides of my board tighter and glanced down at the Channel Islands logo. "I know," he said softly, his voice hoarse. "Dickson's asked me to come."

My gaze popped up. "Really?"

Cooper's brows pulled in and he pinched his lips together.

Then, he gave me a sarcastic smile. "Guess my mum made me important enough to invite," he said.

I flinched and took a deep breath to keep my voice from cracking. "I didn't mean it like that. And I'm so sorry about what happened to your mom. I just—" When the words wouldn't come, I paddled my arms to nudge my board forward.

He came up right beside me, unwilling to let me go. "You just what?" he demanded, his nostrils flaring.

"I wish I'd known who you were before we started this." I arched my body slightly, staring through blurry eyes at the shore. "I wish I'd asked or *something*. I'm so sorry," I whispered. I needed to get away from him. I needed to get away before I shoved my foot further down my throat.

He released an agitated sigh. "It wouldn't have changed what happened to her."

No, it wouldn't have.

"You want to know what the sad part is?" he continued, as he moved his board past mine. He looked over his shoulder and waited for my response.

"What?"

"I still want to take you into my place and bury myself inside of you until I—"

I sat up on my board, straddling the middle of it. "Until you what?" I questioned. He pushed himself up into a sitting position and yanked the front of my surfboard next to his. I gripped the edges firmly between my thighs to steady myself.

"Until I forget myself," he murmured. "Or fuck, get this taste for you out of my mouth."

We were still several feet from reaching the shore, so nobody would be able to see the way his fingertips skimmed my breast through my tankini or how my nipple instantly responded to his touch, hardening. I flushed, held my breath for a drawn-out moment, and then relaxed.

"Is that something you really want to do?" I whispered. His gaze washed over every visible inch of me, starting at the top of my head, and I tugged my bathing suit top down to cover the patch of stomach that was exposed.

"The question is, is that what you really want?" he asked.

"I just want to know if it's bothering you to be around me now that I know about your mom," I said all in one breath. When his eyebrows furrowed together, I squeezed my eyes shut. "Don't make me say it out loud."

"If you want me to answer the damn question, you will."

My eyes flew open and narrowed into a glare. "I've got a history, Cooper, and it's scary when my—" I struggled to find the right word to describe what he was to me at this point and finally heaved a sigh. "I'm scared that you're drawn to me because you feel bad for me."

His expression changed to something unreadable and he pointed down at my board. "Let's go back in before another wave hits."

Clenching my teeth, I stretched out on my board and began paddling back to the shore, my arms and legs tingling the entire time. The moment both our feet hit dry land, though, Cooper gave me a dark look. "Get rid of your bodyguard for a little while. We need to talk." When I didn't budge, he pulled in a deep breath through his nose, crossing his suntanned arms over his chest. "I'll call you out at Dickson's party, Wills, if you don't hear me out."

I was seething when I stalked over to Miller, who was patiently waiting for me on a beach towel, but I coaxed a smile onto my face. "I'm going inside with Cooper to talk for a few minutes." He lifted an eyebrow and I forced a laugh. "About surfing and movie stuff. Can you—I don't know—hang out in the shop with Eric and Paige?"

Even though he never dropped the concerned expression, Miller muttered, "Sure, Willow."

When we stepped into Cooper's house, Miller disappeared into the shop where Eric and Paige were signing up two new students—twins from the look of it. Cooper wrapped his fingers around mine and led me upstairs to his bedroom. As he slammed the door behind us, part of me expected him to put my back up against the wall like he did the other night, but when I saw the look in his eyes, I knew that wasn't going to happen.

Disappointment. Complete and utter disappointment that made me crumple against the wall all on my own.

"Let me make this clear," he said. He took a deep breath, squeezed the bridge of his nose, and turned around for a moment, facing the king-size bed. When he faced me again, his shoulders were squared. "Am I hell-bent on protecting you? Yeah, I'd rip someone apart to keep you safe. Are you a pity-fuck for me? Absolutely not. I've wanted you more than anything."

"I'm fucked-up, Cooper," I said, and when my voice hitched,

he closed the space between us, lifting my eyes until our gazes were equal.

"We'll fix you."

He took both my hands into his and drew me across the room. Sitting on the edge of his bed, he pulled me onto him so that I straddled him. We were both still wet from being in the sea, and his bedspreads dampened beneath our bodies.

"And I'm insecure," I whispered. He touched the side of my face with the tip of his index finger, tracing up the curve of my cheek.

He massaged the area behind my ear, skimming his fingertips along the tattoo, making the skin there—and the scar on my abdomen—burn with the memory. "We'll fix that too."

"I'm selfish, too," I said at last.

"God, Wills, so am I."

The party went down without a hitch. Every time my eyes connected with Cooper's, and it happened more than it should, he gave me that deep-dimpled smile that made my knees feel weak and my heart twist painfully in my chest.

Later that night, after I'd returned to my rental house and lay alone in the dark, staring at the moonlight through partially opened blinds and listening to Ellie Goulding on my laptop, I decided that I wouldn't think about what might happen after the summer went away, when I was done with this movie.

I only wanted the here and now with Cooper.

I left for work the next morning repeating that thought in

my head as Miller drove me to my filming location. Once we arrived, I felt myself being slowly immersed into my old life. The life of someone I couldn't be anymore.

I tried my best to shake away the panic slowly shooting through my veins.

"I can do this," I whispered over and over again, as a makeup artist fussed over me.

"Can you hold your lips still, honey?" the artist asked, blowing a stray lock of her asymmetrical blond bob out of her eye. It was a reminder that I would hear things like that often over the next month or two, and I froze every muscle in my body.

I spent the next hour in hair and makeup, getting M.A.C. caked onto my face so I would look natural on camera, and then another hour arguing with the costume designer about the string bikini I refused to wear. The moment I stepped out of my trailer dressed in the costume we'd finally decided on—a tiny pair of hibiscus-print board shorts and a tight, high-necked Quicksilver rash guard—I felt a weight drive itself down on my chest. Justin, my leading man, only made that feeling worse when I ran into him at a refreshment table.

He tossed an apple into the air before taking a bite out of it, and I rolled my eyes. "We're on Yahoo!'s entertainment page today," he said.

"Let me guess—WilTin?" I asked, grabbing a bottle of water and a doughnut. He laughed.

"Close. Jillow."

I made a disgusted face. "It sounds like a cross between

Jell-O and bodily fluid," I said, and before he could get a word in, I added sweetly, "With you being the bodily fluid."

He scratched the tip of his lightly freckled nose and cocked his head to one side, squinting at me. "Damn, so I don't have a chance."

"Not at all."

He sighed then shrugged. "Can't blame me for trying. There's always the girl who plays—"

But I'd already tuned him out, focusing my attention instead on Dickson, who was coming toward the refreshment table. He clapped his hands together, grinning. "Ready to remake magic?"

I'd almost forgotten that he'd worked as the production manager on the first film. I bobbed my head, shoving away the fear of failure that churned in the pit of my belly. My hair, which had been styled to look careless, ruffled in the stifling late-morning breeze. "I'm ready if Justin is."

"Let's make a movie then," Dickson said cheerfully. He apparently hadn't noticed the way my voice had faltered, and if he did, he didn't say anything about it.

I spent the morning working on a love scene with Justin on the beach. I was numb to the kisses and touching, the way his long hair scratched my face, and found that I was more focused on trying not to develop a lazy eye from all the cameras—of the studio variety—flashing in my face for the sake of promotional stills.

Justin, on the other hand, loved it, especially when I had to lie flat on my back on top of a surfboard to finish up a makeout scene. As he pinned my arms over my head, I waited for him to make some wise-ass remark, but he only spoke his lines.

"I can't live without you, Alyssa," he whispered, his hazel eyes reflecting the emotion of the scene. Then he swooped in to kiss me as an actor, and I did my best to respond to him, to act oblivious to the giant-ass cameras recording us at just about every angle.

A moment later, the scene was called and Justin climbed off of me. He winked before disappearing in search of one of the extras he'd been talking to earlier.

When the crew took a break for lunch, Miller escorted me back to my trailer. He peeked in first and then nodded, giving me the go-ahead to step inside. "I missed an important call," he explained to me, holding up his phone. "You need me I'll be right out here."

"I'll let you know," I said, closing the door. I was in the middle of letting out an exhausted yawn when a voice with a distinctive Australian accent spoke up.

"He didn't check very well." I gasped as Cooper's hands slipped over my eyes. My body automatically moved against his, and I shivered when his warm breath fanned my ear. "First illegal bonfires and now breaking into my girl's trailer. I'm all sorts of bad," he teased.

His girl.

I was his girl.

I licked my mouth, attempting to get rid of the sudden dryness at hearing him say that. "You said you had a lesson," I whispered hoarsely, slowly turning around to face him. "At least that's what I think you told me this morning."

God, he looked so good with his hair all messy and his face still a little red from surfing and I just wanted to—

"I'm here *because* of this morning," he said, his expression tense. He'd showed up at my door at four a.m., grabbing me to him without saying a single word, and had picked me up, taking me to the back of my tiny rental. He'd used his mouth on me for ten agonizing minutes, pulling away each time I came close to release.

"Please," I'd finally panted, struggling up on my elbows to meet his hot gaze. He'd nipped the inside of my thigh, shaking his head, and I'd groaned.

"Please?" I'd said once more, just for him to shake his head again. Then I raveled his blond hair with my hands, jerking up on it. "Cooper—"

A moment later, he'd climbed up, drawing my tongue into his mouth and using his fingers to finish getting me off. When I'd tried to pull down the swim trunks he'd been wearing, he stopped me, catching my hands around his waistband.

"I want an IOU," he'd said right before he kissed me one last time, dizzying me up so that I couldn't return to sleep.

Reluctantly, I shook my head to bring my thoughts back to the present, to where he had me lodged between the mini fridge and the kitchenette table. "You broke into my trailer for an IOU?" I squeaked, and he guided my hand between us, wrapping my fingers around him through his cargo shorts. I squeezed hard, causing him to shudder.

He groaned against the column of my throat. "I broke into your trailer because I wanted to be with you."

I took a couple steps back, until the backs of my thighs rested against the top of the table, and gazed up into his blue eyes. "We've got a surf lesson tonight," I whispered. He cracked a smile, and snarled his fingertips underneath my Quicksilver shirt, pulling it up.

My head swam, but I was conscious enough to grab both of his hands, stilling them by my side. "I can't," I said. I wasn't ready to let him see me completely naked in the light just yet, if I ever would.

"Wills—"

The door to my trailer shook and he drew away from me, groaning dramatically. I straightened my clothes and slid past him, my ass brushing up against his crotch, to open it just enough to see who was there. One of the assistants stood on the bottom step, grinning up at me.

"We're ready for you again, Miss Avery," he said.

The fact that Miller was a foot away looking like a beast with his arms folded over his muscular chest didn't seem to affect this guy in the least.

"Give me a few," I said, closing the door as he opened his mouth to say something else. I turned back to Cooper, who was suppressing a grin. "What?" I asked, through clenched teeth.

"Miss Avery."

"I've got to get to work."

He stared at me for a long time before dipping his gaze to the carpeted floor for a moment. "Seeing you like this just—" I covered his lips before he could say something that would get me any more worked up than I already was. He dragged his teeth gently across my bottom lip before forcing himself to break away from me. Breathing heavily, he shook his head. "You beautiful girl, you fuck with my head like no other."

I didn't tell him that I was glad.

That I wanted to be the only girl on his mind.

CHAPTER SIXTEEN

~~~~~~~~~~~~~~~~~~~~~~~~~~~~~~~~~~~

The next two weeks passed by in a blur of work, surfing, more work, and Cooper.

Deliciously copious amounts of Cooper.

I didn't even realize it was my birthday until my mother called me first thing in the morning on the fifteenth to sing her rendition of "Happy Birthday" in a horribly off-key voice. When she was finished performing, she said, "I know you asked me not to come there, but your dad and I are so proud of you!"

Mom and I had been talking every few nights, and when she'd called me on the Fourth of July, she had brought up coming to Honolulu to spend my birthday with me. I'd told her I already had plans even though I only had my probation meeting.

"Thanks, but Mom, it's six a.m. here and I'm not filming

today." I didn't add that I'd been out late with Paige the night before, at a hibachi grill that she'd sworn was the best on the island. My mother would ask me a million questions about who Paige was and then warn me about the dangers of being around an open flame.

I stifled a sleepy laugh as I imagined Mom saying, *You'll burn your damn face off and then where would you be?"*

Mom didn't take my hint about the time because she continued to talk. "I wanted to call with a birthday present," she said.

I pulled a pillow over my face and groaned. "Please don't sing again," I begged.

"Clay called early this morning," she said. My breath caught as soon as I heard my lawyer's name, and I threw the pillow away from my face. It hit the wall and then fell somewhere beside the bed.

"And?" I asked.

"And he's got a court date for your case against that agency scheduled for the middle of next month." I could tell by the shrillness in her voice that she didn't actually believe this was good news—in fact, it probably scared the hell out of her—but she must have known how much it would mean to me, especially on my twentieth birthday.

My heart hammered in my chest, and I pressed the palm of one hand flat against it, reminding myself that I needed to calm down and take a deep breath.

"Does he think I have a chance?" I asked, my voice sounding fuzzy in my ears.

"Absolutely."

One word. That one word somehow managed to send a flood of emotions rushing through me. Fear and pain and hope all sliced through me at once, and as I sat there shaking, tears trickled down my face. "That's a start, huh?" I asked, keeping my voice calm, level.

"I knew you'd be happy to hear that," Mom said. I heard an inaudible voice murmur something to her, and she laughed. Then, to me she said, "One sec, your dad wants to speak to you."

I hadn't heard my dad's voice in months—since the court date where I was sentenced to Serenity Hills to be precise—so when he came on the line, I had to press the back of my hand against my mouth to hold the sob in. "Happy birthday, baby," he said.

I couldn't decide if I was more excited to speak to him or angrier that it had taken this long for him to pull his head out of his ass, but regardless, I was crying. Pulling in a deep breath to gather my bearings, I said, "Thanks."

"Looks like you've been staying out of trouble," he said, which meant he'd been scouring the gossip columns to see if I'd stepped out of line.

I hadn't.

"Yes, I'm—" I thought of the past month and everything that had happened and gave a tiny sigh. "I love Hawaii," I whispered at last.

He made a little noise in the back of his throat. "Your mom and I would love to come see you when you're ready to have us," he said in a tentative voice.

But I wasn't ready for my parents to visit me. Not now when things were going so well.

I tangled my hands into the corner of my sheets. "Thanks,

Dad, I'll let you know." My voice was polite, but firm enough to let him know that probably wouldn't happen anytime soon.

Our call ended a few minutes later, and I swung out of bed, suddenly high from the news Mom had given me at the beginning of the call. I was too happy to be bothered by the fact Clay had called her instead of me. What my mom had told me was hands-down the best birthday present anyone had ever given me. It was three years too late, but I'd take it.

I was a jittery mess for the remainder of the morning, running on very little food and too much Red Bull and adrenaline, so when I went to my probation meeting in the middle of the afternoon, I was shaking.

Officer Stewart narrowed her eyes at me from across her desk and straightened a stack of papers before saying, "Have you had any run-ins with the police since our last meeting?"

I swept my hand across my forehead, shaking my head. "No," I said. I didn't mention the fact one of Justin's fans—a girl he already had a restraining order against—had snuck onto the set a couple days before and the police had questioned me along with other members of the cast and crew after they arrested her.

Stewart tapped her long, French-manicured nails against the hard surface of her desk. "And everything else is still the same?"

I nodded.

"Nothing special planned for your birthday?" The way she said "special," like I should automatically insert my drug of choice there, made my muscles tense up.

I cleared my throat a few times before answering her. "I've got work in the morning."

She tilted her head to one side thoughtfully, to gauge whether or not I was telling the truth. I wanted to let her know that I'd been too busy to even think about getting messed up, and that the few times it had entered my mind for even a flicker of a moment, I'd automatically flushed the thoughts out and reminded myself of how well I was doing without going numb.

I had friends.

I had a job.

Holy fuck, I had Cooper.

And now, if everything went right with my attorney—

I let out a shaky sigh; for the first time in years, I was golden.

Officer Stewart typed something on her laptop keyboard, twisting her lips to the side as she worked. "You know that if you fail your drug test I'll have no other choice but to have you arrested."

Now it was my turn to narrow my eyes. "I'm not on anything."

"You know I've got to make sure, right?"

I'd loaded up on energy drinks and water for that very reason.

After I passed my screening with flying colors, she ushered me back to her cubicle where she brought up the subject of my community service. "Dave says you've not been back for the last couple weeks," she pointed out.

I linked my thumbs together in my lap, settling my palms on the stiff fabric of my new Rag & Bone skinny jeans. I'd splurged on them a week ago when Paige had dragged me away—with Miller in tow, of course—to go shopping when her younger sister Delilah was in town. To date, the jeans and fluttery chiffon shirt I was wearing were the only things I'd spent any of my work advance money on, aside from food and basics.

Thirty days down and no drugs. It was a record for me.

"Do you plan on finishing your community service?" Officer Stewart asked in a soft voice.

I took a deep breath before answering. "I'm planning on going back once things die down with work. We've been shooting quite a few of my scenes because—"

Because I'm unreliable and Dickson probably thinks I'll bail.

Stewart shook her head slowly, her light-brown hair swinging back and forth around her shoulders as she did. "I understand that, but don't forget that if you don't complete your community service, I'll—"

"Have to report me to the courts. I get it," I answered in a sharp voice.

She sighed and dropped her chin for several seconds. When she lifted it, she was nibbling the corner of her lip. "I'm not doing this to be mean, Willow. This is my job. While you're a very . . . *nice* girl, I have to be thorough when it comes to my career because I like having an apartment and food."

I understood Stewart had to look out for her career, but at the same time, I couldn't help but wonder if some of her coolness toward me had anything to do with her sister and Cooper. I couldn't exactly come right out and say anything to her. For starters, Stewart was my probation officer and I wasn't going there with her, and secondly, confronting her would out my relationship with Cooper.

I wanted him to myself a little longer before that happened.

But as Stewart escorted me out to the lobby she brought up her sister herself. "Miranda said she met you."

"If you count her saying three or four words to me, yes," I

said. I clenched my nails into the hem of my thin top. "I'm pretty sure I could get you fired for talking about a client to your family members."

Stewart's glossy red lips quirked into a shadow of a smile. "Actually she has no clue I've ever met you. We were talking about Willow Avery the actress, not the girl with the criminal record. But if it helps, Miranda said you were nice."

My eyebrow shot straight up. "Nice?" I asked, choosing to ignore her comment about me being the girl with the criminal record.

She shrugged. "For Cooper. Personally, I wouldn't be able to stand it if the guy I loved fell for another girl, but Miranda and I are very different people."

My breath caught but I shrugged it off. I was so used to dealing with jealous ex-girlfriends—like Gavin's psycho ex whose friends had started a nasty YouTube channel blasting everything from my weight to my clothes and even my shade of fingernail polish—that it was a bit of a shock to get a thumbs-up from Cooper's ex-girlfriend.

"Tell her . . . thanks," I said, and Stewart shook her head.

"I can't discuss my clients, remember?" When I gave her a half smile, she continued, "I'll see you again in August and don't forget to finish your community service before then. I'd hate for you to ruin the work you've put in by not following through with the terms of your probation."

I nodded my head understandingly.

Since I'd been given the day off filming, Cooper and I had planned a surf lesson to work on a technique I needed to master for a shot my stuntwoman and I would be working on at the end of the week. But when I arrived at Cooper's house, and Miller told me he had to run an errand, I knew something was up. My bodyguard had made it a point to stick around for all of my surf lessons ever since production began. I told him I'd see him soon, but as I walked into Cooper's place alone, I noticed that Eric's truck was gone too.

The moment I stepped into Cooper's shop, I smelled candle wax intermingling with the usual scent of PlugIns and Banana Boat. Cooper was shirtless when he appeared around the corner, and smiled as soon as our eyes met, making me go a little crazy with the way he was looking at me. "What day is today, it's—"

"Not the singing," I groaned. "My mother already—"

He yanked me to him, bringing our lips together as he reached behind me to lock the front door. "Don't be a party pooper," he murmured against my mouth as he effortlessly lifted me into his arms and carried me through the house into the kitchen. There was a tiny, homemade birthday cake with lavender icing sitting on the counter with two thin birthday candles plunged deep into the frosting.

"Cooper?" I asked when he left me sitting on top of the granite. He glanced over his shoulder as he adjusted the kitchen blinds to make sure they were view proof. "What are we doing?"

"Can you forget yourself for a day?"

"Like you forgot how old I am?" I asked, indicating the candles, when he returned to me. I leaned over and blew out the candles before plucking them out of the cake to lick the icing off the bottom.

He grinned and nudged himself between my legs. He slid his hand up the front of my body, stopping just behind my ear. A strangled moan escaped the back of my throat as his fingers gently threaded through my hair.

"Happy birthday, Willow," he said, his voice serious this time.

I reached out and skimmed the back of my hand along the side of his face, through his hair, before pulling his head down to mine. I laced my fingers through the hair at his crown, and wrapped my ankles around him.

When the kiss turned sweet, it took me a moment to realize he'd dipped his finger into frosting and was sliding it in and out of my mouth as his lips probed mine. I groaned, melting against him, but he shook his head.

"I've got a birthday surprise for you, Wills." Another surprise. I wasn't sure if I could handle another today without bursting into a puddle of waterworks, but I nodded despite myself. His hands slid down the bare skin of my arm, tangling with my fingertips for just a moment before he stepped away. "But first, cake."

We each ate a slice, sitting on the countertop, and then he said it was time to go. I asked him a million questions as he maneuvered his Jeep down Honolulu's back roads, but he wouldn't budge.

"And Paige and Eric know?" I asked. When I'd asked him where they were while we ate our cake, he said they were taking the day off and would be around tonight.

"Paige is a planning goddess," he said, winking as the corners of his lips tugged upward.

I sat back in the seat, crossing my arms over my chest, but I couldn't fight the smile that spread across my lips.

Best. Birthday. Ever.

Our destination turned out to be a small cove a half hour from his house. As I jumped out of the Jeep, taking in the sight of the jewel-green water below the rocks, I said, "I am *so* not skinny-dipping with you." I glanced back at him, where he stood leaning against the front of the Jeep with a giant beach blanket slung across his shoulders.

He clutched at his chest, pretending to be hurt. "God, Wills, you won't even let me see you naked in the lights. I wouldn't dream of trying to get you to strip down in Cockroach Cove."

I froze. "Cockroach Cove?"

He laughed again, coming up beside me to wrap his arm around my waist. I sighed and rubbed the top of my head against his shoulder. "No actual cockroaches," he said, steadying me as we walked down the rocks toward the water. Then he twisted his mouth to the side. "At least I don't think."

Nice to know.

We spent the next hour hiking through the cove, stopping every now and then to step away from the blowholes scattered throughout the place. "What would happen if I jumped in?" I asked at one point, as the salty spray hit my skin, moistening it.

He flicked the tip of his tongue over his full lips. "You would tumble to a certain death."

I turned to him, placing my hand on his chest and biting the inside of my cheek. "Thought you'd always look after me," I said dramatically.

"As much as humanly possible," he replied.

We stretched out in a shadowy portion of the cove, in front of a cave that I refused to go in, and I let the sunlight that occasionally hit our spot warm my bare feet. "We can go diving off that if you really want to jump off something," he said after a long, lazy silence. I followed his pointed finger to a steep collection of rocks that dropped down to whirling white water.

Giving him a sharp look, I shook my head.

I'd been pulled under too many times to count since coming here and that was the last thing I needed.

"I'm not the best swimmer," I whispered, turning my body into his. I rested my cheek on his bicep, and he looked down into my eyes.

"I know." He reached out and stroked my hair back from my forehead. "But I'll catch you when you fall."

My heart skipped a beat, and I glanced down between us at the blanket, messing with a snagged string. I took a shaky breath before replying, "It's hard letting go."

We both knew I wasn't talking about the cliff, and he was silent again for a long time. When he spoke, his voice lowered.

"I'm falling in love with you, Wills." He slid his fingertip over my lips, hushing my response. "You drive me crazy. I mean, it started out as this need to get you out of my head, but the longer I'm with you—" Giving me a sad smile, he lifted his shoulders.

My throat went dry. I'd heard declarations of love from more guys than I could count, the first being Tyler and the last being Gavin, but they'd never looked at me like Cooper did. They hadn't even come close.

I parted my lips to speak, but he replaced his finger with his mouth, kissing me slowly, carefully, as if I'd break. I was barely aware that I was crying until he drew back and my tears had left streaks on his cheeks.

Using the pad of his thumb, he swiped them away from my skin, and then kissed his fingertip.

Why did he have to do things like that?

Why did he have to tell me he was falling in love with me when I had no idea what would happen after this movie was completed?

"This has been the best month of my life and, Cooper, I—"

A half dozen flashes, all from a distance, slammed against my face, making me flinch, exposing me. My heart jumped into my throat as I faced a cameraman several feet away, standing on rocks as he happily snapped pictures of me. Of Cooper and me. I covered my face, but he continued to take photos. Strong arms encircled me and steadied me to my feet.

"Let's go," Cooper said in a rough voice, and I buried my face in his shoulder. I felt him shift. "If you come close to her I'll break that fucking thing in your face."

We left my shoes. And the blanket. And I left behind the words I'd wanted to say to him as we rushed to his Jeep with the sound of the cameras following us.

I'm falling in love with you too, Cooper.

CHAPTER SEVENTEEN

~~~~~~

Finding my photo plastered on the homepage of nearly every gossip blog and magazine in the country had always been a frustrating pill that I'd choked on and swallowed before moving forward, somewhat, with my life. But seeing myself all over the Internet with the guy I was slowly drowning for, finding my face posted beside his dead mother's photo as columnists made comparisons between the two of us was one of the worst feelings in the world.

Inside Cooper and Willow's Love Nest

Willow Avery Trains with Surfing Prodigy Lover on Kailua Beach

Hilary Norton's Son Makes Waves with
Disgraced Actress in Sunny Hawaii

The headlines went on, and each time I read a new one, I just wanted to stick my head into the sand. A week after the run-in with the paparazzi on my birthday, Dickson called a conference with both me and Cooper in his trailer. As we sat across from him, I wrung my hands together.

Cooper reached down, prying my fingers apart with his before giving me a smile meant to calm me down. I tried to return the expression but the only thing I could muster was a clenched jaw as my mouth watered from nausea.

"You've been doing amazing, Willow," Dickson began.

"Thanks," I murmured.

He worked his thumb and forefinger over the bridge of his nose. "But I've got to admit I'm a little worried about the two of you."

I frowned. I'd had producers confront me about everything from showing up late to work to stumbling onto the set too high to remember my lines, but never for dating someone. Especially when that someone wasn't even a member of the cast or crew.

"Why?" I asked, my voice raising an octave.

Dickson leaned forward, resting his elbows on the laminate desk he was working from. A hundred emotions washed over his face as we all sat in complete silence before he finally settled on one: regret.

"I'm terrified that this won't end well," Dickson said. "I'm afraid if that happens, Willow might not be able to fulfill her contractual obligations." He pointed his gaze at Cooper as the words fell from his lips.

"That's the most idiotic bullshit I think I've *ever* heard you say," Cooper muttered, narrowing his blue eyes at Dickson.

I wasn't going to let it go. "Dickson, I'm not sure if you realize it or not but I'm not a sixteen-year-old kid," I said. *Not like I'd been when I fell for Tyler.* "I'm twenty and free to date whoever the hell I want. You're an incredible producer, but please don't turn all fatherly on me. I can take care of myself."

Dickson sighed. "I just want to keep you happy, Willow," he said.

"I am." I squeezed Cooper's hand tight. "I love this role. I love the crew. Fuck, I even adore working with Justin and he's a cocky asshole who's always grabbing at me or talking about himself. Please . . . *please* don't make this awkward. I mean, if you have to, call Kevin and tell him your concerns."

Dickson gave a little jerk of his head and a tight smile. "I understand. I'm so sorry for invading your personal life." Then he refocused his eyes on Cooper. "Willow, can you excuse us for a moment?"

I nodded, ducking my head as I left. I'd barely made it to the end of the trailer to meet up with Miller before the explosion inside began.

"You've got to be fucking kidding me. I ask you to watch out for her and you have sex with her," Dickson's voice filtered outside, and I felt myself flush from head to toe from the shame.

My ears were tingling and Cooper's soft accent made it impossible for me to hear what he said next. Not that I was sure if I even wanted to at this point.

"Come on," Miller said, placing his hands between my shoulder blades and guiding me forward. I cast a gracious look up at him, thankful that he was smart enough to get me away from the situation. That he realized that moments like this—they were the ones that threatened to send me over the edge.

But that night as Cooper and I lounged under the setting sun on his deck, I asked him what Dickson had said to him after I left. He shifted in his beach chair, lifting his shoulders. "Something along the lines of me being a professional fuckup for having taken advantage of you." If he hadn't said it in such a strained voice, I would've believed he hadn't been affected by it.

I winced, rolling to my side to gather my bearings before I met his gaze. When I did, I kept my eyes closed and asked, "You think this will affect you getting another job working for—"

He cut me off quickly. "I don't care whether I ever work for these people again. I just want them to leave you alone."

I let out a shaky laugh, squeezing my closed eyes more tightly together to suppress the moisture that was slowly building. I wouldn't let myself cry over this. I refused to let this fuck with me any more than it already had. "Don't tell me you're going to make a YouTube video crying for the world to leave Willow alone," I said, my voice broken.

"Nah," he said.

I heard him get up from his beach chair and then I felt his hands plant down on either side of my chair. I opened my eyes to see his halo of blond hair in front of my face—his blue eyes staring into mine—and my lips parted. I flushed when he brought my wrists to his lips, rubbing hot kisses on the insides.

A long silence passed and then Cooper's eyebrows knitted together. "On second thought, maybe I will do that YouTube video. Except I'll have to use your real name for dramatic effect." After he said that, the tension clouding the atmosphere around us seemed to fade away and we grabbed our surfboards to go for an evening lesson before Eric returned with pizza.

But if I thought the grief over my relationship with Cooper ended with Dickson, I quickly found out I was mistaken.

The next afternoon, Jessica, who hadn't spoken to me since before my birthday, called to let me know that she thought Cooper was "a delicious piece of Australian goodness" and that she was calling dibs on him once I was through.

To avoid telling her to fuck off, I told her I was busy and would call her back.

At the end of the week, just when Dickson had stopped looking at me like he thought I'd crumble apart at any moment and Kevin had stopped leaving voice mails about tabloid damage control, I returned home after a long day of filming to find an Escalade parked in my driveway. I steadied myself before I climbed out of the Kia, because I already knew who was on the other side of the tinted windows.

Cadillacs are my mother's weakness.

I held my breath as she got out of the SUV and walked toward me on tall heels that hoisted her up to my height. "Fun size" was what my dad had always called her, but there was nothing fun about her expression right now. Even though she was smiling I felt as if she'd swallow me whole at any moment. When Mom stopped in front of me, she pulled me to her, hugging me tight, and I coughed, suffocated by the scent of her strong perfume.

"I've missed you, Willow," she said, sighing.

I lifted my arms from my sides and awkwardly returned her embrace. When she pulled back, she held my shoulders and examined me closely. I studied her too. With her dark, high-lighted hair, wrinkle-free skin, and toned arms thanks to the scary trainer she worked with four times a week, my mom hadn't changed a bit.

"Miller," I said in a distant voice as I heard his heavy foot-steps coming nearer, "this is Tiff . . . my mother."

Miller flicked his hand in an uncomfortable wave and gave me a pitying look. "I'm just going to—" He pointed up at the apartment over the garage, and I lifted my chin, silently praying he'd insist that he needed to stay with me instead.

"I'll call you if I need you," I said.

As soon as Mom and I stepped inside of my rental house, she decided to insult him. "Well, he did a great job escorting us in to make sure there wasn't someone who'd broken in to—"

"Don't start," I snapped. I counted to twenty and then mo-tioned to the couch. She wobbled over to it, smoothing her knee-length skirt as she sat. "Do you want anything?"

Like to tell me why the hell you're here?

But in my heart I already knew, so when she shook her head, I slid down numbly on the edge of the recliner and faced her with my palms rested on my knees.

She started talking, reciting the same spiel addicts' families used on that intervention TV show. "Your dad and I are worried about you, Willow," she said.

This wasn't the first time she'd said as much to me, but dammit, this time I hadn't done anything to deserve it.

"You shouldn't be," I said calmly.

Mom's back stiffened and she released a heavy sigh. "Every time we open an entertainment article online your face is there with that actress's son."

I sucked in a hiss through my teeth. Had she really just said that? Curling my lips into a sneer, I said, "In case you haven't noticed, I'm an actress too. And if it bothers you so much, don't look at trashy-ass gossip sites."

"Don't you think you should be focusing on your career instead of relationships right now? Do you want what happened the last time to happen all over again?"

I dragged my hand down my face, frustrated. "You are unbelievable. I *am* working and focusing on my career but that's not the only thing in my life. You can't expect me not to date or have"—I cringed before I said the next word—"sex or fall in love and—"

Mom's green eyes widened. "You don't love him, Willow." She shook her head slowly to each side, as if doing so would convince me that she was right.

"How can you tell me what I care about and love? You and dad have avoided me like the plague since I fucked up."

Mom winced but effortlessly slid on her poker face again. "We offered to fly out here for the Fourth of July," she reminded me.

"And I didn't want you to because I was fine and happy. I'm still happy. Why would I want you here just so you can tell me what I'm doing wrong every five minutes?"

She threw her hands up and released a sound of frustration from the back of her throat. "You would turn this around on me and your dad, wouldn't you? You're the one who's unbelievable."

I stood up, pacing the length of the small living room frantically as I spoke. "If you want to play the blame game, here we go: Mom, what you did to me when I needed you, sending me away so that nobody would find out about my little *problem,* that was fucked-up." Mom began to say something but then pressed her lips together into a thin, colorless line.

I wished I had the energy to scream at her, to cry.

The corners of Mom's mouth tightened. "You left out that you waited several months to tell me and your dad."

I dragged my hands through my hair. "God, Mom. Seriously?"

She took a deep breath and then another. "Willow, I'm sorry for hurting you. I'm sorry for what happened, but please don't ruin yourself again over a boy you barely know."

I sat back down on the recliner, this time relaxing all the way back. "I'm not ruining myself," I said, emphasizing each word in a dangerous tone.

"I'm planning on staying at the Four Seasons so I can—"

I knew exactly where this was going, and I also realized I needed to end it right now.

"Mom, I don't want you here. You want me to work? You want me to be normal? Then let me do what normal adults do; they don't have their parents overseeing every aspect of their life. I'm not above asking Miller to remove you or having you banned from coming anywhere near the set."

She gasped and her entire body trembled. "You don't mean that."

I gave her a pointed look. "A long time ago you told me I needed to learn to make adult decisions," I said. I remembered the day well because it was a phone conversation we'd had a few days after I'd been released from the hospital, when I could barely move. "Let me do that. And if you love me, if you really want me to be happy, don't try to get custody of me. Because I know that's what you want to do next," I said.

There were giant tears gliding down Mom's high cheeks, and when she swiped them away she took a handful of makeup along with them. "What happens when you get hurt again?" she asked in a quiet voice. "Do you go back to the drugs and the partying?"

"I—" When I paused, my words catching in the back of my throat, she gave me a sad smile.

"That's what I thought." She stood and hobbled to the front door, never looking behind her when she said, "If you want to grab lunch before I leave to go back to Los Angeles tomorrow, call me."

Then she left, and I curled up into the corner of the couch, hugging myself close.

Wanting nothing more than to forget this moment had ever happened.

Wanting to drown quickly.

Paige showed up an hour and a half later, and when I told her to go away, she shook her head and held up a handful of DVDs—a season of *Adventure Time* and both volumes of *Kill Bill.* "Don't ask me to leave or I'll sit outside blasting the *Gears of War* soundtrack." I lifted my eyebrow and she nodded slowly, her hazel eyes gleaming. "And yes, I've actually got it inside of my van."

I shuffled aside so she could come in, crossing my arms as she tossed the DVDs on the coffee table and sat down in one corner of the couch.

"Miller called you?" I asked, dragging myself across the room to sit on the opposite end.

She cricked her neck to one side and then raced her fingers through her short black hair. "Don't be mad at him," she said.

My upper lip curled. "My bodyguard is calling my friend to come sit with me to make sure I won't do something stupid and you're telling me not to be mad at him. I've been burned enough already by people I trust and now he's going behind my back." I clenched my hands by my side and glared up at the ceiling, in the general direction of Miller's apartment. "I should fire him."

"Now you're just being a bitch. He called someone he knows won't throw a ninja star into your back the moment you turn around. You should be thankful."

I turned my dark gaze on her. She narrowed her hazel eyes, challenging me. Frustrated and dizzy, I raked both hands through my brown hair. There was no point telling her the entire story of what had happened with Mom so I leaned forward, burying my face in my hands, and went for the Cliff's Notes version. "My mom brings out the worst in me," I said, my voice catching. "She hopes doing it'll help me change."

And like always, I'd let it get to me to the point where I'd brought up her very worst, hurling it back at her angrily. When I told Paige she nibbled her lower lip thoughtfully for a few seconds and then stood up, disappeared into the kitchen, and returned a moment later with two Diet Cokes that she wrinkled her nose at. She handed me one and then sat down, popped hers open, and took a long swig.

"You know that most people ask before making themselves at home, right?" I demanded, running the hem of my T-shirt across my sweaty forehead.

She leaned forward, placed her can on the coffee table, then sat back to scratch one of the tattoos on her shoulder—a vintage pinup on a surfboard. "Does it work?" she asked.

"What? Not rifling through someone else's refrigerator?"

She snorted. "No. Turning the tables on your parents."

I shook my head slowly. "If anything it just makes me realize what a fucked-up mess I've made of things." When she raised her eyebrow in concern, I released a frustrated groan. "I'm not taking pills again if that's what you're wondering. I just—"

She released something that sounded like a sigh and a groan. "What?"

"It's hard. When they bring Cooper into it. And it's not just my parents—it's the paparazzi and my friend Jessica and, hell, even my producer."

Her lips curled downward sympathetically. "Cooper told me what happened with Dickson."

"See. Shit like that just makes me want to black out."

Her breath caught and she moved closer, trying to get a good look at my face so she could gauge my expression. "Willow, it scares me when you say things like that."

"It's the truth," I said, dipping my head so I didn't have to meet her gaze. "That's what you wanted from me, right? I've been acting since I was a kid. I'm tired of the bullshit that comes along with it sometimes. Ninety percent of the world thinks I can handle anything they sling at me, and the rest—everyone who knows me—believe I'll relapse at any moment."

"What do *you* think?"

"I think I'll be all right," I lied. "But it still doesn't make me feel any better that I can't go for a fucking burger with my boyfriend without getting my weight picked apart. It doesn't make me feel better to see old pictures of myself sloppy drunk and kissing some stranger reposted on gossip sites for shits and giggles."

"Quit acting then," Paige suggested. She took another sip of her Diet Coke and shuddered. "At least for a little while until you fix *you*."

A bitter laugh came from my throat. "The whole time I was in my last rehab I kept promising myself that I wouldn't do any acting anymore, and the day I came out I accepted this role. I can't let Dickson down."

"Then quit afterward. You know what I majored in?" she asked, and when I lifted an eyebrow, she said, "Psychology. My parents thought I'd be in graduate school by now, and maybe I will go someday, but not right now. Hell, look at my sister. Delilah flat-out told my mom she was only nineteen and shouldn't be expected to know what she wants to do. You know what my mother did?"

"Hmmm?"

"She got the hell over it," she said.

"I wish it were that easy."

Paige leaned in to me, as if she were sharing a secret. "It is."

CHAPTER EIGHTEEN

Paige's words stuck with me for the rest of the night and into the next morning. My mom left Honolulu without seeing me—hell, without calling me—again, and I hadn't made an effort to contact her either. As Cooper and I worked on a new technique a few days later, he pointed out that he thought I should call my parents.

"Not yet," I said, after half an hour of going back and forth with him. I was careful the entire conversation because of his own parents; he said he hadn't talked to his father since he and his mother had left Australia more than ten years ago. Before I could press further, he immediately turned the conversation back to my own mom and dad.

"You're being childish," he said, as we walked back up the beach toward his stucco house after our lesson.

"No, I'm trying to figure myself out," I told him. And I was.

He opened the door for me, grasping the frame, and raised his eyebrow. "At least the cameras have eased up on you."

Considering my attorney hadn't returned any of my calls about the status of our court date, the fact that I was no longer front-page tabloid fodder was the best thing that had happened to me in a while. For the first few days after our relationship made it into the news, the paparazzi had showed up at random times outside his house and on the beach, snapping photos and hounding Paige and Eric, but for the last couple days, everything had died down.

On Wednesday evening as we shot an indoor scene with my on-screen dad—the guy who'd played the role of Chad in the original movie—Justin told me the paparazzi's sudden disinterest in my love life was due to some actress who was twice as famous and five times more screwed-up than me "accidentally" running the Bentley she was joyriding into a cameraman.

"He's all right," Justin quickly assured me, digging his fingers into his dreadlocked hair and making me itch all over. When was the last time he washed that mess? "But she was coked up."

My costar gossiped more than Jessica did, and I rolled my eyes. "I've finally figured out why you refuse to cut that shit." I pointed up at his long hair. Then I dropped my voice to a whisper. "It's full of secrets."

The *Mean Girls* quote flew right over his head, and he continued speaking, staring up at the grip who was fixing a lighting issue. "How much time do you think she'll get?"

I shrugged and sat down on the prop couch, resting my elbows on my lap. He followed, much to my irritation, and sat in the exact same position. I slid my teeth together irritably as his gaze burned into the side of my face. Finally, I turned toward him. "How would I know how much time she'll get?"

"Don't you get arrested like once a year?"

"Don't you know when to shut up?" I retorted. When his expression faltered, I sighed, and said, "Who knows, okay?"

He leaned back, kicking his sandaled foot up on the coffee table and gave me a smirk. "You make work interesting," he said, winking.

I tilted my head to the side and gave him a sickly sweet smile. "Don't you have an extra ready to go down on you in the Porta-Potty?"

He stretched his long arms up and shook his head, swinging his hair in the process. "Not today. Besides, I'd much rather talk to you."

Someone shouted that it was time to get back to work and I got up, glancing over my shoulder at Justin. "Me and some of the makeup artists have a bet going whether or not your character will get the silver bullet next season on your show," I said, referring to the werewolf show he costarred in. "And from what I hear there's no Sam-and-Dean-esque twists that will bring your ass back if they do."

His mouth fell open and I felt myself smile as he followed behind me, asking if I'd ever even watched the damn show.

Even though I was tired to the bone after work, I had Miller take me to the homeless shelter. There were four hours left in my community service and I was determined to get them done this afternoon; my probation ended in seven days. Dave, my boss, looked generally excited to see me, stopping me when I passed by his office to thank me for a bunch of my old clothing I'd bugged Miller to drop off a couple days ago.

"Your donation means a lot to me, and to the residents." He tilted his head back for a second and closed his eyes. When he lowered it, a genuine smile pulled across his face. "Thank you, Willow."

"I've got more stuff in storage," I told him. "When I go back to Los Angeles, I'll have them shipped here." I ignored the lump in my throat that formed when I thought about going back to L.A.

We'd been shooting my scenes too quickly for my liking, which meant that at any moment my time here could be over and I'd have no other choice but to go back home.

Dave thanked me a few more times, and then I finally managed to slink out of his office. I went into the dining room and dug around for the cleaning supplies in the storage closet, filling the mop bucket with hot water and hanging a bottle of cleaner and a cloth over the side of it. I dragged the bucket out into the dining room, and nearly screamed when I turned around to come nose-to-nose with a small, familiar face.

"You look like you just shit your pants," Hannah said, lifting her eyebrow as I stumbled backward.

I recovered, giving her a look. "Aren't you a little young to say 'shit'?" I lugged the bucket full of water into the middle of the dining-room floor and she acted as my shadow, following a few steps behind me. "And besides, anyone would freak out when someone's creeping up on them."

She grinned at me as I started spraying the tables with a cleaner-filled bottle. "Sorry I scared you, but you seriously looked like you thought I was going to kick your butt."

I paused. "Are you kidding? I fight like a girl," I said. "You'd probably head-butt me in the chest and I'd be out like that." I snapped my fingers, and she laughed, sliding into a chair across from where I was cleaning.

She rested her chin in her hands and twisted her lips to the side. "You haven't been around a lot."

"I've been working." I wrinkled my nose. "Boring movie stuff."

"I bet it's awesome."

I glanced up from scrubbing a SpaghettiOs stain and then relaxed my face into a smile. "It's very tiring, but I've gotten to work with some . . . *interesting* people."

"Like who?"

I knew I wasn't supposed to be carrying on a conversation with Hannah—even though Dave was happy with me for giving the shelter thousands of dollars' worth of my clothes, he'd probably flip out if he knew I was—but I wasn't going to shrug off her question. Hannah clapped her hands over her mouth when I said, "Justin Davies."

"Are you kidding? You have the best job ever!"

After the stressful few weeks I'd had, who would have thought that talking to a little kid would make me feel better? The corners of my mouth dragged up into a smile and I shook my head. "Not kidding. I'll tell him he has a fan," I said, and she beamed. My grip loosened on the rag I held. People like Hannah—they were the ones who reminded me why I'd loved my job in the first place. I lowered my gaze back to the table.

"Guess what?"

I lifted an eyebrow but didn't raise my head. "Hmmm?"

"My mom got a job." There was so much pride in her voice that I felt my heart contract. I didn't know her story any more than she knew mine, but I grinned down at the bleach-soaked cloth.

"I'm glad," I said, finally meeting her brown eyes. "My fingers are crossed for you guys."

"Mom says we'll probably get to move to our own apartment in a few months. I'll get my own room and won't have to share with my older brother." She wrinkled her nose and I laughed.

"You've got a brother?"

"He sucks."

"It'll get better," I promised, and she tilted her head skeptically.

"You've got one?"

"Nope, only child." My mom and dad had always said that having me was enough, although now I wasn't sure if that was a good thing or a bad thing. Before Hannah could issue a sharp retort, I added, "But I've played a little sister more times than I can count."

My cell phone vibrated in the back pocket of my shorts, but I ignored it. I also ignored the part of my brain that kept telling me to stop talking to this kid before Dave found me. Hannah was lonely, like I'd been so many times before. I'd restart the entire fifty hours of community service—and finish before the deadline—if it meant I wouldn't have to shrug her off.

I sat down a few seats away from her and glanced over, folding my hands on the table. "Know how you're going to decorate your room yet?" I asked and her brown eyes lit up in excitement.

She spent the next fifteen minutes telling me about the Justin Bieber bedding set she'd coveted at Walmart and how her mom had promised her she'd have it by Christmas. When a tall, wiry boy with light-brown hair and dark eyes poked his head into the dining room to yell for her, she rolled her eyes theatrically and I knew he was her brother.

I'd done the same eye roll on-screen too many times to count.

"I've got to go. Shots for school," she explained, making a face. "Will you be back tomorrow?"

I thought of the few hours I had left and, not wanting to lie to her, shook my head. Her face fell for a moment, and then she held up a finger. "Be right back."

She raced over to the boy in the doorway, her sneakers skidding on the slick floor, and argued with him for a minute about something. She returned with a miniature sketchbook and a black pen. I watched, biting my lower lip, as Hannah flipped to a blank page at the back of the sketchbook.

Handing it to me, she gave me a hopeful smile. "Please?"

I signed my name across the page slowly, not quite wanting to let go when I was finished. "Stay out of trouble," I said to her when she finally pried the book from my fingertips.

She rolled her eyes dramatically. "Does this look like the face of a troublemaker?" She gave me a sweet smile, and I swallowed hard.

That smile—I'd seen it too many times to count, on the promotional images of my movies from ten years ago.

"Ugh, I'm not even going to answer that," I said, laughing despite the painful churning in my stomach. "Try not to kill him, okay?" I nodded my head toward the skinny boy at the door and Hannah flashed me a thumbs-up. As she left the D-hall, arguing with her brother about her using the paper in his sketchbook, my shoulders slumped and I had to sit down for a minute to catch my breath.

My phone vibrated once more, pulling me away from my thoughts. When I dug it out of my pocket, I saw the photo of a drunken Jessica holding up a shot glass. Groaning, I positioned my finger over ignore, but then I sighed.

What the hell, right?

"Hello?" I answered, and she released a long sigh.

"Willow, I miss you!"

I pushed myself away from the table and stood up, pacing the length of the space between it and the wall. "Sorry I haven't called."

But I wasn't.

She snorted. "Ugh, I probably wouldn't call either if I was dating *that* guy." I clenched my hand by my side, picking up speed. Jessica and I'd gone after each other's ex-boyfriends repeatedly in the past, not really giving a shit. But Cooper wouldn't be one of them. Ever. I pinched my mouth, hoping like hell she wouldn't bring him up again.

"How's that new show you were shooting for going?" I asked in a strained voice.

She ignored my question and I heard a squeaky noise in the background. Her bed, maybe? "I'm dying to see you, woman. What are you doing this weekend?"

"I've got to study up for a scene next week. Sorry, babe, but I can't fly to L.A. to see you," I said. It was partly true—the part about the scene, that is.

Jessica sniffled. "Actually, I just finished shooting a guest appearance and wanted to take time to see my best friend. I haven't been to Hawaii since I was a kid."

I froze in place. I should have felt excitement about seeing the girl who'd been my best friend since I was thirteen, but instead, a chill crept down my spine.

"We can meet up when I come home in the next month or so," I suggested, but she quickly brushed that off.

"I want to see you now. I won't take no for an answer."

No, I was sure she wouldn't, but that didn't stop me from saying it over and over again. I came up with a half-dozen excuses not to see her until finally a guttural sound bubbled from the back of her throat. "Do you just not want to see me?"

"That's not it," I said.

"Then what the hell is it?"

"I—"

I could practically see her eyes rolling when she said, "Then I'll see you this weekend. Call you tomorrow to let you know when my flight will be there. Love you!" Then she squealed, making the spot between my eyes hurt, and hung up before I could get another word in.

I was still seething five hours later as Cooper and I watched an Andy Samberg and Adam Sandler movie at my rental house. We'd thrown around the idea of going out to dinner with Paige and Eric and a few of their other friends (including Miranda), but I'd said I had a headache. Now my head lay on his lap, and I held on to the hem of his long cargo shorts as he stroked his fingertips across my skin.

"You know, Wills, if you want to rip my clothes off, just ask," he teased, staring down into my green eyes.

Groaning, I sat up, sliding my hands through my long hair and pulling it into the band that I'd put around my wrist earlier. It'd left a deep indentation in my skin, and I rubbed it as I bit the inside of my cheek.

Cooper moved closer, his blond eyebrows knitted in concern. "You've been scary quiet. What's up?"

"Jessica wants to come visit me," I said. He twisted his face, like he was trying to remember who she was. Finally he shook his head, waiting for me to elaborate, and I groaned. "Sparkly pastie girl," I said.

That got his attention; I felt his body go rigid. A smart-ass friend of a friend had posted a picture of me and Jessica at some party a year and a half ago on Cooper's Facebook wall. We'd been flashing whoever wielded the camera phone, red-faced and laughing.

Cooper touched his fingertips to his full lips, and I licked my own, feeling that pull between my legs. "And you said?" he asked.

I stared down at my hands. "I can't stop her from coming to Hawaii."

He groaned, but motioned me to him. I locked my legs

around his hips, one at a time, my breath catching when I saw the need in his blue eyes. "You'll be fine," he said. He'd been saying that to me more often than usual and I'd started to wonder if it was more for his benefit than my own.

But I nodded, touching my forehead to his as his fingertips skimmed under the elastic of my panties to slip inside of me. "We're filming too fast," I moaned, ready to get the thought of Jessica out of my head for now. I'd worry about her later or hell, once she showed up in Hawaii.

Cooper murmured something against my collarbone, then traced the tip of his tongue across the delicate bone there. "It doesn't matter."

"I don't want to go," I whispered, my voice heavy. I closed my eyes, my head falling forward, my hair falling over his shoulder, as his fingers picked up speed inside of me.

He was unraveling me.

Driving me crazy.

"We won't have to let go," he said, raking his teeth gently across my flesh as I came for him.

I slid down his body a moment later, undoing his shorts and wrapping my hands, my mouth, around him as the floor bruised my knees. I caught his gaze, and the corners of his lips lifted, his blue eyes softened.

Then I lost myself in him.

CHAPTER NINETEEN

In a move that was so typically Jessica, she changed her mind about coming to Hawaii at the last minute, claiming that she'd been brought on to act as the love interest in a music video. But instead of canceling her plans altogether, she changed her flight to nine days later. By the time Miller and I met her at the airport Thursday afternoon, I was a bundle of stress. I waited for her, chewing on the inside of my lip and squinting at the escalator through my giant sunglasses. Then I saw her, carrying her signature Louis Vuitton bag and looking like she was bored out of her fucking mind.

Jessica squealed once her eyes landed on me, and she wobbled forward on four-inch heels that had to make her at least six feet tall and threw her arms around me. I sucked in a deep breath. She smelled like too much booze and too little perfume.

"I've missed you," she cried, kissing me right beside my lips. Miller stared down at the airport floor.

"I've missed you too. We're parked in short-term parking so we should hurry this up," I said, and she slid her fingers into mine.

Her mouth dropped open and she gave me a surprised look. "No limo?"

I laughed. "No, actually it's a Kia."

She snorted but said nothing as she collected her luggage from baggage claim. When she tried to pass the bags off to Miller, I bit the inside of my cheek and lunged forward to grab them myself. There was a look of determination on his tanned face, and he shook his head.

"I've got this, Willow." I didn't miss the dark look he shot at Jessica, who was rapidly typing a text on her Samsung tablet.

As we walked a couple feet in front of Miller, she peeked over her shoulder and gave him an appreciative twice-over. "You lucky bitch," she said, shaking her head. When I raised my eyebrow, she continued, "You're fucking two gorgeous guys, and I've been too swamped to do anything fun."

I froze and looked her directly in the eye. The last thing I needed was for her to think Miller and I were sleeping together, or even worse, that Cooper and I *and* Miller were sleeping together. I shuddered at the thought. "It's not like that, Jess. I'm . . ." I paused before saying happy. It felt wrong to admit that to her. "I've been busy, too. With work."

Her lips parted slightly and she took another look at Miller. "So, the bodyguard—"

"Has a girlfriend," I replied sharply.

As we drove her to her hotel—a fancy five-star place over-looking Waikiki Beach—she chatted about the flight and all the clubs she'd found online in Honolulu. "We're going dancing at Moose's tonight," she said, and I noticed a muscle tic in Miller's cheek.

He was playing the role of big brother again, but this time I was glad. I glanced back at Jessica and gave her an apologetic smile. "I've got a scene to shoot first thing in the morning," I explained, and she threw her long strawberry-blond hair back and laughed.

She caught Miller's eye in the rearview mirror. "Is she fuck-ing serious?" Then she held up a purple-manicured hand and shook her head. "You know what, never mind. We'll have plenty of time to go dancing."

"Dickson will skin me if I'm late," I said. My producer had seemed detached ever since that day in his trailer when he'd ad-monished Cooper and me; I felt like I was walking on thin glass whenever I was around him.

I couldn't screw up and come to work late.

After we dropped Jessica off at her hotel, declining her invite up to her room, Miller drove me to Cooper's place for my lesson. He was in the middle of instructing a small group of ten-year-olds, so I sat on the beach with Paige, watching him. All of his gestures were over the top and dramatic and the kids were laughing at something he was saying.

Cooper caught me staring and gave me a chest-clenching smile that I returned.

"How'd picking up your friend go?" Paige asked, breaking my daze. I glanced over to see she was holding her hand over her eyes like a visor, studying me.

I shrugged. "She wanted to know if she could move in on my bodyguard."

Paige let out a laugh. "Hulk? God, I can't imagine what he said about that."

I hugged my knees, focusing my gaze back on Cooper as he showed the ten-year-olds how to pop up in the sand. I couldn't resist thinking about my first day—okay, first few days—doing the same thing with him two months ago. I sighed. "Miller didn't say anything because he probably doesn't want to piss me off," I admitted.

Paige lifted an eyebrow, ignoring Eric, who had come out on the deck to yell for her. "My phone call can wait," she said. She tilted her head to each side for a few seconds, biting her lower lip, before asking, "*Would* it piss you off?"

I swallowed hard. "No. Guess it makes me a shit friend that I want Jessica to leave already, huh?"

Paige rose to her feet, dusting the sand from the back of her bright-red Billabong board shorts. "Sometimes I realize that those things that make me feel like a dickwad usually pop into my head for the best reasons."

Leave it to Paige to mix in a giant dose of psychology.

When Cooper's group lesson ended, he lifted his hand, grinning so that his dimple showed. He crooked his finger for me to join him at the shoreline and I gravitated to him, feeling the sand squish into my flip-flops.

Jerking me flush to his body, he slid his hands down my shoulders. "You look like you're ready to strangle someone," he said. His fingertips pressed into the small of my back to close the gap between our bodies.

"Just tired," I said.

"Want me to talk to Dickson about giving you some time off?" he asked teasingly and I shook my head.

"You're not his favorite person," I said, and he shrugged, releasing me.

"Story of my goddamn life."

As we pushed our boards out into the white water, we talked about his surfing competition coming up in October. Every time I mentioned Jessica, he steered the conversation away to anything else. We talked about my work, his work, and even the new shipment of promo tees Blue Flame had gotten in earlier that day. By the time he volunteered to take me back to my rental house a few hours later, after the lesson, my irritation had migrated from Jessica to him.

"Please don't tell me you're turning into one of those possessive dickheads," I said, as I stalked through the house to my bedroom. I pulled the band from my hair, shaking the long strands out, and then flipped each of my flip-flops off, kicking them beneath the bed.

He turned on the radio by the bed and made a face when a Ke$ha song blasted throughout the tiny room. He slid the dial over until he found another station—this one with nothing but commercials.

"I've never been a big fan of toxic friends," he said, and I stiffened halfway to my closet. Taking a breath, I dragged a pair of shorts and a tank top down, tossed them onto the bed, and spun around to face him.

"Cooper, she just got here. She hasn't done anything to make you dislike her yet."

But even as I said the words, they didn't feel quite right. They sounded like I was trying to convince myself.

Cooper sneered. "Don't be ridiculous, Wills. Every picture I've ever seen of the two of you makes me think she's just waiting for the perfect moment to bury a hatchet in your throat."

"Now you're being dramatic," I said. I still didn't know how to handle this whole relationship thing where the guy I was dating actually gave a shit about what I was doing and where I was going. I sank down on the opposite end of the bed and placed my head between my knees. "Part of me is glad she's here and the other part is—"

"My mum had this friend when I was a kid who'd come to Australia every now and then. Wanted me to call her Auntie Amy."

Cooper rarely spoke about his mom. I slowly lifted myself back up, mussing the blankets as I turned around to face him. I crossed my legs over each other, leaned forward, and waited for him to finish. "And?"

"Mum would disappear for a few days, leaving me with him." He shuddered, clenched the soft cotton comforter, and then said, "And when she came back she'd be coming off a high."

I rubbed my hand over my chest hoping it would ease the burning sensation in my heart, but it didn't. "And you think because Jessica's come here for vacation I'm going to fall off the wagon?" I asked in a soft voice.

"There are still pics of you two on TMZ with your shirts raised and little silver stars over your tits. So sorry that I'm a little worried."

I slid closer to him, so that my knees nudged against his side. Touching his face, I stared him straight in the eye. "Have more faith in me."

"Come here," he whispered, his voice deep, and he pulled me in to him. His hands were gentle as they hooked under the denim waistband of my shorts, but mine were desperate, dragging up the front of his polo shirt and pulling at his collar.

One button hit the hardwood floor—then the other—and I felt him smile under our kiss and murmur something against my lips about liking it rough. We were partially naked in a matter of seconds, with me on my back and his fingers pushing inside of me.

"What you've done to me is—" he started, but I tangled my hands around his back, devouring his lips. I flicked my tongue at each corner. "You're tearing me down," he said, dragging away from me.

"I never said I was an angel," I whispered, closing my eyes as he fished through the bedside drawer for a condom.

When I felt his body against mine again, Cooper blew his minty breath against my collarbone. "Bend over, Wills," he ordered, and when I did, he pressed a kiss to the small of my back.

When we collapsed in a pile of sweat a while later, I whispered, "You were right." He swallowed hard and turned to me, his eyebrows pulling together. I cleared my throat. "Our first lesson you said you intended to see me like that."

He laughed and slipped his fingers under the ribbed cotton of my tank top. He'd pushed the neck of it down earlier when we undressed, exposing my breasts. Guess he'd gotten used to me refusing to get completely naked.

After a long time of lying still, he murmured, "Why won't you let me see all of you?"

"You have seen all of me."

He made a little noise in the back of his throat. "With the lights off."

My shoulders stiffened. "Because I'm messed up," I whispered at last. He propped himself up to look into my eyes, and I brushed back a sweaty strand of golden hair from his forehead. "Don't look at me like that."

"Like what?" he asked. "I've told you a million times you're perfect. We've been going at this for what? More than a month?"

"Don't be fucking pushy," I said.

He held up his hands in surrender. "This is me, dropping it."

"Good," I said.

The next morning, Friday, Jessica called me bright and early, claiming she was still stuck in L.A. time. She mentioned a bunch of Honolulu sights she was dying to see and from the monotone voice she used, I was pretty sure she'd only found those five minutes before calling me and was reading them from Google as we spoke.

"I'm shooting in a little bit," I said.

She gasped, excited. "Do you think James would mind if I watched?" she asked, and I hesitated. Dickson wasn't the biggest fan of guests on set but then again, she'd worked with him before, on a movie a couple years before I shot *Sleepless.*

But when she greeted him an hour and a half later, smiling, he didn't look too happy to see her.

"You look great," he told her, giving her the once-over he'd given me two months ago at Junction. But now the words didn't carry to his eyes.

Jessica amused herself by flirting with Justin as I shot an emotional scene with my on-screen parents. Every now and then, I felt her blue eyes watching me, taking me in, but when I met hers full-on she grinned, waving.

And I found myself rubbing my throat more than once, imagining that hatchet Cooper had mentioned last night.

As soon as Dickson declared my scene a success, he took me aside. "Is everything okay, Willow?" he asked. I was getting tired of hearing that everywhere I turned, but I swallowed hard and nodded politely.

I placed my hand on his forearm and gave him a meaningful look. "I'm great."

"And Cooper is—"

My producer was veering toward the awkward again, and I groaned aloud, holding my hands out in front of me to stop this conversation before it took that turn. "I'm *great.*"

Dickson cast a sideways glance at Jessica, who was talking to one of the supporting actresses—they apparently knew each other from a movie they'd done together two years ago. Jessica lifted her head, flipping her strawberry-blond hair over one shoulder, and gave us a long, examining stare.

"I'm half tempted to schedule a scene for you tomorrow so that—" Dickson started but then he caught himself. He clenched his hands out in front of him, bobbing his head slowly as he said, "Just be careful, Willow."

Suppressing an exasperated grunt, I nodded and swore to him that I would. As I walked over to join Jessica, and her smile widened, I felt Dickson's eyes following me.

Miller drove us back to my rental house, and Jessica quickly undid her seat belt, placing her chin on the back of my seat. "We're going out tonight, yes?" I jabbed my tongue inside my cheek and gripped the door handle.

"Miller can take us to dinner?" I asked her at last, and she sighed.

"Whatever."

As we entered the house, I told Miller I'd text him as soon as we were ready. He nodded, replying, "I'm going to hit the gym for a little but I'll be waiting."

Then I took Jessica inside, and as she threw herself down on the suede couch, she gave me a smile that showed nearly all of her straight white teeth. "This place is cute." I'd known Jessica long enough to know that "cute" meant she utterly loathed whatever she was talking about. I picked up handfuls of clothing off the arm of the recliner and gritted my teeth.

She'll be gone in two days, I reminded myself.

A moment later I heard the sound of something hitting the table, and every muscle in my body tightened. I turned slowly, staring in horror at the baggie sitting atop the stack of magazines on the edge of the table. "What's that?" I asked, feeling my heart skip a beat. Of course I already knew exactly what *that* was. I could probably even guess how much the bag of Roxies had cost her.

She lifted the corners of her lips. "Happy belated birthday, Willow. I celebrated without you, but hey, it's never too late to—"

I jabbed my finger at the bag and shook my head. "Get rid of them," I growled. Her smile faded and her dark-blue eyes narrowed into tight slits.

"Don't be stupid."

I redirected my finger to the door and said in a tight voice, "Jess, I'm not above telling you to get the fuck out. Throw them away, flush them, I don't give a shit—just don't give them to me."

She gave me a long, hard look and then swooped up the bag of Roxies, dumping it back into her Vuitton bag. Sitting upright, she flexed her hands on either side of her body. "All right, Willow." She slid her tongue from side to side between her teeth. "What now then?"

"Dinner," I reminded her.

"Fun," she said, emphasizing the word.

Her movements were jerky when I excused myself to take a shower and I stood under the hot water, gripping the shower wall for support. I hated myself for my reaction to what Jessica had brought—for wanting it for a split second—just about as much as I hated her for bringing it to me in the first place.

After my shower, I sat on the edge of my bed, listening to the muted sound of Jessica's laughter and the Andy Samberg movie Cooper and I had watched the week before drifting from the living room.

"I can do this," I whispered. I picked my phone up from the nightstand to check the time and found a text message from Cooper.

> 6:18 p.m.: Still going out for dinner with Pastie tonight?

I sighed, lifting up off the bed to go in search of clothes as I messaged him back.

> 6:29 p.m.: Yes. Do you want me to have Miller drop me off afterward?

He texted me back as I sifted through underwear.

> 6:29 p.m.: You can have him drop you off now if you'd like. Or I can just come get you. Or . . .

I bit my bottom lip, feeling the stress slowly lift off my shoulders.

> You do know that I hate ellipses because of the implication behind them, right?

I shimmied my panties on and my bra and set about finding something to wear. I opted for a pair of skinny jeans and a blue-and-red flannel top with a white tank top beneath. My phone vibrated as I buttoned my jeans. Sliding my feet into a pair of sneakers, I flopped over to the bed to answer Cooper's call.

Except it wasn't Cooper, it was my parents. I gripped the phone tightly, staring at the neon text rotating around the screen as the phone continued to shudder in my hand. They hadn't called me since the fallout with Mom a week after my birthday and I honestly wasn't ready to talk. When the phone stopped vibrating, I threw it down on the bed and finished getting dressed. I combed my long dark hair into a high ponytail and rubbed on lip gloss before sliding my phone and credit card into my back pocket.

Jessica wrinkled the tip of her nose when she saw me. "You look—" She paused, cocking her head to one side and raking her gaze up my body and back down, from head to toe. I tensed up under her scrutiny as I waited for her to say something. Then she gave me a mock disgusted glare. "Ugh, I need to start surfing. You look hot."

Relaxing, I grinned at her. "It's an ass-kicker."

She licked her lips nonchalantly. "Speaking of ass-kickers—am I going to get to meet Surfer Boy while I'm here?"

I focused my attention on fishing my phone out of my back pocket as I said, "He's got a competition he's training for so I'm not even getting to see him this weekend."

Jessica groaned. "Well that sucks."

I closed my grip around my phone, fighting the urge to hurl it across the room at her. "Very much," I said sweetly.

I texted Miller that we were ready whenever he got back from his workout. Right after I hit send, my phone vibrated yet again. My mother. I groaned and shot Jessica a look. "Be right back. My mom won't stop until I take this."

Slipping out the front door, I paced the lanai as I answered. "Hey, sorry I missed your call before, I—"

"Willow, I've got bad news."

My heart flew into my throat. "Dad?" I gasped.

She made a strangled noise, and I leaned against one of the wooden beams of the house. What if something had happened to him? What if—

"Willow, Clay called a little while ago."

My heart slunk away from where it was lodged inside of my throat, and for a moment it felt as if it had dropped out of my body completely.

Because the moment Mom had said my attorney's name— even before she started saying things like "agency" and "appeals process" and "new court date sometime next year"—I knew it was over.

CHAPTER TWENTY

~~~~~~

The first drink I took that night scorched my throat, making me choke, making my eyes water. I didn't know if the tears were from the pretty blue bottle of SKYY vodka or the sobs I'd been swallowing back ever since Miller had picked me up and I told him my plans had changed for the night—that I wanted to go back to Jessica's hotel room.

So since I couldn't figure it out, I took another shot and then one more, just to be sure.

Jessica lay beside me, her blue eyes glazed as she stared at the recessed lighting above our faces, which cast a reddish glow. "You sure you don't want it?" she whispered, gesturing her hand toward the nightstand, to where the other half of the blue pill she'd downed an hour ago sat.

Of course I wanted it, but I shook my head. My phone vibrated in my back pocket—probably Cooper again. I ignored it.

She traced her tongue over her lips and sat up for a moment to look at the door to her room. Miller was on the other side, waiting for me as I'd asked. "We can still get him to take us to that club," she said, dropping back down and giving me a little smile. She scooted her hips across the memory foam, closing the space between us until our hips brushed. "It'll be fun."

"I'm fine here," I argued. But I wasn't fine. My head was spinning and my stomach pitched violently because I'd left my dinner untouched. I felt myself slowly slipping farther under.

And yet, I caught myself sitting up, swinging my legs over the side of the bed to pour yet another shot.

Because I'd lost.

Because I wanted to escape.

Jessica murmured something inaudible and I half turned to see that she'd closed her eyes. "My show isn't going to work out," she said at last, referring to the pilot she'd shot earlier in the summer.

I lost. I'm never going to see him again. I lost.

I massaged my temples, trying to get that thought out of my head. I'd think about it tomorrow or the next day. I'd think about it when it didn't hurt so bad to think. Instead, I'd focus on Jessica. "You don't know that," I said, and she opened her eyes, turning her head to me to give me a cold look.

"Let me Willow it down for you—I got fired. I'm not going anywhere with it," she said, and my mouth pinched together. I crossed my arms tightly over my chest, turning my back to her once again, as she continued, "You're lucky."

Sucking in a harsh, nauseating breath, I clenched my hands into the fabric under either side of my arms. "I'm not."

She snorted, and then coughed, and I saw her come up on her elbows again in my peripheral vision. She gave me an incredulous look. "Of course you are. You've got a good role and—" Then she paused, laughter taking over her body as she rolled onto her stomach. Placing her cheek on the smooth comforter, she reached out and hooked her fingertip in one of my belt loops. "You've got a boy with more daddy issues than you've got."

I flinched the moment she mentioned Cooper, snapping my gaze around to meet her eyes full-on. "Don't talk about him like that, Jess." She could say whatever she wanted about me, but I didn't want his name mentioned tonight. Not when I was doing this.

Jessica wouldn't drop it. "Oh come on, I'm sure Sunday dinner has been a fucking disaster at his place when you add you and James Dickson to the equation." She resumed her glaring match with the ceiling and the lighting, waiting for me to say something.

"What are you talking about?"

She made a hysterical sound that was part laugh, part sob, before demanding, "Don't you see it?"

She was talking in circles and the vodka was making its way to my head, to the rest of my body. The only thing I saw were the spots that would eventually become the darkness I wanted so badly.

When I didn't answer her she rolled her eyes. "James Dickson's his dad."

I rolled off the bed, stumbling a little on one of the shoes she'd left at the foot of it. My breathing was harsh and labored as I steadied myself, gripping one of the wooden posts for support. "Don't be an idiot, Jess. You've never even met the guy." And she never would as long as I had anything to do with it.

She sat upright in the middle of the bed and hugged her knees. She raked her hand through her strawberry-blond hair, making each movement seem like it was an effort. "There was a picture of them together on Leah Dishes." When I slid my teeth together, giving her a hard look, she added, "But let me guess, you've been too caught up in Willow problems to even notice the resemblance."

I turned my back to her. "I've got to pee."

The moment I slammed the bathroom door behind me, I pulled my phone out, exiting out of the missed text messages from Cooper and my mother. I stood in the center of the enormous bathroom, fumbling through pages of a shitty gossip site I never visited, but once I found what I was looking for, I sank down beside the oversize bathtub, staring down at it.

The photo had been taken at the meet and greet we'd done the evening after I found out who Cooper's mother was. Cooper and Dickson were side by side, smiling, and the caption under the picture read

Tidal producer (James Dickson) greets the man
behind the surfer (Cooper Taylor).

I would have shrugged Jessica's comment off and immediately turned off my phone if I hadn't stared closer—if I hadn't realized just how tense their body language was.

And the dimple in Dickson's left cheek.

I slid my phone away from me, to the far corner of the porcelain tub, so I wouldn't hurl it against the wall. Cooper had lied to me. He had fucking lied and—

Then I remembered the scar on his back. The long, jagged scar that he'd told me his father had given him when he was a kid.

My hands trembled as I grabbed my phone and sent him a message.

11:23 p.m.: I'm coming over. Are you home?

He responded quickly.

11:23 p.m.: I'm here. Are you okay?

I didn't answer, shoving the phone inside the back pocket of my tight jeans. Taking a deep breath to clear my head, I walked into the bedroom to face Jessica, who now lay back on a mound of pillows with her legs crossed, eating from a plate of fries that had gone cold hours before.

"I've got to go home," I said.

The corners of her lips quirked up but she never moved, never even turned her gaze on me. "I won't see you after this, will I?"

I reached the door. And I didn't stop to look back at her when I said, "No, you won't."

Miller escorted me to Cooper's front door, his gaze never meeting mine. He'd been quiet as he drove me from Jessica's hotel, opening his mouth and then slamming it closed every couple minutes, and I knew he was disappointed in me. Hell, I was disappointed in me. And I was furious.

Furious at Cooper and at Dickson and at myself.

Eric answered the door in his boxers, holding a remote control and scratching his beard. He propped one arm up against the wood frame to support his tall, lanky body. He started to make one of his usual remarks but Miller shook his head. Then Eric leaned forward a little and inhaled.

The easygoing expression slipped from his face, giving way to the worry I'd seen hundreds of times, and Eric dropped his gaze to the foyer floor. He moved aside so I could step through the doorway. "Cooper's upstairs showering."

I turned to Miller, holding my stomach. "Wait for me in the car." The order sounded harsh when it came out so shaky and unsure, but he lifted his chin.

Before Eric could say another word, I stalked past him, stumbling up the stairs and into Cooper's bedroom, which was steamed up from his shower. He was coming out of the bathroom wrapped in a towel when I lunged at him, shoving him square in the chest. He barely budged, and when I went at him again, he grabbed my wrists, not seeming to care that the towel fell to the floor.

"Goddamn it, Wills, calm down. Calm down and"—his body froze and he dragged me closer to him, despite my struggling—"you're drunk. Holy fuck, you're drunk."

I didn't deny it. "You lied to me."

He released me, scooping up his towel. Turning his back to me, he leaned up against the dresser, sliding his hand back and forth over his forehead. "You're drunk and you're accusing *me* of lying?"

I backed up against the wall next to the dresser, sliding down it until I crumpled on the floor. "Is James Dickson your dad?" I demanded. When Cooper's eyes went hard and the muscles in his neck tightened, I balled my hands into my flannel shirt. "So he beat the shit out of you and you decide to work for him? You let me go on believing he's this good guy after he did that to you?"

Letting out a frustrated moan, he pushed away from the cherry wood. He kneeled in front of me a second later to touch my face, and I flinched. "He's not the one who hit me, Wills." Then, raking his fingers through his wet blond hair, he took a deep breath. "My mother was married to Colin Taylor when she got pregnant with me, Wills, and James Dickson . . . he's had the same wife forever."

I bit the inside of my cheek but said nothing, compelling him with my eyes to continue.

"Mum passed me off as Colin's for years but he always knew. He knew the whole damn time and tortured me for it."

My lungs constricted, making it hard for me to catch my breath. "Did Dickson know?" I asked in a hoarse voice. When he didn't immediately answer, I spoke louder, more desperately. "Did he?"

Cooper shook his head and sat down beside me. "Not until after the shit with the fishing pole and even after that I didn't meet Dickson until I was seventeen, at Mum's funeral." Cooper raised one of his knees as he stared at the wall across from us. "I wanted to hit him. I wanted to kill him that day."

I gave him a pained look. "Cooper—"

"She loved him. And all she ever got from him were a million excuses."

And suddenly, what he'd said to me days, weeks, ago about his mother loving him and everything he'd represented to her made sense.

"I'm so sorry," I stuttered.

Cooper held up his hand, shaking his head. "Don't be. Dickson and I have been trying this father-son bullshit for years. It probably won't ever work, but I'll keep trying because despite what a selfish ass he's been, Mum genuinely loved him."

Then he reached out, cupping my face with his damp palm. Our eyes touched, and I suddenly felt like the room was closing in on us. "Wills, why are you drinking?" When I started to climb to my feet, he locked his fingertips gently around my wrist. "You wanted me to spill my shit so I did. There's no way in hell I'm letting you leave this room tonight without you coming out with yours."

And though I wanted to fight him, though I just wanted to

escape, I eased back down on my bottom, feeling every inch of my body go numb as I said in a monotone voice, "I lost my baby."

He dropped wide blue eyes to my stomach. "What?"

"Tyler and me. We had a baby and I lost him."

He was quiet for a long moment, a muscle twitching in his jaw. "So he got you pregnant and you had a miscarriage?" When I shook my head, he continued, "You had an abortion?" The last word was spoken in a whisper.

I didn't deny it and I didn't acknowledge it; I just let out a thick sigh. "When I told my mom and dad they freaked out. I mean, I was sixteen and"—I hugged my arms around my stomach, as the memories hit me—"we went to this little clinic in Washington and I'm lying there getting an ultrasound, scared out of my mind. The sonographer looks up at my mom and says, 'Looks like you're going to have a baby in four months.'"

"Wills—"

"I'd hidden it from them for too long to get the abortion, so my mom sent me to live with her stepmother in Oregon until he was born."

Cooper sucked in a long, hard breath through his teeth. "And you gave him up for adoption?"

I nodded. "Tyler didn't care. He was more worried about being charged with statutory rape than whether or not I was okay. My parents and Kevin kept telling me it was my choice—that they weren't making me do anything even though I knew they were. So I signed him away when he was born. I signed a closed adoption and was too fucking stupid to realize that that meant I'd never see him again."

Cooper came close to me, trying to draw me into him, but I shoved him away, staggering to my feet. Yanking my jeans down around my hips, I turned to him. When I pulled up my tank top, his electric-blue eyes narrowed.

And my heart broke. My whole body was shaking but I didn't make an effort to straighten my clothes. There was no point. "There you go. That's why I won't let you fuck me with the lights on."

He reached forward and grabbed my hips hard, tugging me to him and burying his damp head into my bare skin. "Don't say it like that," he said in a low growl.

"Why?"

"Because you've never just been a fuck to me. I love you, Wills."

And then I slid down on the floor with him again, and I was crying into his bare chest. "I found out tonight that I lost my suit against the adoption agency and then I just lost myself. All I wanted to do was black out and forget. Forget myself and the baby."

"I'm so sorry, Wills," he whispered into my hair, and I sobbed harder. When there was nothing left inside of me, I dragged myself away from him, suddenly aware of smelling like alcohol. I'd never been more ashamed of myself. "I'm a wreck," I said.

"We'll fix you."

He kept saying that, and it left a bitter pang in my chest each time. "How can you talk about fixing me when you've got your own issues?" I demanded, lifting bleary eyes to look up at him.

He closed his eyes for a moment. "When my mum died I realized that it's possible to live without someone you love." When I asked him what he meant, he wrapped me back in his arms. "I love you, Willow, but I *can* live without you. I just refuse to."

We lay there on the floor for what seemed like an eternity before Eric tentatively knocked on the door saying that Miller was downstairs and wouldn't budge until he knew I was okay. Drying away the tears with the backs of my hands I started to get up, but Cooper held me back.

"Stay," he said. "I don't care if you messed up and got drunk with Jessica. I just need you with me."

I nodded, gently pulling my hand from his as I stood. Eric had an awkward expression on his face before he turned away from me to jog down the steps. Miller met me at the very bottom and I took a deep breath. "I'm all right," I said.

He slid his tongue over the tiny gap in his front teeth. "You're crying."

"There were some things that needed to be said."

"And you're leaving now?" he asked.

I shook my head, looking back over my shoulder to where the light strained out of Cooper's bedroom door. "No, I'm staying."

CHAPTER TWENTY-ONE

~~~~~~~~~~~~~~~~~~~~~~~

After a dreamless night, I panicked the next morning when I felt a feather-soft kiss touch the scar on my stomach. My eyes flew open and I caught Cooper's messy blond hair in my fingers. Shaking my head frantically to each side, I whispered, "Don't."

He didn't move but rested his hands on either side of my belly button, digging the tips of his fingers softly into my skin until I moaned. "I'm sorry about everything that's happened to you, Wills."

I released a bitter laugh. "I should be the one apologizing. I've been selfish and you've been hurting just as much as I have. "

He lifted his head, furrowing his brow. "I'm fine. Maybe Dickson and I will eventually work things out, maybe not. The point is that I've learned to deal with it."

Sighing, I closed my eyes, arching my back a little when he trailed little kisses from my hip bones to my scar and to my breasts. He settled himself between my legs and groaned when my phone vibrated in the pocket of my jeans, which I'd left on the floor the night before. At first I ignored it, dragging his mouth down to mine, but when it continued to buzz, I pulled away from him.

"Leave Willow alone," Cooper said, grinning, and he slouched back against the pillows, watching me as I plucked my phone out of my pants.

There were several missed calls from my mother, a few from Kevin, and a cryptic text from Jessica.

11:16 a.m.: Have fun explaining this one. Leaving today. Don't ever call me again.

My parents called again before I could even exit out of the message. I answered, and it was my father who spoke. "There's a fifteen-minute phone call that you made to one of your friends on Leah Dishes," Dad said in a numb voice.

I felt the air slowly leave my body. "What?"

"Everything is there, kiddo. Everything about the baby and Tyler Leonard and your boyfriend's secret," he said. "What the hell were you think—"

I disconnected the call before Dad could get another word in and fumbled anxiously through my call records. My breath was puffing in and out of my chest in choppy gasps, and Cooper sat up in bed, his brows knitted in concern. His hand brushed my shoulder blades, but I shoved it away. Finally, I found the last call I'd made. It was to Jessica from 12:18 a.m. to 12:41 a.m.

After I'd gotten to Cooper's place the night before.

Cooper touched my shoulder again, shaking it, and I flinched. "Willow, what's wrong?"

"I fucked up."

I punched in the web address for Leah's blog with prickling fingers, ignoring Cooper's questions. When the homepage popped up on the screen of my phone, I dry heaved. There I was at the top—the same photo of Tyler and me that had been posted on the site a few weeks ago—with the headline AVERY SPILLS ALL ON LEONARD LOVE CHILD.

Even though I shouldn't have, I pressed the triangular play button over the audio clip. I released a cry when I heard myself freaking out at Cooper the night before.

His face froze. "What the fuck is that?"

"I must've accidentally called Jessica while we were arguing."

We listened to it for a long time—to ourselves letting out secrets we'd never told another soul—and we didn't say a single word. Twelve minutes into the audio clip, a commotion from downstairs brought Cooper to his feet. Too numb to move, I sat there, half listening to the recorded call and half to the sounds of Cooper's footsteps as he shrugged into a pair of shorts and bounded out of the room. I heard him yelling and then Paige's voice, and when he returned to me a few minutes later, his face was drawn.

"There are cameramen setting up on the beach," he said. "In front of my fucking house. Jesus, Wills, I—" He caught himself when my face fell, holding his hands out in front of him. "It's going to be all right. We're going to . . ."

I buried my face into my hands, but he pulled them away. "I've got to call Miller and—"

"He's already here."

I didn't dare look at any of the faces that surrounded me when I walked downstairs a half hour later wearing the same jeans I'd worn the night before and one of Cooper's T-shirts. Paige, Eric, Miller, and I sat around in the giant living room, while Cooper argued with someone—Dickson from the sound of it—in the next room.

"Evie will be okay, all right? I—" Cooper raged, and my shoulders sagged even more at the mention of Dickson's wife. He paused for a moment and said, "I don't know if she'll be. I don't know anything right now."

"I want to go home," I said.

Paige moved hesitantly forward, kneeling down so her hazel eyes could take me in. "I think you should stick around, Willow," she said in a soothing voice.

"Miller, please just take me home."

Cooper was still in the other room talking to Dickson when I left, and I didn't interrupt to tell him I was leaving. I put on my poker face, letting Miller guide me through the throng of cameramen flashing their Nikons at me—once when we left Cooper's place and then again when we returned to my house.

But the second I locked the door behind me, I burst into

tears again. I dragged my hands through my hair and buried my face into the suede fabric of the couch so the paparazzi around my rental house couldn't hear me as I screamed.

I screamed at myself for being so stupid and as I sat there, rocking back and forth, I screamed at Jessica not just for recording such an intimate conversation but for the tiny blue bag she'd left on my coffee table. I balled up in the corner of the couch and stared at it, biting my lip so hard it bled.

When Kevin called a few minutes later, I answered the phone, relieved at the distraction. "I'm sorry," I said simply, because there was just nothing else to say. "I've hurt Cooper and Dickson, and I—"

Kevin hushed me, speaking in a gentle voice he'd used on me only a few times before. "We're going to do damage control," he said. "We're getting the studio and your publicist and Tyler's—"

I shook my head, hugging myself tighter. "There's no damage control for this."

He let out a heavy sigh. "There's always damage control," he said.

"I'm not doing this anymore."

"You've got to."

"I'm not," I said. "Let them talk. Let them say whatever. It's the truth."

Kevin missed a beat and then groaned. "I'm not going to let you do that, Willow."

"You don't have a choice. I'll call you soon," I promised, before dropping the call.

I grabbed the bag Jessica had left, slid it into my pocket, and walked down the hall to my bedroom. I sat on the edge of the bed, gripping my MacBook so hard it was bound to break. My fingers felt numb as I went to Leah's website and clicked the contact link. Leah's grinning caricature stared up at me, and I glared at it as I started my message.

August 17

My name is Willow Avery.

Yes, THAT Willow Avery—THAT actress. The one who went off the deep end three years ago. The one whose face is plastered all over the tabloids this morning. They don't give a shit if there's more to me than meets the eye, that there's so much more to my fall from grace, even if nobody— other than my parents and agent—knows what that is. Well, at least nobody knew until a few hours ago.

And the thing is I've ALWAYS cared about what everyone thought of me, even when it seemed like I didn't. No matter how much my need for approval has hurt me, there's always been this sick part of me that refuses to let it go. That still desperately craves it. It's just that now, I'm not sure if I mind that everyone knows the truth about me. Now, there's this guy and he's not waiting for me to screw up. He doesn't care that I HAVE screwed up.

I typed until I couldn't see anymore, and when I hit send I pushed my laptop aside. Then I rushed to the bathroom to vomit up the remnants of the vodka I'd drunk the night before.

Cooper found me there an hour later, with my eyes closed, dried tears burning the corners and making the sides of my face feel as if they were cracking into a million pieces.

Just like the girl herself, I thought.

I heard him stumble across the room and felt his body sink down next to me on the cold tile. It sounded like his heart was in his throat as he said over and over, "Wills. Willow. Wills."

"I'm not high," I whispered in a voice rubbed completely raw from the crying. He sighed, falling back hard against something. My eyelashes were sticky as I pulled them apart to squint at him. He was by the tub, his expression tight as he worked his fingers against his temples. "But I wanted to be," I said.

"But you're not," he told me, cupping my face between his hands. He kissed me hard and desperately. "You're all right."

I cried out and he pulled back. "Cooper, I'm fucked-up."

"Jessica screwed you over. Just because you wanted to—"

I pushed him away from me, scooted back to the wall, and hugged my knees. For a long time, our breathing was the only sound in the bathroom. "Wills?" he whispered at last, hesitantly.

I dug into my pocket, pulling the bag of Roxies out and tossing them across to him. "My birthday present."

He looked at the bag as if it would rot his hand off if he touched it, then dragged his hands over his face. "Rick?"

It took me a moment to figure out whom he was talking about and then I realized it was Eric's dad, the pill dealer. I shook my head. "I've never even met the guy. Jessica brought those for me last night as a belated birthday gift and left them."

He clenched his hands, his features, but he didn't ask me about Jessica; he simply said, "What do we do now?"

"I wrote an email to Leah's blog a little while ago." When he groaned and started to say something, I shook my head fiercely, cutting him off. "They've already put out everything that could hurt me. Everything that could hurt you and your da—Dickson. What else can they do besides mock my grammar?"

"Wills—"

When I cut him off again, I looked away so I wouldn't have to see his face when I asked him my question. "If I go away—if I go to be fixed—will you still be here?"

He was quiet for a long time, and I knew it was over. That he was going to rip me apart like Tyler did, but wouldn't leave a single bit of me to salvage. I wouldn't cry. I'd already wept so much that even if Cooper told me to fuck off, I didn't think it was possible for me to shed another tear. I would not cry. I would not.

And suddenly, he was coming over to me, wrapping his arms around me, and burying his face in my hair.

"Don't ever doubt me again, Willow. The whole time you've been here I've told you two things until I was blue in the face— that I'll look after you and that I'm not wishy-washy. If you've got to go fix yourself, nothing I feel for you changes. I won't stop loving you."

I was wrong. There were still tears left in me.

Dickson sent a car, and an extra bodyguard, a half hour later and we met him at a secluded beach house he said belonged to a friend. The three of us were tense, as we talked about what would happen next. When my producer assured me that he had enough footage of me to make the movie work, my head popped up.

"I'm not going to bail on you, Dickson," I said. Dickson shook his head and touched my shoulder.

"You're not. We'll give Justin a few extra scenes if we have to—that kid will love that. What I want you to do is go get yourself help, Willow." Not once did Dickson look at me angrily, even though his name was being smeared too, and I caught Cooper giving him an appreciative nod when he added, "I know of a good place in L.A. and I'll gladly foot the bill."

That night, once Cooper went to bed and the cameras outside his place finally left, I slunk away to the hallway that led out to the deck so I could call my parents. It was two in the morning in Los Angeles, but my mom answered almost as soon as I hit the call button, her voice anxious.

"Where have you been all day? We've been worried sick. Your dad and I have scheduled a morning flight to come to Hawaii and—"

"Don't," I said, pacing, my bare feet tapping softly on the cold floor.

"Don't? Please don't push us away this time—" She paused

and I heard my dad say something to her. I heard the sound of her hand scratching against the receiver, and a second later my father came on the line.

"Willow, don't be difficult," Dad said.

Don't be difficult. Don't. Be. Fucking. Difficult.

I bit the inside of my cheek before telling him, "I wrote a letter to Leah's blog."

Dad sucked in a breath of air. "I'm aware," he said. Of course he already knew what I'd done. There was no doubt in my mind that my e-mail had been published on the site almost as soon as I'd sent it.

"I'm going back to rehab, Dad. Dickson says he's gotten everything out of me that he needs to make this film a success."

"Willow—"

"Just listen to me for once!" I snapped, and then I heard nothing but silence on the other end. "Cooper's flying me home tomorrow or the next day—hell, I don't know—but the point is, I'm coming back to do what I should have done eight months ago. And hopefully, the next time I see you, I'll be okay. I'll be . . . right."

Dad murmured something to my mother and I heard her make a strangled noise. "What about your career? What about your acting?"

"Hollywood has survived twice without me before. I don't think the industry will shut down if I disappear."

"Do you need—"

"I don't need money," I said, and then I sat down on the floor across from the laundry-room door and told him about Dickson finding me a rehab and paying for it. When I was finished, I sighed. "I'll call you. Or write you. And Dad?"

"Yeah, kiddo?" he asked, his voice heavy with emotion.

"For once, it would be nice if you didn't have something planned when I come out. If you could just let me ease back into regular life. If you could give me that respect."

When I placed the phone down on its screen a moment later, a sound from the end of the hallway startled me, and I looked up to see Cooper leaning against the wall, looking so much like he did that first night a couple months ago when he'd kissed me senseless in the doorway at my rental.

I smiled sadly as I got to my feet and gravitated to him. Our bodies were flush, and he threaded his fingertips into the hair near my temples.

And then, he kissed me again, as if it were the last time we'd say good-bye.

CHAPTER TWENTY-TWO

My new home for the next sixty days was called Seaside, even though it wasn't anywhere near the sea. It was not nearly as luxurious as the first one I'd been to, nor was it as plain as Serenity Hills. The Monday after Leah Dishes Hollywood first broke the story about me and Tyler, and Dickson and Cooper, Cooper helped me check in. After I filled out a packet of paperwork a good two inches thick, we stood in front of the staff station because he wasn't allowed beyond that point.

"A couple months ago I never thought I'd say this," he said in a low voice, his fingertips skimming the sides of my face, "but I'm actually going to miss you, Wills." He was grinning, but it didn't reach his eyes, and I knew he was just trying to make me smile.

This will be hard.

I refused to say that aloud. So I forced the corners of my lips up into a smile and dragged in a deep breath between my teeth to keep from crumpling. I didn't want to be here. Two months ago I'd sworn to myself that I'd never go back to rehab and now here I was again, checking myself in. All I knew was that I needed help—I didn't want to feel like I needed to drown my sorrows every time I read about myself online or whenever I had a bad dream. I could do this. It was only sixty days.

People had been separated for so much longer.

A desperate exhale slipped from my lips as I pulled his mouth down to cover mine. The kiss was entirely too short and I shivered when our mouths broke apart. A member of the staff called my name and Cooper cast a grim look in his direction, tightening his grip on my fingers.

"I feel like—" he started and then dragged his free hand through his blond hair.

"Like what?"

The corners of his lips quirked up for a moment into a painful grimace. "Like I've failed you, Wills."

He hadn't; he'd done just the opposite. I shook my head. "This will be worth it," I said. Then, reluctantly, I pulled away from Cooper and went in the direction of the man saying my name.

"I can do this," I said under my breath. "I'll be fine."

I quickly discovered that I wasn't a celebrity at Seaside. The staff didn't treat me as if I were a god or some idiot assigned to them by a judge or *anything* other than a patient. My room had a window and my roommate, Nora, wasn't famous—she was a hairdresser whose wealthy grandparents were paying for her to be there. When I introduced myself to her she cocked an eyebrow and bit her bottom lip before reaching out to take my hand.

"I'd hoped I wouldn't get a roomie," she said.

I smiled. "Sorry. You can pretend I don't exist if you want." She winked and stopped chewing her lip long enough to give me a half smile.

"I was already planning on it."

When I was given phone privileges two weeks after I arrived, and I called Cooper, I told him that Seaside was the baby bear of rehabs.

"I don't get it, Wills," he said, but I could tell he was smiling.

I slid down on one of the floral-printed couches in the empty common room. "They don't have fables in Australia?" I teased, squeezing my eyes shut as I listened to the sound of his breathing. He'd sent letters—every day—but parting with a voice I'd heard every day for months had been difficult.

He cleared his throat. "I'm pretty sure the bear one is a fairy tale."

"Same difference," I choked out.

His voice grew serious. "How are you holding up?"

So I told him, as fast as my fifteen minutes would allow. I told him about Nora. I didn't add that she'd been in and out of rehab for the last sixteen years—since she was eighteen—or that she had a family who never wrote her. I'd started getting letters from my parents a week ago and I hid them under my pillow because I didn't want to see the hurt look on her face.

"She's good to you?"

"One of the sweetest people I've ever met," I said honestly.

I heard noises in the background and then Paige's voice came on the line. "I miss you, Avery!"

Swallowing hard, I said, "I miss you too. And Eric. Your piece-of-shit Grand Caravan still holding up?"

She made a noise that sounded like a hybrid of a laugh and a hiss. "You shut your dirty mouth." Then she said, "Cooper's flailing—and no I'm not even kidding—for the phone. We love you, Willow. Me and Eric and the boy with the coconut shampoo."

I wasn't used to friends telling me they loved me when we weren't drunk, so when I said it back to her, it sounded awkward. "Love you too, Paige."

It was the truth, so that was all that mattered.

I had three minutes left when I heard Cooper's voice return to the line. We spent all of it talking about his surfing competition in October, the one he'd told me about earlier in the summer. As he gave me the dates, I felt something sink in the pit of my stomach.

He'd be in the Canary Islands from the seventeenth through the twenty-third. I was set to be released from Seaside on October 19. Cooper and I'd never actually talked about my release date. Entering rehab with my thoughts centered on when I'd get out just seemed like the easiest way to set myself up for failure, and at the time, the only thing I needed to focus on was healing.

Now I felt a wave of regret.

"Why are you so quiet?" he whispered.

I rubbed my hand roughly across my chest. "Because I miss you," I said. Then, in an attempt to lighten the conversation—it was all I could do not to break down—I added, "And because I think your accent is hot when your voice drops like that."

I could hear a sound buzzing at the side of my ear, and it took me a long time to realize that a staff member was saying my name—my actual first name—in a soft voice to let me know my call was up. If I stayed on track, I'd get another call next week.

"I've got to go," I said. "I'll write, okay?"

"Mm-hmm." As I prepared to hang up he dropped his voice again and said softly, "Wills, I love you."

I pushed past the lump in my throat to say, "You too."

When I hit the round button to end the call, I gave the cordless phone back to the smiling woman waiting for it. "You're on the schedule for a meeting with Doctor Nelson in ten minutes. Will you be—"

"Yes," I answered, thinking of the man I'd just hung up from. Of his friends who'd been writing me just as much as he did, and of my bodyguard, who'd become closer to me than any friend I'd made since becoming an actress. I thought of myself and how I'd spent my last session with Dr. Nelson in a puddle of tears as we talked about everything, from the baby to the lawsuits to my parents.

And we'd talked about Cooper.

I held up the gazillion-page book I'd been reading over the past couple days. "I'm just going to put this in my room before seeing Doctor Nelson," I said. The book was the same one that had been passed around the last time I was in rehab.

It was so much better than the script for the movie had been.

The first time I realized that I no longer wanted Roxies or anything else to drown away the pain was at the end of September. I woke up at six a.m. after a bad dream and didn't want to black out the memory of it ever happening, of the baby ever happening. All I wanted to do was climb into the shower and then go to breakfast so I could start my day.

When I told Dr. Nelson about my epiphany at our session at the end of the week, he beamed, tapping the end of his pen against the corner of his desk. He gave me a pointed look before asking, "Does that mean you're checking out early?"

Placing my elbows on the desk, I rested my forehead against my clenched hands. God, if this had been eight months ago, I would have checked myself out as soon as he asked me that, especially when I had Cooper waiting for me somewhere under a palm tree or on a paddleboard.

Instead, I shook my head. "I'll stick it out the full sixty days."

Dr. Nelson nodded his bald head carefully, his expression never changing. "Do you know what you'll do after you leave here?"

It wasn't the first time the question had come up since I'd come to Seaside almost a month before, but it was mostly in my parents' letters. *"Will you go back to acting?" "Will you come to live with me and your dad?" "Are you going to use your payment from* Tidal *to get your own place?"*

I'd written them back each time without answering their questions because I didn't want to act. God knew the last thing I wanted to do was live with my parents. And to be honest, it really wasn't any of their business what I planned to do with the money I made filming the movie.

"Maybe I'll go to college," I told Dr. Nelson. The moment I said it, I felt my heartbeat pick up. Felt that thrill of excitement I used to feel when I scored a dream role or a glowing review. Maybe I would go to school. It would be my first go at a normal education since I was in fourth or fifth grade.

Dr. Nelson lifted one of his eyebrows and leaned forward. "You look surprised."

"I am. I mean, I didn't realize I wanted to do it."

"Do you know what you want to major in?"

I lifted my shoulders. "No clue. The only thing I've ever done was act." But I remembered what Paige had told me about her sister, Delilah. That she'd told their parents she was only nineteen and shouldn't be expected to know what she wants to do.

The corners of Dr. Nelson's lips twisted in concern. "Have you told Cooper yet?"

Shaking my head, I swallowed in an attempt to clear the tightness from my throat. Since our first call, I'd gotten to talk to Cooper only two more times on the phone and the last time I'd called he was in the middle of having dinner with Dickson and his wife. He'd insisted that he'd much rather speak to me but after ten minutes, I lied and said my time was up.

He needed to fix his relationship with his dad as much as I needed to fix myself.

"I'll tell him when I get out."

"He's coming to pick you up? You'd mentioned during our first session your frustration with your family for never being around once you reach the end of your treatment—"

Pulling my arms off the desk, I dropped them by my sides and stared down at my lap. Mom had written me a letter last week, swearing that she and Dad would be here to pick me up on October 19, even if they had to walk. It was dramatic and typical of my mother, but I believed her. Flicking my tongue over dry lips, I said, "No, my mom and dad are coming to get me."

I had no plans to tell Cooper; I wasn't going to be selfish and make him choose between me and the competition.

I would be okay if I had to wait a week more to see him.

And as I sat in front of my therapist talking about how I'd handle the paparazzi once I was released in a couple weeks, I knew that even though what had happened three years ago would always remain one of those what-ifs for me—even though I'd probably always have nightmares and would never be rid of the scar in my heart—that I'd live.

CHAPTER TWENTY-THREE

~~~~~~~~~~~~~~~~~~~~~~~~

October 19

On the day of my release from Seaside, I woke up a few minutes after eight a.m., smiling.

My parents had sent me a care package with new clothes the week before and I tried to get dressed quietly, hoping not to wake Nora. She woke up anyway, flipping on the little light above her twin-size bed to stare across the room at me. "You scared?" she asked.

She and I had stayed up late the night before, talking about everything from her kids—her oldest was a few years younger than me—to movies and finally to surfing. I'd spent the last couple months gushing about it, and she said that once she left Seaside next month she might give it a try.

I pulled on one of my long leather boots and shook my head. "Not this time."

"Excited?"

I glanced up at her and smiled. "More than anything."

She slid up into a sitting position and crossed her arms over her thin chest. "You should have told your boyfriend you were getting out," she said, and I shot her a look. She'd been on my ass since last week when Cooper and I had spoken and I still hadn't said anything to him about my release date.

"It's not a big deal," I said, despite the lump in my throat. "I'll fly out to Hawaii next week to see him."

Nora shook her head but gave me a wistful smile. "I hate surprises." My roommate was the type of person who read the last chapter of books first and refused to watch a movie without spoiling it, so I rolled my eyes.

"I'll keep that in mind," I said, the edges of my lips pulling up. I stood and buttoned my skinny jeans and grabbed my bag from atop the dresser. Then I crossed the room and sat on the corner of her bed.

"Personal space," she reminded me, but she was laughing.

"I'm going to miss you," I said.

Groaning, she demanded, "You're not going to cry all over me, are you?"

But when I hugged her, she squeezed me tightly. It was only when I reached the door to our room that she asked in a husky voice, "You'll write?"

My throat felt dry. Nora's family still hadn't written her—she said they were trying to teach her a lesson this time around. I pushed past the discomfort and turned partially around to glance at her.

"Every day, if you want."

She snorted and rolled her light-brown eyes. "Don't be a lame ass. You be good, Mouse Ears," she said, even though I'd told her a hundred times I'd never acted in a Disney production in my entire life.

"I will. And you'll try not to harass the hot counselor anymore?"

She didn't respond until I stepped out into the cold hallway. "Yeah, probably not."

I hugged myself close as I walked toward the staff station. When I turned the corner, I half expected to see Kevin waving at me with news that my parents couldn't make it and that they'd accepted a new role on my behalf, but then I saw my mother. She was pacing, her heels clacking hard on the linoleum floor, and biting her bottom lip.

"Mom," I said, and although I thought I'd accepted the fact that she might not show up, my voice cracked.

She stopped and turned to me, and her face stretched into a Botox smile. She rushed toward me, meeting me just outside the staff station and wrapping me in a tight embrace. "It feels like it's been years since I saw you!" she exclaimed when she finally let me go.

I gave a little laugh. "Yeah, well, me too." Frowning, I looked over her shoulder. "Where's Dad?"

Mom took a couple steps back, smoothing her hand over her highlighted hair. "He was on a trip in Boston, but we're picking him up on the way home." She checked her watch and cringed. "Right now, actually."

"I've just got to check out and—"

She took my bag from me, sliding the strap onto her shoulder, and nodded. "You do that and I'll call your dad to let him know we'll be there soon."

I was grinning like an idiot as I signed out of Seaside. The counselor in admissions gave me my phone back, then I signed a few forms and the staff wished me the best of luck. The whole process took all of fifteen minutes, and then Mom and I went out to the parking lot where her red Cadillac CTS-V was waiting. I slid into the passenger seat, immediately reaching for the radio dial as she cranked the engine.

I sighed when I caught the middle of a Jason Mraz song and sang along off-key, sounding as horrible as my mom had when she called me on my birthday back in July. She shot me a look as she navigated the Cadillac into traffic.

"Jesus, Willow, I don't remember you being like this at nine in the morning *ever*," she said.

"It's a good feeling," I admitted, resting my head against the headrest and looking out the window at an orange Metro bus a couple lanes over. Seeing it brought back the memory of myself back in June, and I slid my phone back and forth between my hands, wishing I could call Cooper.

The song switched to Paramore and I nearly choked when my mother joined in with me, singing loudly. Our eyes connected across the center console and though I knew we had a long ways to go, this was a start. When the song ended, she brought up my attorney and where he was in the appeals process. Clay had flat-out told Mom that he didn't think we stood a chance but he was willing to keep trying.

I was silent for a long time and then I nodded. "I'd appreciate it if he did."

When we arrived at LAX twenty minutes later, Mom gave me an apologetic smile. "I'm going to park." She glanced down at her phone, flipped through her messages, and told me the American Airlines flight number, before saying, "He's already here. Can you go in and—"

I was already getting out of the car, grabbing a pair of sunglasses from the center console as I did so. "Got it."

It was the first time in years that I'd been in this airport without a bodyguard standing over me, and as I made my way to the gate I felt like a million pounds had been lifted off my shoulders. It wasn't like I'd been forgotten—I was 100 percent sure I'd show up again on some gossip site with a poll on when I'd fuck up again—but today I was normal.

I arrived at the baggage carousel for the flight number Mom had given me, but when I glanced up at the scrolling text on the digital sign, my breath caught. It wasn't Boston, but Honolulu.

"What? No lei?" a voice with an Australian accent said from behind me, and I turned slowly to face Cooper. He was wearing jeans, Chuck Taylors, and a blue T-shirt that brought out his eyes, and I felt my mouth go dry as I drank in the sight of him.

"What are you doing here?" My voice came out in a whisper.

One corner of his mouth lifted. "Remember how I said that I like to study up on my clients?" he asked, and I lifted my chin slightly. He'd said that in this very airport actually. "Did you really think I wouldn't show up?"

"I didn't want to be selfish," I said honestly.

He took four long strides to me and gripped me to his body. An elderly woman collecting her baggage from a nearby carousel did a double take, but Cooper didn't seem to notice. "God, Wills, you can be as selfish as you want with me."

I shivered when our lips touched, and my body responded to his, moving closer so that I could slide my arms around his shoulders. I'd missed this. I'd missed him so fucking much that now that he was here, it hurt.

Groaning, he finally pulled back, massaging my neck with the pads of his thumbs. "Do you know how hard it was to coordinate things with your mum? She's the scariest person I've ever met, you know."

My laughter was mixed with a sob as I nodded. "She told me we had to pick up my dad."

He shook his head, chuckling. "Nah, he's at some fancy restaurant waiting for us to show. My fucking flight was delayed an hour or I would've been there to get you first thing."

I took a deep breath. "What about your competition?"

He kissed the center of my forehead, brushing strands of my dark hair away from it. "What about it?"

"You didn't have to miss it for me and I—"

Pressing three fingers over my mouth, he released a sigh. "You talk way too much, Wills. I'm where I need to be, okay?

And for what it's worth, the answer to the question you asked a few months ago is thirty-four. I've won thirty-four competitions."

I drew back and ran my tongue over my teeth. "Bit of an overachiever, aren't you?"

He laughed and wrapped his arm around my shoulders, guiding me toward the exit. "I love you, Willow."

"I love you too."

He paused, stopping a few inches from the automatic door. "Before I forget"—he opened his duffel bag and pulled a necklace of crushed flowers from the top—"I owe you a lei."

I choked on a sob, dipping my head so that he could drop it around my neck. "You do realize that this is exactly the way they'd do it in the movies, right?"

His arms encircled me again and I sighed into his T-shirt, breathing in the scent of sunblock and coconut shampoo. "Guess I don't hate the film industry as much as I let on."

EPILOGUE

~~~~~~~~~~~~~~~~~~~~~~~~~~~~

Two Years Later

Cooper and I weren't perfect. It took us nearly six months to figure out where we wanted to live, and even then, it wasn't the
perfect solution careerwise—we would alternate between Hawaii
and California.

Somehow, it worked for us.

The first time he'd asked me to marry him was right after
the release of *Tidal,* a year after we met. The second time was
at Paige and Eric's wedding six months later. When I'd told him
that I was still thinking, he'd given me that dimpled smile that I
fell all over myself for and told me he'd wait a few more months.

When those three months passed, I realized he probably wouldn't ask again.

"You look cold," he said, as we walked through Central Park. He had insisted we go to New York City for the second anniversary of our first date, and even though I had midterms in two weeks, I'd agreed.

I wrapped my coat around myself a little tighter and grinned. "This is definitely *not* Honolulu."

He led me to a small picnic table and we sat across from each other, clasping hands. "I've got a surprise for you, but I want you to close your eyes," he said. I nodded, biting the inside of my cheek as I heard him shuffle around.

After a couple minutes, I felt him behind me, breathing in my ear. "Open them, Wills."

When I did, nothing had changed, and I glanced over my shoulder, cocking an eyebrow. "Okay, I must be a dumb-ass. What is it?"

Touching the back of my head, he turned it until my gaze landed on a couple and a little kid by a statue of three bears. "So, I may have resorted to extreme bribery to get this, but there's someone over there you'd probably want to meet."

I felt my body go numb and my voice didn't sound like my own when I demanded, "Wait—what?"

He pinched the bridge of his nose, laughing. "Put it this way, somewhere there's a lady who works for an adoption agency who—"

"No, I know what you mean, but . . . Are you fucking serious?"

His hands slipped under my arms, lifting me up and compelling me forward. My heart slammed between my rib cage with each step, and when we reached the couple, Cooper nudged me forward. "Wills, these are the McKays and that"—he pointed to the little boy swinging upside down from one of the bears—"is Parker."

Parker.

My kid's name was Parker.

Cooper had found him.

"This is that friend of Mommy's that we told you about," Mr. McKay told him, tugging on the sleeve of his coat, and Parker stopped playing to give me a green-eyed once-over.

And then I was crying. Because of what Cooper had done. Because Parker had run over to me, his small hands stretching the hem of my shirt. He smelled like chocolate and the nontoxic dough stuff little kids liked to eat. I was crying because Parker was here, period.

"Hey," he said.

Dabbing my eyes, I knelt down so our gazes could meet. "Hey," I said. It was so hard to keep my voice steady as he grinned at me, revealing two missing teeth.

"You're the girl from Kaylee's movies."

Before I could look over at them for an explanation, Mrs. McKay spoke up, clearing her throat. "Kaylee is our fourteen-year-old—she's a . . . fan of your movies. And Parker *loves* his big sister."

I nodded, my gaze never leaving his. "Yes, I'm that girl," I said.

Parker tilted his head to one side. "You're crying."

"Yes," I said. "Because it's . . . a good day. The best day, actually."

He dug inside his coat pocket for something, and when he pulled his hand out, he held the ring box Cooper had tried to give me twice before. Parker gave Cooper a big grin. "Told you I wouldn't lose it."

I took it from him, my fingertips skimming his gloved ones, and I held my breath.

Cooper cleared his throat behind me. "It doesn't have to be tomorrow or even a year from now, Wills. Just say that—"

I glanced over my shoulder, meeting his blue eyes, and nodded quickly. Unquestionably.

"Yes," I said.

I had never been more certain of anything in my life.

THE END

ACKNOWLEDGMENTS

To my amazing agent, Rebecca Friedman, and her assistant, Abby Schulman—thank you ladies so much for your support and guidance, and for putting up with my millions of emails!

To the ladies in the "Naughty Mafia"—Ava Black, Kelli Maine, Kristen Proby, and Michelle Valentine—you all rock. I'm so blessed to be a part of such a talented group of ladies and I'm so thankful for your friendship!

Thanks so much, Katie Ashley, for your amazing eye for grammar. Your notes and comments have helped me so much, and I'm so grateful for your big red pen!

Lisa Pantano Kane, Kim Box Person, Lisa Rutledge, Crystal Spears, and Marilyn Medina: You guys rock! Thank you for beta-reading my book and for the kick-ass feedback. I love you guys!

ACKNOWLEDGMENTS

To the wonderful bloggers who've read, reviewed, and promoted my books, THANK YOU! You guys have made this experience absolutely amazing for me.

Thank you so much to my family for supporting my writing and believing in me. You guys often eat Subway three nights (okay, *five* nights) a week so I can write, and I love you. Another big thanks to my best friend for reading my chapters over and over and over again!

And to my readers . . . you guys have made my dreams come true. Thank you, thank you, THANK YOU for reading my books and showing so much love and support. I love you guys!

ABOUT THE AUTHOR

Emily Snow is the *New York Times* and *USA Today* bestselling author of the erotic romance series *Devoured*. She loves books, sexy bad boys, and really loud rock music, so naturally, she writes stories about all three. She lives in Virginia.

Visit her online at emilysnowbooks.blogspot.com, or follow her on Twitter @EmilySnowBks.

Turn the page to read the first chapter
of Emily Snow's bestselling novel

Devoured

Available now from Touchstone Books

1

"Your baby brother called. Three times."

My gaze snaps up from the mail I'm holding to meet Tori's dark eyes. She's ten feet away me, sitting behind the Formica countertop in the kitchen that we share. My cool, confident roommate—whom I met four years ago when she rescued me from a wasted and touch-happy frat boy—fidgets anxiously with the rim of a supersized shot glass that boasts a raunchy quote: LIQUOR GOGGLES: MAKING FUGLY GUYS HOT SINCE THE 19TH CENTURY. Tori knows my brother well enough to realize something is going on. It must be important because Seth wouldn't stop avoiding me for anything else. He's owed me two grand since July, seven months ago, and the last time I actually spoke to him was Labor Day.

Even when Seth had backed out of visiting me for Christmas break, he'd done so via e-mail.

God . . . this can't be good.

"Did he say what he wants?" I croak. I press my body up against the steel door behind me, the long row of deadbolts poking hard into my back. Crisp envelopes crumple between my fingertips, but I'm powerless to stop myself from obliterating the stack of shared bills and postcards for Tori, from her parents who are vacationing in Mexico. I'm much too worried about why Seth has called me.

Three times.

Tori shrugs her bare, shimmery shoulders, squints down at the splash of clear liquid in her glass, and then downs the shot in one swift flick of her wrist. There's no bottle in sight, but I know she's drinking peppermint schnapps. Her telltale bottle of chaser (Hershey's sugar-free chocolate syrup) sits next to her phone. Plus, schnapps is her usual Friday night pregamer. Sometimes—when my boss has an off week that inevitably rubs off on me—I let Tori talk me into drinking a little. I'm in no mood to even consider touching the stuff right now, though.

There's already a migraine building in that frustrating spot between my eyes.

"He just said call him . . ." she says. But as her voice trails off, I know she's thinking the same thing I am.

What the hell has my mom done this time?

Because last time I received a frantic call from Seth, a year and a half ago, he'd told me that Mom had made a suicide attempt. I'd taken the first available flight out of Los Angeles, only to discover that she had lied to my brother and grandma for attention. Even now, I can vividly recall how Mom had laughed at me for being naïve and stupid enough to come running, and I ball my hands into tight fists.

"Always so quick to please," she'd said in her thick Southern accent. Then she took a long drag of a cigarette for which she'd probably had to do unmentionable things to earn, and blew the smoke over my head.

Forcing thoughts of my mother out of my mind for the time being, I offer Tori a strained smile that I know isn't fooling anybody. "You going out tonight?" I ask.

The answer is obvious. It *is* Friday night, and even though only her upper body is visible, I can tell Tori is dressed to kill. Immaculate long black hair and makeup that would make Megan Fox weep, check. Strapless red dress that's probably no longer than my top, double-check. I can almost guarantee she's wearing a pair of her mile-high, "screw-me" shoes, too.

"Vanguard with Ben, Stacy, and Micah." Her jet-black, perfectly arched eyebrows knit together as she parts her lips to say something else. I shake my head stubbornly and she snaps her mouth shut. We both know it is pointless for her to invite me. Tonight, no amount of sweet-talking will convince me to leave the apartment. There's a good chance that whatever Seth is about to tell me will ruin my night and the rest of my year, too.

I swallow, over and over again, in my best attempt to get rid of the sudden dryness in the back of my mouth.

It doesn't help.

"That's it," Tori snaps. She reaches across the counter to grab her phone. "I'm calling to cance—" But I lunge forward and pluck her massive Samsung Galaxy out of her hand. I drop the balled-up pile of mail beside her empty glass. Thanks to my sweaty palms, it's practically fused together.

"Please, just . . . *don't*. You look way too hot to spend your night with me. I-I swear I'll be fine." She doesn't seem too convinced because she presses her full lips into a thin, scarlet line. I slide her phone into her hands, curling her fingers around it. I coax my face into an even brighter smile and tell her in the most chipper voice I can muster, "Go, and have a good time."

She's talking, protesting, but I can barely hear her exact words. I'm already walking down the narrow hallway to my bedroom, my own phone clutched in a death grip as I dial my brother's number.

Seth picks up on the second ring. On those rare occasions that we speak, he always lets my call go to voicemail and then responds to me five or six hours later.

This is *definitely* not good.

"Is everything okay, Tori said that—" I begin, ducking into my bedroom and shutting the door behind me.

"Thank God," he hisses before I can get another syllable out. "Where've you been, Si? And why the hell didn't I have this number?"

Less than ten seconds into our conversation and my brother is already arguing with me. I slam my oversized bag onto my bed. My wallet along with a bunch of tampons and makeup spill out onto my lavender cotton sheets and some fall on the carpeted floor. I'll clean it up later, even though clutter annoys me.

"I work. And I've tried to call you from this number several times. You just didn't answer," I point out.

I don't sound angry, which is how I feel, but like I'm explaining myself to my brother. Like I'm the one who should be sorry for *him* ignoring me.

I really hate myself for sounding like that.

"Sienna, it's Gram," Seth says.

And this—*this* is when I literally freeze in place, standing between my bed and desk. I must look like one of those tragic, serious statues in the cemeteries back home in Tennessee. My heart feels as if it's stopped. The first thing I'd assumed when Tori told me Seth was trying to reach me was that my mom had somehow gotten herself in trouble again. I hadn't even thought of my grandmother because she's so strong and resilient and wonderful.

She's also seventy-nine years old.

I try to say something, anything, but there's a lump the size of a lint-flavored golf ball clogging up the back of my throat. Is Gram sick? Is she—?

I can't even bring myself to think *that* word.

I'm still choking and wheezing when Seth finally releases an exasperated sigh and snaps, "She's fine, Si. Well, physically fine."

I don't get a chance to exhale in relief or yell at my brother for scaring the hell out of me before he launches into the story of what's going on. Seth says words like *foreclosure* and *eviction notice. New owner*—some douchebag musician from California. *Court on Monday.* And then he tells me that I need to be there for her, for him.

"I have to work," I whisper. Tomas, my boss, is like the Michael Bay of wardrobe, and he's been telling me ever since he hired me how many people would literally kill to work with him. I can't imagine what he'll say if I ask for time off for anything besides a funeral or the certain impending demise of an immediate family member. I might get fired. Or worse, my boss could possibly give me a horrible reference and I'll never get another wardrobe job for the rest of my life.

"No, you've *got* to be here," Seth says stubbornly.

"I can't just . . ." But I'm already sitting in front of my laptop with my bank statement pulled up on one tab and a discount airline Web site on another. I'm already entering in my debit card information for an early Monday morning flight, biting down so hard on my lower lip that I taste blood. I'm broke. Half of what's in my account—half of my *total* savings—will have to go to Tori for my share of the bills.

And before I hang up with my little brother, I'm already shoving my belongings inside the beaten Coach suitcase my grandparents had given me five years ago as an eighteenth birthday present.

It's mind-numbingly cold in Nashville—thirty-three degrees, to be precise—and snowing lightly when I scoot into Seth's messy Dodge Ram 1500 on Monday afternoon. From the way I'm sweating, though, you would think it was the middle of August and that I'd arrived in Nashville dressed from head to toe in wool. The flutter-sleeve top I'd so carefully selected because I thought it would make me look professional, clings uncomfortably to my skin and the tops of my thigh-high tights sag to just above my knees.

The sudden spike in perspiration is my own fault. I spent the majority of the four-hour flight from Los Angeles to Nashville fretting over how I'd convince Gram to come back to California with me. And the more I thought about it, the more doubtful I became. My granddad had given her that cabin and land as a gift after my mother was born, back in the early seventies. There's no way in hell Gram's giving it up without a fight, even though from what Seth has said, the house is already gone.

"What'd your boss say?" my brother asks as he turns onto the interstate. He slams on the brakes to avoid hitting another car. The Dodge skids on the slippery road, jostling us around, but Seth manages to get the pickup truck under control halfway into my frantic gasp.

My brother doesn't so much as flinch. He squints straight ahead, the same way our dad always does when he drives in crappy weather, and rubs the tips of his thumbs on either side of the steering wheel—yet another Dad trait. With his dark blond hair, brown eyes, and year-round tan that puts my easily burned skin to shame, Seth even looks like Dad now.

I've got red hair and what Tori calls "Amazon height" and don't resemble either my mom or my dad. Not that I mind.

"Damn, Si, you going to answer me or just sit there with your mouth wide open?" Seth demands.

Digging my hands into the hem of the dark tweed pencil skirt I'm wearing, I shrug my shoulders. "I worked through Christmas and New Year's, so he didn't have much of a problem. Besides, I'm just an assistant." I don't add that I had to beg Tomas for the time off and that he'd pointedly said I better take care of my family drama and have my ass back in L.A. before the end of the month—two and a half weeks later.

"Echo Falls is ranked first in females aged eighteen to thirty-four. There are people willing to trade their own offspring for a chance to work on this series. Replacing you with a new wardrobe assistant who covets this career won't be too hard a feat," Tomas had said, punching something into the iPad he carried around everywhere. *He never even spared me a glance, so when he shoved a newly inventoried wardrobe rack against a brick slab wall, he didn't see me startle. "Don't force me to find that person, Jensen."*

"I'll wrap it up in two weeks, Tomas," I'd promised.

"You'd better."

Telling Seth any of that is simply a waste of oxygen. He would either not get why I can't neglect my job whenever I please or simply not care. Knowing my brother, it would be both.

"Got anything I can wipe my face with?" I ask.

Seth twitches his head to the right side, toward the center console. "In there."

I find a package of wet wipes in between a half-empty thirty-count box of condoms and a completely empty bottle of Jose Cuervo. Before I can stop myself, I whirl on my brother and blurt, "I hope you're not stupid enough to drink and drive. You're only nineteen and you—"

"Don't start, Si, okay? Today is not the day for your bitching."

I could remind Seth that I am older than he is. That out of

just about everyone in his life—aside from our grandmother—I care about him the most. I could keep talking in an attempt to get my point across.

I don't.

Instead, sinking my teeth down on the inside of my cheek until the nauseating taste of copper floods my mouth, I turn my attention to the bumper stickers plastered on the little Ford Escort in front of us. HONK IF YOU HATE PEOPLE, TOO one of them says. How fitting.

There's only eight miles between the airport and the courthouse, but the drive takes forty-five minutes due to the traffic and snow. Seth and I spend just about every minute of the ride in silence, like we usually do when we're around each other. The only time he says something to me is after I switch the radio on. Seth lets The Black Keys serenade us for a minute and a half and then abruptly cuts the volume.

"I can't listen to this and drive," he grumbles.

"Fine."

As I dab at my face with wipes and smooth my long red hair back into a low ponytail, I mentally kick myself for being such a dumbass and lending him money. Not only has he been nothing but terse toward me since I got in his car, he hasn't mentioned the cash I gave him.

I doubt he will.

Seth's smart enough to realize that I'll never bring up the money he owes me because I'd rather gouge myself in the eye than get into a confrontation with him.

There's a reason, actually a few reasons, why I rarely come to town and baby brother is just the smallest part of them.

By the time Seth and I arrive at the courthouse and find the correct courtroom, the hearing is coming to an end. My brother and I sit on opposite ends of one of the wooden benches at the back of the room. He's got his arms crossed tightly over his chest, staring ahead with a stony look in his dark eyes. I hate that he's irritated at me, but there's nothing I can do about it. Giving him a sad smile, I lean forward until my chin brushes the top of the next pew up and listen attentively to what's being said.

From what I manage to piece together, this is the second hearing. The new owner, whom I've decided to refer to as Asshat, and his lawyers are both here, and they're seeking a formal eviction. My grandmother and her attorney Mr. Nielson (the same one she's had since before I can remember) are across from them on the left side of the room. Even though I know I shouldn't be angry with him, I find myself glaring death rays at Asshat.

Then again, I shouldn't be checking him out, either.

Since his back is turned to me, there's a depressing limit to what I'm able to ogle, but I know that he's *built*. And with a backside like his, the rest of him is bound to be equally as gorgeous. Dressed in an impeccable black business suit that molds a little too perfectly to every inch of his body, he's got dark, tousled hair that brushes his neck and long fingers. He taps them rapidly in some type of rhythm on the mahogany table in front of him. I'm tall, but this guy must tower over me by a good six inches—he's easily six foot three or six foot four.

And his ass . . .

Ugh, I'd bet the last thousand dollars in my account (and would even overdraw it a few hundred bucks) that the attorney who's standing beside him would be staring at it, too, if she could get away with doing so. Or if she could stop beaming up at him with her chest thrust out for longer than five seconds.

Hot-faced and utterly reluctant, I drag my gaze back to Gram's side of the courtroom. If Seth catches me staring at Asshat, he'll never let me live it down. Knowing him, he'll probably accuse me of conspiring with the enemy.

I frown, because I know that's *exactly* what Seth would say to me.

"Mr. Nielson, your client has ten days before the court issues a possession order," the judge is telling my grandmother's lawyer in a deep Southern accent that rivals the one I used to have. "After that, the sheriff will carry out the eviction within a week."

When she hears those words, my grandmother's shoulders sag. She grips Nielson's shoulder for support so hard that even from the back row, I can see her knuckles turn white. It takes every ounce of my willpower not to bolt out of my seat. I hate this. I hate my mother for this, because at the heart of things, it really is all her fault.

I was right when I assumed she'd done something stupid. Mom's the reason my grandmother is losing her home. She is the reason everything in this family turns to shit.

And then the hearing is over. Gram's bright blue eyes widen

in stunned surprise as she makes her way toward me and Seth, and her drawn expression softens. She gives me a melancholy smile that's full of defeat. I've only seen her look at me like this once before. There's a sour taste in my mouth when I realize it was in this exact courthouse. Before Gram has a chance to utter a single word, I pull her to me and bury my face into her puff of gray hair, inhaling her familiar scent of vanilla and Chanel No. 5.

"Did you drive?" I ask. I won't say anything about what just happened—not in here, at least—because I don't exactly trust my emotions or Gram's. She nods into my shoulder, so I say, "I'll take you back home then." Loosening my grip, I glare over her shoulder at Asshat. Now his back is no longer turned to me. Instead, I have a side view that's just as nauseatingly sexy as the back.

He's speaking to his female attorney, and they're both laughing. She's got her hand on his arm and her boobs are still jutted out. If we were *anywhere* else I'd snort aloud at how ridiculous she looks. He's probably thanking her. And she's more than likely suggesting they celebrate the easy win against an old woman and her equally ancient lawyer over drinks and then a quick screw at her place. I'm about to draw away from Gram and lead her out of the courtroom when the man turns his face, lifts his eyes. Our gazes connect. His hazel eyes challenge my blue.

Predator and prey.

He draws himself up to his full height.

My chest seizes up. I was right, the full package is devastatingly handsome. And when I decided to nickname him Asshat I was being much too lenient.

I pray my grandmother doesn't feel the change in my heart-beat, the sudden hitch in the way that I'm breathing. This exchange isn't one of those love-at-first sight moments. No, it's nothing at all like that. This is one of those moments where fate has roundhouse kicked me in the face yet again. Why is *he* here in Nashville? In the same courtroom as *me*?

God, please, please *don't let this man remember me.*

For a moment, I'm sure he has no clue who I am, that he'll go back to chatting it up with Boobs McBeal. *By now there would've been tens,* hundreds, *of other girls. I'm nothing to him. I'm the only one who remembers,* I tell myself.

But then, a slow, animalistic smile of realization stretches across Lucas Wolfe's face.

It makes me feel like he'll devour me whole at any second.

That grin—it's the exact same one he gave me two years ago, right after I refused to let him cuff me to his bed, and just before he literally told me to get the fuck out of his house.

Also by Emily Snow, the *New York Times* and *USA TODAY* bestselling Devoured series!

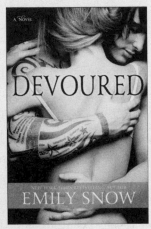

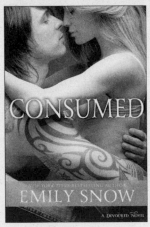